The Terror of Living

Urban Waite

W F HOWES LTD

This large print edition published in 2011 by
W F Howes Ltd
Unit 4, Rearsby Business Park, Gaddesby Lane,
Rearsby, Leicester LE7 4YH

1 3 5 7 9 10 8 6 4 2

First published in the United Kingdom in 2011
by Simon & Schuster

A CIP catalogue record for this book is available
from the British Library

ISBN 978 1 40747 057 3

Typeset by Palimpsest Book Production Limited,
Falkirk, Stirlingshire
Printed and bound in Great Britain
by MPG Books Ltd, Bodmin, Cornwall

LP

For Karen

'Do you ever just think of just doing a criminal thing sometime? Just doing something terrible. Change everything.'

—Richard Ford, *Rock Springs*, from
the story 'Winterkill'

'We can never know what to want, because, living only one life, we can neither compare it with our previous lives nor perfect it in our lives to come.'

—Milan Kundera,
The Unbearable Lightness of Being

PART I

BY AIR

The kid had taken a bus north from Seattle and stood outside studying the bar for a long time, weighing the options. A gust of wind brought the smell of sun-warmed tar from a patch of cracked pavement, the day changing warm to cold, airplanes passing overhead in the afternoon, the sound of jet engines firing and planes taking off from the nearby field. The bar wasn't much to look at, just a two-story clapboard with a rock-and-pebble parking strip. He toed a piece of gravel, thinking it over, then went in.

He took a drink off his beer, looked around the bar, and put the glass back down. With his elbows pushed out on either side, he was leaning hard up against the bar. It was the type of place he used to come to when he was underage – a short bar, dim light, with customers of questionable means – using his older brother's ID and hoping to get laid. He'd been out of the world for two years on a vehicular manslaughter charge. He'd been lucky about it, too; young as he was, the judge had gone easy on him. On his thin frame he wore a red shirt, so worn the material had turned the color of a dried peach. Locked up, he hadn't worn the old shirt in years. The smell of him, in his new old clothes, was something of dust, something of mildew and dark, locked-away places, so deep it seemed to come from his skin itself.

He looked the beer over, better than the piss-pot stuff they brewed in Monroe, half-fruit, half-saliva, like some sort of Amazon moonshine. He took another swallow. It was his first legal drink and he sat staring at it, watching how the air condensed against the side of the glass and collected around the base in a watery circle.

Don't fuck this up, he said to himself, looking around at the other customers. Don't do a stupid thing like that.

When Eddie came up to the bar and sat down, the kid was taking in that dreamy glow of being somewhere he'd never been before. The two were separated by a seat between them, the kid looking down into his beer, staring hard at the way the bubbles bounced against the surface, then sloughed off to one side and collected.

Eddie ordered a beer from the bartender and waited for the man to pour it. The kid raised an eye to study Eddie, watching him as he waited for the beer to be delivered. After the bartender had gone, Eddie turned to look out on the bar and take it all in. There were two pool tables in the back, one occupied, an assortment of low tables near the wall with two or three chairs at each.

4

Eddie turned back and spoke to the beer in front of him. 'I guess you're my man.'

The kid stared at Eddie for a moment and then looked away. Eddie wasn't what the kid had been expecting, a squat, dark-skinned Mexican, his cheeks chewed up with acne scars, and a thin trail of hair along his lip.

'Kind of young, aren't you?' Eddie said.

'Old enough,' the kid said, drawing himself up on the stool. He knew what he looked like, a kid of twenty-two, barely old enough to be there. Two years of prison had thinned him out, tightened up his muscles. His time there had toughened him, but he knew he still looked like a kid, Adam's apple big as a newborn's fist, the patch of a beard below his chin, drawn in like a child's scribblings.

'I don't think I need to tell you this,' Eddie said, 'but it's best you understand from the start that there are no mistakes. I was told you were looking for something and here I am. I wouldn't even be here if someone hadn't put his own life out there for you. You understand?'

The kid nodded and looked straight on at the liquor bottles behind the bar. His older brother had been the one to put him up to it. He'd been in the driver's seat two years ago, and the kid had slid over, taking the blame. Scared shitless, but taking the blame for his older brother so he wouldn't go back in. It was a stupid thing to do, but he had done it and his brother had walked away. And now his brother would help him out and it would all be even.

'You don't have to worry about me,' the kid said. 'There won't be any accidents. I'm as good as they come.'

Eddie smiled. 'You don't need to tell me. As far as I'm concerned you're in business for yourself. You're a contractor working for a percentage. You don't have to answer to me. I'm just here to tell you that it's in your own best interest not to fuck this up.' Eddie got up from the bar, thanked the bartender, and went out through the front door.

On the barstool where he'd been sitting was a set of car keys. The kid leaned over as casually as he could and swiped them off the vinyl. He kept them below the bar, and as he finished his beer he fit his finger into the metal key ring and rolled them over and over again, feeling them swing loose in the air.

Deputy Bobby Drake gave the car another look. Drugs had always been a problem north of Silver Lake, but these days, smugglers would have to be real idiots to take anything across the border crossings. Security had doubled, a real task force going now, after all the years of people passing on through. For a time it was as if the two countries were one, a driver's license the only thing necessary to get up into British Columbia.

The drugs just spread out, finding other ways of crossing, as the borders tightened. If you had the experience or the know-how, it could be a good business. Drake knew that. His father, the former sheriff – locked up now – had known that. This land, these mountains and valleys, carved by glacier and erosion, were about all Drake had left of a former life. A life that had seen horses raised in his father's field, now taken and gone. A life built of apple orchards and fall harvests, sold off and forgotten, nothing there now but a wooden fence melted away with age into the ground, trees left behind as withered and bony as skeletal hands.

From one side to the other, Drake's life so cleanly cut in half as to be unrecognizable.

He took out his binoculars and scanned the clear-cut. It was all forestry land, leased out to the big lumber companies. Everything a patchwork of fresh-cut brown or newly planted green. Hills stretched off and became mountains, the white tip of Mount Baker poking up into the high blue. Jumbo jets could get lost in a place like this, he thought.

The deputy propped his door open, letting the mountain air into the cab of the cruiser, sticky smell of pine needles, resin, and damp, windblown earth. He left one leg outside and worked an old basketball injury in his lower thigh. He was tall for the cruiser, and his leg stretched out onto the gravel. Sharp chinned, with thinning brown hair. He was still young enough to push the ball up the court and keep in shape, but he was starting to lose it, starting to get comfortable in this job.

The license plate had come back clean. He stared at the onboard computer, then got up and walked over to the car. There was nothing out of the ordinary about it. No forced entry. It was in the middle of nowhere, just a car on the side of the road. He knelt and fingered the raised edges of a wide double tire track in the soft ground. Drake traced it back to where the tires had come off the road and then walked to the other side and saw how they caught the far edge and made the turn to go back up the road. He guessed it to be something big, a semi without a trailer, or a big Chevy or Ford, something with a tow. He couldn't put his finger on it, couldn't say, but he did know – judging from how the larger tire tracks lay across the smaller – that whatever it was had come after the car had been there, and he knew from driving this road every twenty-four hours that the car hadn't been there for more than a day.

Drake walked back across the road and looked the car over. He cupped his hands and put them to the window. The car was clean. Not even a gum wrapper on the floor. He'd expected an old McDonald's bag, a grocery bag, even a receipt, something.

He watched the wind come down from the mountains along the trees. Heard the rush of it through the branches, evergreens moving all at once, like cresting water on the tip of a wave, rolling smooth and fast down the face. The sky marvelous and clear above, he felt the wind play at the back of his neck. He didn't know what he was doing, why he couldn't just let it go, this car, this feeling, everything. He was battling an old, familiar sense of unease, some loneliness he'd been left with. Just he and his wife living up this way, in his father's house, now theirs, left to them for the keeping while his father was away.

He looked back up into the mountains, glassed them with his binoculars. Running his vision along the ridges, pausing to focus, then running on. He stood for a while next to the car. The wind came up off the lake and whipped some of the gravel dust into a dervish. He walked back to the cruiser and called the ranger's station over at Baker.

'You got anyone up from Seattle in the Silver Lake area?'

'No one up there, Deputy.'

He read the ranger the license plate. 'Anything?'

'That's all clear-cut and logging roads. Don't know why anyone would want to see that.'

'Don't know either,' Drake said, thanking the ranger.

The trail climbed steep and jagged in front of them. It was not a place for the kid, someone who couldn't ride and sat straight-backed in the saddle, unyielding to the horse's steps. Phil Hunt turned to look the kid over. The horses would follow each other up one hill and down the next, but the kid made him nervous.

'You been in this line of work long?' Hunt asked.

'Not long.'

'How old are you?'

'Twenty-seven.'

'That a lie?'

'Yes.'

'I'd say you don't look older than twenty-two, twenty-three?'

'That's about right,' the kid said. He turned in his saddle to look back down on what had passed before, hemlock and fir trees stretched into the narrow valley. Farther on, a patch of clear-cut and a newborn forest sprouting up in rows. The kid began to drift off to the left.

'Careful now,' Hunt said, lowering his hat to shield his eyes from the sun and watching the kid.

'Didn't expect this when I signed up.'

Hunt rolled this around in his head and let it rest. The kid couldn't have had much experience for the thing, riding up one ridge, then down into the following valley, just to do it again. Still, the kid reminded him a bit of himself at that age, thirty years ago, a head of brown hair, skin tanned brown as desert soil, a little too cocky, too sure of himself, body lean as a razor blade and with a mouth like one, too. 'It's not all cigarette boats and fancy parties,' Hunt said. 'Maybe down in the Keys that's how they do it. But up here it's a bit different.'

'It's been an education.'

Hunt thought he heard the kid laugh, but he didn't turn around. It was the last run of the season; soon the mountains would be covered in snow. What had Eddie been thinking, sending the kid up here? A big job like this, and some kid who doesn't know the first thing about the business. He could get killed just riding a horse; one mistake and he'd come up short and throw himself face-first over a cliff.

The horses were Hunt's, two roans he'd raised on the back acre of his property, Hunt feeding them and letting them run – chestnut brown with flecks of white, muscles as beautiful and sculpted as carved rock, rounding the field, divots of earth kicked up under the pounding of their hooves – his wife, Nora, and he taking turns every morning, casting hay through the field, standing at the fence, arms resting, enjoying the playful nicker and whinny of the horses. He didn't know where they'd have been without them. He hated that he needed them for this, that he let them be pulled up one hill and down the next, led by the inexperienced hands of this kid.

Hunt cast a wary eye at the kid, half expecting him to be riding backward in the saddle. Weather beginning to turn cold and the kid wearing nothing but jeans, tennis shoes, and a black nylon jacket that snapped and fluttered in the wind as they came up over the hump of the ridge and descended along a line into the next valley. Hunt wore a pair of leather gloves, jeans, and a thick, padded hunting jacket to keep out the cold, the jacket mottled green to blend in with the forest. On his head he wore a cowboy hat he kept in the back of his truck for jobs like this one. It made him feel official and he liked to tip his hat for his wife and see the smile come across her face. He felt young in the thing, the short-cropped gray of his hair covered by the hat, and the strong lines of his face shadowed by the brim. He'd given the kid one of his baseball caps, an adjustable Mariners cap, and left it at that.

'You been at this long?' the kid asked, leaning back in the saddle as they came down off the ridge, trying to keep himself from tumbling frontwise over the nose of the horse.

'Only thing I can do that makes any money.'

'How so?'

'Not much work out there for a man of my history.'

'I'd imagine we've been in the same line of work,' the kid said, a smile creeping across his face.

Deputy Bobby Drake hooked the rifle strap with his thumb and brought it around. He carried a pair of regulation binoculars, but the sight on the rifle was stronger. He carried a .270 for hunting and wore a pair of good mountaineering boots, strong enough for crampons in the winter and light enough to wear in the summer. He carried the pack over his back, lungs working for every step. He was young, just thirty years old. Heart trained for endurance, trained for the long haul of the mountains. Skin colored dark as the earth from a summer of swimming and hiking.

He'd come back to the car the next day, his day off, early. Looked the plates over again. Nothing. He stood out there next to the car, with the big blue waters of Silver Lake stretched out beyond him and the windblown dust from the edge of the road coming up and rolling along the cement. He rapped absently on the glass, perhaps just to make sure the car existed at all, that it wasn't some phantom mirage. He stood there and peered down inside. Nothing had changed. The whole thing made him uneasy.

As he walked, parting bear grass and the low-lying tops of mountain blueberries, his thoughts turned to his wife, whom he'd left behind that morning, Sheri sitting there at the breakfast table, a bowl of Cheerios, the milk turning yellow, sick and sweet in the air. She'd wanted to know what he was doing, what it mattered. He knew what she would say if he told her. They were newlyweds still and the idea of her there every morning, double-checking his life, hadn't quite set in. He couldn't explain why he had packed up his car, strapped on the tent, his rifle, and enough food and clothes to get him through the night. It wasn't like him. None of it was, just running off like that. It was something his father would have done. He walked on, thinking about what type of man he was becoming.

He'd grown up in these mountains. His father had brought him up in them, taking him on weekend trips. The valley leveled off at around two or three thousand, and as Drake hiked through fields of sedge and bluegrass, following the little streams that cut the base of the valley, he looked up to scan the ridges.

He could smell the scent of fall mountain bells, and as he passed he drifted a finger beneath the flowers and caught the wilted pink petals in his hand. He needed to get higher.

Hunt took out the topographical map and held it in his gloved hand, giving it a once-over. He checked his watch and found their altitude. They had camped the night before in a thicket of white birch and he'd slept all wrong, with a pebble digging into his back on the uneven ground. For a moment he'd dreamed of being back in prison, that locked-away, lonely feeling worse in his dreams than it had been twenty years ago. Hollow sounds of voices echoing down cement hallways. The poor, eaten-away souls residing there, the weak and starved, blubbering nonsense, rib cages like two claws come together across their sternum. He woke, stunned, his tongue pulled back in his throat, floating back there like something meant to suffocate him. He rolled over, breathing the cool mountain air.

Hunt had parked his truck and trailer a day's ride behind them, far enough back that they wouldn't be found. He held the map in one hand, guiding his horse forward with the other. As they rode, cutting through a stand of fir, he bent to avoid branches, taking in the smell of the horse's coat, the thick sheen of it, dust and oil rising off her and commingling with the air. She was a beautiful girl. He felt pride in her, in what she'd become.

They came down through a tangle of black raspberries, following the edge of a scree chute, the kid eating as he went. Hunt got down off his horse, shielded his eyes, and looked toward the sun. He judged there to be about three more hours of light. 'Come on now, get down off your horse and help me out here.'

The kid swung his leg over and half slid, half fell off the saddle, holding on the whole while to the pommel.

Hunt took a GPS from his saddlebag and gave the map another look. They were standing in a thicket of low alder, the white bark shining around them and the green moss floating off the trees with the wind. 'We're too low,' Hunt said, checking the altimeter on the GPS, then looking at his watch to make sure. He handed the GPS to the kid and began walking.

Thick and crooked, the alder stand stretched on up the valley, following a small stream, and this is the way they went, leading the horses.

The kid swore and lifted his foot off a soggy mess of lowland marsh.

'Careful now.'

'I didn't think I'd say this, but it would be nice to get back on the horse.'

'All we need to do is find an open meadow with a view to the north, we'll set camp and let the horses out for a little while. Just keep your eye on the GPS. We want to keep this latitude if we can.'

'There a pot of gold at the end of this rainbow?'

Hunt looked back at the kid, but smiled and said, 'If we're lucky there'll be a couple pots.'

'Hope you're good at sharing,' the kid said.

'Not particularly.'

They walked on in silence, leading the horses, Hunt thinking about what could be done with the money ahead. He walked on, adding dollar figures in his head. He thought about this for some time, thinking of his wife, Nora, of their life together, picking his steps with an absent mind. He thought about how they were, about how they'd been in the early years, when they couldn't keep their hands off each other, night and day hot as blood in the vein, famished and pulsing its way back to the heart.

Afterward, in the middle years, life had felt as if they had been trying to fill something in, pour it like cement over the questions of their lives, the answers down there, but the liquid rock just flowing in. Again and again they'd been to the doctor, looking for answers, just to return to the same house, the same spare bedrooms and empty space.

'Do you blame me?' Nora had asked, the two of them lying there in the coal black of their room, shades drawn and not a light on anywhere to tell him the voice he heard was his wife's at all. Turned away from her in the dark, he pretended to be asleep, his eyes wide open, feeling his cowardice grow deep within him, not saying anything. He didn't know what to say. She'd left him then, just got up from bed and left. He heard the car start up and he lay there listening to the night sounds beyond their window, cars passing on the road nearby, the rush of wind wrestling its way through the alder branches. This is it, this is how it ends, he thought. No desperate run for the driveway, no pulling the door open and begging her to come back. Staring up into the darkened room, he felt as if hours passed, and when he got up to wander the house, to find some salvation in the life he'd led, he saw Nora out there beyond the windows, engine running, headlights on, but the car still there.

They'd had nothing then; it had felt as if everything had been taken from them. And the truth – had he anyone to tell it to – was that the possibility of success scared him. They'd worked through much of what had come between them, much of the trouble he'd felt that night, watching her out there in the car.

In the years that followed, he knew they'd reached some plateau of understanding, some partnership that kept them there together. He knew also that money could change things, he knew this, knew it could change for the better or change for the worse. Following the small mountain stream through the woods, thinking this over, he found a line of higher ground and led the kid forward, climbing up until they came into thick stands of pine. It wouldn't be long now, not long at all.

The trees gave way to an open meadow, the stream winding down from somewhere high above and nothing but grass to look at, flat and wide in front of them. From somewhere far away he heard the shrill call of a marmot announcing them to the valley. There was no speaking, just the two men leading the horses, and the gray rock faces of mountains looking down on them, sparse clumps of tree and rock climbing like vines along the tip of the ridge.

The kid looked around, taking it all in. 'You always work alone?' he asked, bringing his horse parallel with Hunt's.

'Most of the time,' Hunt said, looking for a place to hide their camp beneath the trees. 'Why do you ask?'

'I can tell.'

'It's not human resources, kid.'

'No, it's not,' the kid said. 'This is a whole different skill set.'

When he came up out of the trees and found a place to set up, Drake laid the .270 out on the ground, took a sleeping pad from his pack, and put it down under him. He checked the sun and then he checked his watch. It was nearly fifteen past five and he hadn't eaten a thing in more than six hours. On the far ridge he could see a hawk or an eagle climbing in the updraft, marmots calling to each other as the predator's shadow passed over the rock. He ate one of his packed sandwiches and brought out his binoculars. 'What did you expect?' he said, feeling the contempt rise up. He looked the map over and guessed at where he was on the ridge. He didn't have anything but his own intuition to tell him if he was right or not.

There was a good view of the valley below and the valley he'd just climbed out of. He looked back down the way he'd come and found the little stream and the patch of mountain bells he'd walked through. From where he was lying he had a good view all the way back to Silver Lake. The clear-cut stood out on the far hills, marked with little strips of gravel and dirt where the logging roads passed. He put the binoculars aside and sighted with the rifle, squinting into the scope and hoping to pick out a nice buck shot.

The light overhead was fading and it left ghostly shadows in the meadows below him, whole fields taken up as the jagged fall of light swept across them. His eyes adjusted. The low sun crept onto the edge of the rifle sight, and he found that by shielding the end of the scope and bracing the rifle on a rock, he could better see into the shadows. He figured he had almost twenty hours before he'd need to be back at the station, enough time to buckle down and wait for something to skitter out of the bush. A whole forest and not a thing but the treetops moving.

T he Sundowner rose past the ridge, then steadied, dipping its wings as the wind hit and the body of the plane shuddered without warning, everything in night shades of gray and blue, the cockpit blacked out, a thin film of green from the display clinging to the faces of the pilot and co-pilot. Well past midnight, the plane had taken off from a private runway near Reclaim, just north of the border, and flown low and tight to the ground for nearly fifty miles. The pilot checked his GPS, signaling the co-pilot to approach the door and prepare the load.

For a brief moment, all the pilot could see was the next ridge rising up and the blue black night ahead. He bent from side to side, looking down, marking the potential and trying to guess at what lay below. He pulled the controls back and made a wide, looping turn through the valley, high-lighting the plane for a moment against the white glaciers farther out. As he came around he could see the flare go up, red and full, sputtering in the cross-wind but climbing all the same.

He eased down on the throttle and signaled the

co-pilot. The cabin filled with the red beacon light marking the package, and the door opened. Wind rushed in for a moment, and there was the brief bounce as the weight left the aircraft and the co-pilot rolled the door closed. The pilot gave one more turn over the valley, watching the load drift with the wind, the parachute like a giant jellyfish hanging there in the air. The silent red blink of the beacon floating down.

Drake woke in the middle of the night for no reason. He lay watching the wind rustle the tent walls. He'd always thought, This is how it will be. This is how I will die, in a tent with the wind all around me and no one to know it happened. He stared at the tent a while longer, listening. There was always the idea of being hunted, the nagging indecision about what lay just out of sight. He had been coming into the woods since he was a boy, but never without that fear that clung to him. Bears, cougars, those things that were bigger than him, that could hunt him down. He lay there listening to his own breathing; then he heard it, far out on the wind rising off the valley. The low humming sound of an engine. He heard the throttle drop an octave and he was sure of it now, the thing was climbing, bending out across the valley like a boomerang.

He unzipped the tent and stood barefoot on the cold grass, watching the valley. He heard it again, the whine of an engine. It could have been a lawn mower for all he knew, but he knew it wasn't, not here. The moon was out, brilliant white in a navy sky. Shrouding all the stars into mere dots of light. He could see it now, a plane, running low to the trees, curving around until its dark shape broke free over the glaciers and dipped back into the blackness.

Wind came and lifted his clothes about him, the sensation so alive on his skin and him so alone, standing there over the dark shadow of the valley below. Hadn't he been expecting this? Wasn't this why he was here, some desperate urge to set things right, to capture some piece of a life left behind? From the valley floor a flare shot up, climbing in a spiral into the air. The plane seemed to veer towards it like a trout in the water, inspecting. He heard the chute catch, the big wallop of air as the thing filled and the package floated free, red blinking lights strapped to the side and a dark cloud hanging over it. The plane ducked once through the valley, then headed north, dipping over the ridge. No lights, nothing. The silent darkness out there and the blinking red of the package floating over the valley.

Hunt led the kid crashing through the underbrush. The chute had caught a crosswind and was pulling for the ridge. They'd left the horses in the meadow and climbed, sometimes on hands and knees, sometimes with their arms spread out in front of them to catch the branches and shrubs that lay before them.

It could happen this way. It wasn't fine art. They could only guess at how it would play out – one chance, and if it didn't play, that was it. There was always the danger it would get hung up. But Hunt was careful, he'd given the pilot fair warning, shot the flare wide so the pilot could circle and get his bearings.

'This is how it is?' the kid asked after they'd slowed and sat, watching the load – big as a metal desk and looking just as heavy – where it lay on the ground in front of them.

'What do you want me to tell you, kid?'

'Cigarette boats and palm trees would be nice,' the kid joked. He was sweating and he moved his sleeve over his forehead to wipe the grit.

'You cut me in on that deal,' Hunt said, the white of his teeth showing. He took a knife from his belt and began to slice the cords away. The parachute caught in the wind, and as he cut, the upright sides pulled over and lay down, revealing the packages beneath, each one of them the size of a fifty-pound bag of flour.

'Shit,' the kid said, 'that's a lot of coke.'

'I'll guarantee they know it down to the gram.'

'I'm just saying.'

'That's fine,' Hunt said. 'Just don't think too much about it. It'll get you all twisted up inside.'

The two of them worked for fifteen minutes, hefting bags the size of pillowcases over their shoulders and bringing them down into the meadow.

'How much you think this is worth?' the kid said. 'Honestly, how much?'

'Is there a reason you're asking?'

'No reason. Just curiosity.'

'I wouldn't worry about a thing like that. Don't worry about it. We'll be paid enough. You don't want all the trouble a thing like this can bring.'

'You've never thought—'

'Never.'

'What is it you do for a living again?'

'You're looking at it.'

'And it's never crossed your mind.'

'Not once. Like I said, I can't do much with a history like mine. But I can do a little, and what little I have I'm happy to hold on to.'

'Two horses and one busted-up life.'

'Not everyone that plays the lottery wins. You understand me, kid?'

'Yeah, I get you. But it's like putting the winning ticket in my hand and asking me not to cash it in.'

'Are we going to have a problem here?'

'No problem, man. I'm just saying. Just saying is all.'

D rake took the scree chute in bounds, holding the .270 by the stock and letting his thighs take his weight. The rocks scattered out in front of him, clattered off each other and followed him down. What did you expect? he thought. So what if they hear me, they're probably half-gone as it is. It's probably better that way.

He paused to watch the thing in the air. The package pulled out over the forest and hung there for a moment. He didn't wait to see what it would do; he was already running. It was a long ways. He figured he'd dropped a thousand feet already and he still had another five hundred or so before he reached the bottom. He stopped again, listened, giving the forest a long stare. He didn't know what he would find.

He felt foolish, the feeling coming over him as fast as anything. Someone else could be here, someone else could do this. Why him, a guy on his day off? But he knew he couldn't let that sit, and he headed off through the forest at a dead run, anticipating the dips in the damp ground before they came.

After they'd loaded the bags onto the horses, Hunt went through, tightening the straps. The kid had walked off a ways, and he stood in the meadow rubbing his arms and looking up at the glacier. When he came back he was smiling. 'What now?' he said.

Hunt remembered being a kid once, years ago, before he went away. So much of his life seemed to be divided by the time he'd lost, as if a wall had been built during those ten years. He could remember waiting at home with his mother, a promise his father had made to take him to the races, and just waiting for his return, as if it was the only thing that mattered, though Hunt knew now that it wasn't.

The choices he'd made had brought him here. He could look back on them now, rationalize them, yet he still felt that dim excitement of possibility growing inside him like an old piece of charred wood, burned long ago and pushed aside, taking on a miraculous light.

Hunt watched the edge of the forest. There was no time for the kid's excitement, or his own, no time to stop or dream or hope for things that might or might not turn out. The lacquered moonlight coated their faces, everything slate blue, the shimmer of the light catching on the bridles. He hated this part of it. Better to be done with it than wait around here. He twisted the reins over his hand and told the kid to come on.

Hunt had never adjusted to the night forest. Better to be out of it, he thought. Better to be home in bed. A memory came to him of Nora, the cut of her nightgown as she lay in bed, her back turned and the light coming in through the blinds. Better to be home, he thought. Better to be far away from here.

Hunt and the kid walked on a ways, leading the horses and parting the grass in front of them. There was no reason to be worried. No reason at all.

When Drake broke out into the meadow, he could see the two men at the far side, leading horses. He dropped to one knee, felt the damp of the dew-covered grass come through the fabric of his pants and rise onto his thigh. Through the scope the men were nearly straight on, their backs turned, facing away from him, their horses loaded with large bags. Drake couldn't tell what was in them, but he could guess.

As he looked on, he talked to himself: 'Don't move. Don't make a fool mistake and get yourself shot.' He couldn't see any weapons on the men, but he knew that didn't mean there weren't any.

With his hand in the soft earth, he pushed himself up and circled into the forest, following the edge of the trees around until he was almost parallel to the men. He took his steps carefully, toe to heel, slipping from tree to tree. He could hear the draw of the horses' lungs, the sound of the grass parting and then coming back together. He had the gun in his hands, held close with the barrel pointed upward and the butt at his belt. He took a big breath, he pulled in something gigantic, pressure and fear, and he felt it there in his lungs aching to get out.

How many times had he pictured himself here, gun drawn, taking sight along the barrel? He couldn't say. Didn't even know if he could go through with it. His father had been the one to show him how to shoot a gun, ten years old, elbows raised over the alder fence out back of their property, his father in the old cop browns of the department. Four apples set there amid the grass. 'Careful now,' his father had said. 'Take your time, you may only get one chance.'

He stepped from beneath the shadow of the trees and leveled the rifle. There was no plan. His father slipped back into memory. No one to tell him this was how it was done or to tell him otherwise. The silver light of the moon was on him, and he stood there with the rifle leveled and the two men looking at him, not knowing what to make of him.

One of the men began to speak, the older, a voice rough and bumpy as cobblestones. With his hand Drake shushed him. Told him to shut up, told him to just be quiet. Drake was saying a million different things, identifying himself and holding the rifle in his hands and yelling and not knowing anything. Just making it up as he went along. He kept his hand on the rifle and watched the steam break from the nostrils of the horses, everybody just staring at each other, waiting for what came next.

Hunt was the first to make the assumption. There was a good two hundred feet between him and the cop, and he guessed the man could make a nice shot. Could hollow out his head with that .270, but he wouldn't. Hunt wasn't going back to jail. It was reckless and he knew it. He was shivering all over, and he could feel his muscles tightening up and a million other things beginning to go wrong. But he had made his mind up a long while ago, when it had all started to happen for him, and Eddie had come to him and given him the job, which had been his ever since: he didn't intend to go back to jail.

The deputy could see what was happening and Hunt knew it. Let him see it. They were in an open meadow, with the forest only a few steps off. Things were dark in the forest, and Hunt could see he might make it if he could get in there, the deputy just standing in the meadow, holding the rifle on him and yelling. Hunt didn't know what to make of it. It didn't make much sense. He wasn't listening and the kid was starting to back away and it was all going to shit.

With one quick movement, Hunt was behind the horse and had the buckle undone, the weight of the drugs carrying the saddle off. The man was yelling, but Hunt was yelling, too, not knowing what to say, but telling the kid all the while what to do. The kid stood there like some stupid scarecrow, stuffed up with straw and hay and not real guts like he should have been. Simply dumbfounded. Hunt was pulling on the reins, pulling the horse down by its mouth, leading it down until it was kneeling there in the grass. The kid was fumbling with the strap under the belly of his horse, the deputy coming on in a straight line across the field, the rifle held out in front of him. He was yelling something the kid couldn't understand, and Hunt was rising up on the back of the horse, his gloved hands gripping the mane and the horse surging forward through the meadow.

There was a shot, and Hunt ducked, nearly falling from the horse. The kid's horse startled and bucked back, and the kid stepped away, watching the hooves catch the air. Then he turned and ran head-down across the field, trying to keep the horse between him and the rifle. He ran wildly, not looking, keeping his head planted and his feet going. The meadow raced away under him, but he didn't have any true plan except escape, and even that seemed a tough decision.

D rake watched the kid go, weaving through the grass in an absurd fashion. It seemed to Drake that he was running a football pattern, juking left, then faking right. Drake raised the rifle and fired into the night. He listened as the echo caught high up in the valley and bounced back to him. 'I don't have a problem shooting you in the back,' he yelled, cradling the rifle again and sighting the kid. 'Stop, goddamn it!' He shucked the shell casing and loaded another. The shot hit the meadow in front of the kid, and a cloud of dust bounced up like a little atomic explosion, pale and blue in the moonlight. The kid stopped, raised his hands, and waited. Drake shucked another shell casing and pushed the bolt forward.

He didn't say anything when he got to the kid. What was there to say? No words could help him. The adrenaline was beginning to fade and he could feel his arms go loose and ropy, the shudders coming over him. One smuggler shy of a hole in one. He was sure the kid could hear his feet in the grass, the slow crunch as he stepped forward and bent the stalks. Somewhere out there, riding hard, was the other man, and Drake had all the best intentions of catching up to him.

With the butt of the rifle he struck the kid in the back of the head and knocked him unconscious. It was a clean shot, and he didn't think the kid saw it coming. Drake was sorry the minute he did it. But he couldn't take it back and he didn't think he would even if he could. He checked the kid's pulse, then used the knife from his belt to cut two strips from his shirt to tie the kid's hands and legs. He felt around in the kid's pockets for a wallet but didn't find one. The horse was still standing nearby and he walked the short distance over to it and cut the packages away.

The horse shied and watched him out of the corner of its eye but didn't present any trouble when he swung his leg over and gave it a nudge with his heels. The strap of the .270 across his chest, he kicked the horse again and felt the power of the animal take him. From the way the other man had handled himself, he'd thought him a very good rider. And Drake himself knew he couldn't compete with that. There was just no way. He kicked the horse and led it up onto the ridge overlooking the surrounding valleys and waited, watching the clearings and listening for any sound.

The sun rose at the edge of the Cascades and the pink light was everywhere. He turned to look back down into the meadow and saw the kid lying there and the big white packages that looked like pillows nearby.

Hunt pushed hard on the horse, his fingers wrapped up in the mane and holding tight. He kicked the horse, but there was no real control; he just let the girl go and take him away. It was impossible to ride bareback with any real control. If he'd practiced it, maybe, but he hadn't and he couldn't spare the thought now. He'd heard three shots, one he expected was for him, the other two for the kid. For a moment he'd pulled the horse around and listened to the echo of the second shot, wondering if it would make any real difference to turn back. The horse swayed and he could feel the big muscles at the top of the forelegs as they shifted. 'Please let him get away,' he was saying. 'Please let him.'

He heard the next shot three seconds later and he figured it would be the last. If the kid wasn't dead he was in a whole shitload of trouble, and Hunt didn't want to be anywhere near it when it hit. He kicked the horse and pointed her in a general downhill direction.

When he came out of the trees and followed along by the side of a river, his arms ached from pushing away tree boughs. His gloves and sleeves were covered in sap. He paused and looked up the cut of the river, trying to find his bearings. The map had been in the saddle pocket, along with the GPS, and he didn't have any true reasoning to tell him where he was going. There was a map in the truck and he could figure his way off this mountain by sticking to the logging roads.

He wanted to think it had been a fluke, but it probably wasn't. The man had said he was law, he'd said a whole lot of things, but Hunt couldn't have told a soul what they were, at least not in any reasonable order. There was a primal drone going in his ears and it wouldn't have made sense no matter what the man had said. One thing had, and it was to get away, because he knew he wasn't going back, not now, not ever, and it was the one thing he was sure of.

By using his watch and sighting the glow from the rising sun, he could estimate a rough grid of his position. He didn't know what the river was called, though he thought he remembered it from the map. The truck and trailer lay roughly in a southerly direction, near the Silver Lake area, and he thought it best to stay hidden, riding the long way and avoiding the ridges. Once he reached the truck it would be a three-hour drive into Seattle, and he thought he could make that, he thought it wouldn't be a problem. The problem was getting off the mountain before the deputy did. If the deputy had a radio, Hunt imagined a helicopter would be called in, but he didn't think the man did. He didn't think the man even expected a day like this, showing up half-dressed and leveling the rifle on them.

The bullet caught the horse below the ear. Blood everywhere. The horse was stunned for a moment, teetering over some unseen abyss, her front legs buckling beneath her. With only time enough to swing free and push himself clear, Hunt was on his feet and running before he heard the next shot. It was a good shot or a bad shot, Hunt couldn't tell. Either the man had meant to hit him, or he'd meant to hit the horse; perhaps he'd just meant to buck the horse and hoped Hunt would fall. It was all unclear and Hunt kept running. He thought the shot had come from the far ridge, but he couldn't be sure. It seemed by the echo of the gun that the shot had come from a distance, but everything was happening outside the boundaries of time.

He had been riding in the dry cut of the river, where the water flowed in the spring and left loamy soil behind. A stand of young cottonwood and ash sat before him and he ran for that. Another bullet hit and he heard the earth crack and the bullet go in. Again, the sound didn't reach him for a second or more. He ducked in behind the trees and leaned back on the bank, hoping his legs and feet were covered. He looked back at his horse and saw how the sand had gone black there. The horse did not move and he looked away.

The world seemed to have gone volatile and unpredictable, the catalyst of a chemical reaction he couldn't stop. The horse lay there, still as a rock, blood seeping from a hole drilled clean through her head. He closed his eyes, tried to put the image out of his mind, warm morning sun on his eyelids, the red glow of light beyond. Close by, water rushed over river stones, the buzz of an insect gliding through the air. Open your eyes, he thought, keep moving. Bright sunshine everywhere. What was he doing, what was he doing here?

He tried to remember what the range was on a rifle like that. Even at a run he'd have no chance if the deputy was riding the other horse. Hunt looked back to where the horse lay and swore under his breath, cursed himself and didn't stop for the better part of a minute.

Somewhere in that long-ago time, back when he'd just been a man living in a prison cell, he'd realized there was no going back, as much as he'd wanted it all to disappear, for his life just to start over, like pushing a reset button. Life wouldn't give him that pleasure. He'd gone through a door that only swung one way. He thought about this now, held up under the stretch of cottonwood and ash branches, a bank of earth his only protection. He had to keep going.

The river ran wide and flat and he guessed the depth to be about three feet at its maximum. He was running for it before he knew what he was doing. He knew it flowed down toward Silver Lake, close enough to the truck. The cold hit him in his ankles first and sunk into his boots. The rocks were slippery, and he fell, catching himself with his hand and going forward. The water was up to his shins and it didn't seem to be growing deeper. He went on, keeping himself low to the river's surface, his hands outstretched and the water shooting out in front of him as he ran.

Deputy Bobby Drake sat for a long time looking down from the ridge, long enough for the chill of the mountains to sink beneath his clothes, long enough for it to get beneath his skin. He lowered his head and pressed his forehead to the wooden stock of the .270, feeling the cold hardness of the rifle on his temple, the blood in his veins calming, his pulse steadying. For a while, after it was done, he just lay there, looking down at the valley. The man was gone now, escaped. Fir and hemlock stretched as far as he could see, the dull red brown of trees burning up with the season. The dead horse lay down there in the river-bed, the other was waiting close by, waiting to take him back to the kid and the drugs, and Drake had no real idea what he would do.

He hadn't asked for this life. He hadn't asked for any of this. It was given. He looked out on the forest below, the auburn haze of the light rising in the east and all of it starting anew once again. He'd accepted a kind of guilt for what his father had done; he knew that, knew he had to earn the name back, earn it back for himself and for his father.

He ran the scope along the river but saw nothing. Just the pale blue sheen of the river and the sun playing along as the water bumped on past. He thought about how something like this might change his life. How it already had, his father put away in prison, Drake pulled out of school to come home and tend to things. He'd thought he'd known who he was then, back in college, away from this place, away from his father. But he didn't really know, not really. This would change a few things, he thought, it would surely do that.

PART II

BY SEA

G rady slipped off one glove, then the other. The gloves, each one of them a clear latex, were covered in a pink sheen. Using a white dish towel to wipe his pale hands, he turned to find the noise. His phone sat vibrating on the stainless steel prep table. He picked it up and checked the display. Five a.m. He'd been working with knives, and in front of him sat the half-dissected carcass of a pig, its intestines ripped out, the heart and liver saved, the kidneys sitting in a loose container to his right. The whole thing open to him, the ribs gaping, and the cold smell of a table cleaned with bleach and water. With the gloves off, he ran a hand through his hair and pulled it back away from his face. He was younger than he looked, his hair almost blond and his sleep-starved eyes red as hazard signs. It was still early in the morning, earlier than most expected to be out of bed, and he'd picked the pig up at the market while the trucks were still rolling in with cartons of milk, eggs, fresh-baked breads, and produce. In the next hour, he'd break the body down piece by

49

piece, using a hacksaw he'd bought at the local hardware store.

He answered, saying his full name: 'Grady Fisher.' Around his neck he wore a white apron, soiled with his own bloody handprints. 'Yes, sir, I know Phil Hunt,' he said. 'He was getting out of Monroe as I was going in. We passed ways.' Grady picked up one of the knives and checked the tip. 'Yes, I don't think that would be a problem. I think that would suit me fine. I can pick the package up at the airport, then have it delivered before I go to see Hunt. It shouldn't be a problem. Yes, sir, it would be my usual rate, plus expenses. Yes, I understand.' The whole conversation had taken less than a minute.

Wherever Grady went, he carried with him his case of knives. Over the years he'd added to it as new situations presented themselves. If the job allowed, he preferred using knives, just as he preferred to see the face of the animal he was butchering. He worked a few odd jobs as a prep cook when he found the time, sectioning out meat, practicing his work, seeing what he could do. This bloodlust seemed to make sense to him. He felt a certain intimacy for the thing. A wonder that he thought had disappeared with his childhood. Disappeared with his time in Monroe, prison shrinks, and medication. But in recent years he had started to feel that wonder again, explore it, and enjoy it.

He believed truly and gave himself completely

to the expression 'The eyes are the windows to the soul.' He wanted to see those eyes, he wanted to step close and feel the life of that other. And he hoped that one day it would come down to that, face to face with his eyes open. He'd cut the head of the pig off using the hacksaw, and it sat looking back at him on the table, the eyes cold and dark as open jelly jars.

When he was finished he washed the knives one at a time. Those that saw him work might have used the word 'meticulous'; others may not have had the chance to say anything at all. He'd been using a carving knife for the skin, a small three-and-a-half-inch boning knife, and a utility knife that was slightly longer. He was aware at all times that pigs were not as delicate as the human body, but they came close, and they were good practice for the real thing.

With care, he opened the bag and found the button clasp for each of the knives. Afterward, he cleaned the sinew from the hacksaw, then began to prepare the table once again.

Hunt paced the living room, looking out through the big framed window onto his lawn, where he could see the pines farther out. He still wore his boots, double-laced around his ankles. They had almost drowned him. But then, he thought, so had the river.

He'd never made good money. There was always the hope, but it had never come, not in the past twenty years. It was always one job away, always just beyond his reach. And though he thought often about it, money was not his main concern. His life had been scarred by one remarkable event, remarkable not in a way that he was proud of, but rather in a way he could, even after all the time that had passed, only half believe – that he had shot a man once in a bait shop, for a sum as small as forty dollars, killed him with a spray of buckshot.

He'd done time for that, ten years. Every bit of it he'd wished he could take back. From the time he'd got out, twenty years ago, to the present day, pacing his living room, thinking how life had led him here to this moment, his mind going a million different places, time and time again coming back to the same conclusion – that it was his fault life hadn't turned out different.

He walked circles, keeping his eyes on the gravel drive and beyond, past the trees to the black asphalt of the road. His wife, Nora, came to the living room door to look him over. She was a tall, thin thing with overdrawn eyes and hair curled out like cotton candy. Hunt knew that their life with horses had changed her, five foot six with thin, muscular legs and strong, callused hands. He could see their life together in her face, just as he could see his own in the mirror, both of them lean in the cheekbones, their bodies defined by straight edges and bone-sharp points extending from their elbows down to their knees. Hard work had stripped the beauty from her too soon, but then, looking at her now, there was a different sort of beauty after all these years. He loved her, and when she just stood there looking at him, he smiled, walked the five or so steps from where he had been standing near the window, and gave her a playful kiss beneath her chin. 'Don't worry,' he said, his voice as rough as river rapids. 'We'll get this all straightened out with Eddie.' She gave him a doubtful look, like he was a misbehaving child who kept making promises he couldn't keep.

'I worry,' she said, 'but it's what I do and you can't help that.'

'No,' he said. 'Though I wish I could.'

Nora stood looking at him a moment longer.

Maybe just to look him over. Maybe just to know if everything would be okay. She had felt his clothes when he came in, worn and crusted with dirt, so stiff and starched with mud, Hunt knew they felt as if they'd been washed in a bog, then hung from tree limbs to dry. He'd smelled it all the way home, jeans and shirt smoky with the odor of the forest, lichen and moss and something else, something he knew she hadn't smelled in years, something that he could see troubled her but that Hunt knew was fear.

His eyes gave the place a quick once-over while she tried to settle him. 'I'm going to trust you,' she said. 'I'm going to trust you and I don't want you to tell me different.'

'Don't worry,' he said again. 'Eddie's going to come by and we're going to work this out.'

Nora stared at him a second longer. He could see she was unsure of herself, had no idea what to do or how to react. He'd never been the kind to stare out the window before. Always sure of himself, always in control. 'I'll put some coffee on,' she said.

After she'd gone, Hunt went back to the window. When he straightened he could feel the cold metal of the Browning touch his back, the muzzle wedged between his underwear and his jeans. It made him shiver, and briefly he had a vision of himself and Nora running, hands clasped tight, into an unknown darkness.

'I didn't say I guaranteed it,' Eddie said. He sat there alone with his phone pressed to his face. The Lincoln rested on the side of the road, midway to Hunt's place, flashers on. The only things coming down the road were container trucks and flatbeds. 'I've worked with these guys for twenty years now. I didn't say I'd guarantee it, but I trust them. It was some hero deputy. No. I wish I could tell you that, but I can't. We can work something out. Yes, I remember. No, I don't think that's necessary. It's a good crew. There must be something that can be done.' His voice lowered. 'Yes, I understand. I'll call back later.'

Eddie threw the phone and it bounced off the windshield. He pressed his palms to his eyes before he even heard the phone fall and clatter on the plastic dash. His breaths came one at a time, filling his cheeks, then bursting out. His hands were still at his eyes, his fingers stretching up into his hair. He knew what would happen now. This had all been explained to him. But twenty years had made him confident. Made him think it wouldn't happen this way. That it couldn't.

The lawyer's voice had been very clear. Eddie didn't think the man was on the level. Probably cooled out on some real expensive drugs. Some laboratory stuff that didn't let him feel. Made him think of people the way he did. Nothing made sense, and maybe Eddie had been here his whole life, stuck in the middle, because he'd tried to make sense of money and friendship and a million other things that were never meant to be.

There were other things to think of now, other things he could do. He looked at the clock on the dash and figured the time. Hunt had called nearly two hours before. He'd be expecting him, waiting for him, angry and alone, and it was how it would have to be. Hunt would have to get used to that. Would have to understand he couldn't go back to the life he'd led, to what he'd built.

Around noon, Hunt saw Eddie take the turn off the main drive and pull down into the gravel. Hunt had taken to sitting in the big red chair, the back faced into the corner so that he could see the road. Sometime during the morning, while he was cursing Eddie and calling him on his cell phone, he'd started a fire in the fireplace. The shivers had come over him again and it was all he could do to light the fire and kneel next to it with his big, clay-colored hands held out.

He watched Eddie turn down off the main road, the gravel popping beneath his tires. He drove a big Lincoln, one of the new ones meant to look like a Cadillac. Hunt watched him for a moment, then went into the kitchen, where Nora was standing over the sink looking out the windows. She was dressed for the house in a favorite pair of faded jeans and an old oversize undershirt that hung loose on her slender frame. 'Can you give him a wave when he gets out?' Hunt said, touching the grip of the Browning and trying to look like he was merely adjusting the fold of his belt. 'I'm going to go out the back for a moment.'

Nora gave him a worried look but didn't say anything.

'If you can, let him in through the garage and bring him in the side door here.'

They owned five acres south of Seattle on the outskirts of a place called Auburn. When they were young they'd taken out loans to build stables, and they raised and boarded horses on the back acre of their property. On Sunday nights they could see the big lights from the horse races and hear the cheers coming off the crowd as the horses neared the finish. Mostly, though, it was cow pastures and scrap lots filled with old car parts, refrigerators, and stacked tires. The fecal smell of dairy animals – mud and cow droppings always the first thing. Most days he didn't even smell it. Either he'd gotten used to it or the wind was blowing from the north and carrying the scent south toward Tacoma. A light rain had fallen the night before and he could smell the scents coming off the cows, smell them in the grass and on the trees, coating everything.

He took the back steps quickly, in a hurry to get down onto the lawn, but then turned around, remembering the spring on the screen door and the clapping aluminum sound it would make. From where he stood holding the door, he could hear cars passing on the highway next to the horse track, the bump and gurgle of a small irrigation stream behind the house. Most of their property was wooded, but a good acre of it – around the house, where they had a small pasture set up for the horses – was open, and he could see clearly into the birch and pine that surrounded his house.

Hunt and Eddie had met twenty years before when Eddie had come into the bar where Hunt was drinking, looking for a junkie named Stone. Hunt ran the numbers on the local horse races, and though he made good picks, his drinking got in the way of his profits and he'd reached the point where he was so broke he felt there were bottomless holes in his pockets. 'If you find him,' Hunt had said, feeling a little drunk from a string of shot glasses laid out in front of him, 'tell him he owes me twenty dollars.'

'He owes me a lot more than that,' Eddie said, looking down the bar toward Hunt. 'Give you a percentage if you can show me where he lives.'

Hunt knew where Stone lived. But he didn't know Eddie. 'How much?'

'Enough.'

'Isn't that always the answer,' Hunt said, sliding off the barstool and giving Eddie a smile.

'Tell you what,' Eddie said. 'If you can show me where he lives, you'll make yourself a lot more than twenty.'

It took them ten minutes to drive from the bar to the house where Stone lived. Late summer, the clouds braided up and flat as a rug across the sky above. No wind, and the stillness of the summer heat all around them. Eddie parked the car in an alley around back. 'If he tries to come through

59

here,' Eddie said, making things sound as simple as possible, 'just stop him.'

Hunt gave Eddie a doubting look. 'With what?'

'You want your twenty bucks, right? Figure it out.'

Eddie got out and closed the door with his hip. Hunt still remembered the smell of that back alley. Acrid smell of food, Dumpsters stuffed up with furniture and half-eaten pizza crusts, produce boxes from the nearby store lining the alley, their waxen bottoms colored in vegetal funk.

A minute passed and then Stone appeared, rounding the Dumpster at a full run with Eddie close behind him. Hunt sat in Eddie's passenger seat, still dazed from the bar – not expecting any of it. Hunt didn't have any clear idea what to do, Stone running straight at him. Hunt opened the door and meant to tackle Stone, but Stone, with his head turned back toward Eddie, wasn't looking and ran straight into the open car door. The clap of Stone's body as it bounced, then hit the ground. Hunt stood there looking down. Eddie drew up, breathing hard. Stone was laid out on the stained cement alleyway, looking up at the two of them. 'Fuck, man. Dealers and bookies unite,' Stone muttered.

Eddie kicked Stone twice in the stomach, hard enough that Hunt heard the air burst from the man's lips. With Stone doubled up on the cement, Eddie reached down and took Stone's wallet from him, along with a bag Hunt recognized as heroin.

'Here's your twenty,' Eddie said, taking a weathered bill from the wallet and giving it to Hunt. 'What did we say for a percentage?'

Hunt looked down at the man crumpled up at their feet. 'We didn't,' Hunt said.

Eddie took a wad of bills from his pocket and thumbed two hundred out and then replaced the wad in his pocket. 'Thirty percent sounds right to me.' He handed the two bills to Hunt.

Over the past twenty years they'd both gone on to bigger and better things, Hunt's standard 30 percent paying for his first date with Nora, a down payment on his house and property, and even a few young horses they had jokingly called their kids after they found out they couldn't have children. Nothing in his life had ever arisen that would make him think Eddie wasn't playing straight with him. There was no reason Hunt could think of to be worried about his welfare. Eddie had never had a reason to take his frustrations out on him. They were friends after years of doing business together, backyard barbecues, horse races, and bets. Hunt trusted Eddie because there was no other option and because Eddie had always played straight with him. Hunt could see how everything might change. He'd never messed up this bad, never screwed up, never been in the position Stone had found himself in, laid out and helpless, turtled on his backside in some foul alley waiting to see what would happen next.

Now, Hunt heard the electric whir of his garage

door opening – Nora letting Eddie into the garage. As Hunt went around the house, he was careful to duck his head below the frame of the garage window, taking his steps with caution so as not to upset the small line of garden pebbles they'd put in around the foundation for drainage. He felt for the Browning and brought it out, holding it in front of him as he went along the length of the garage. He'd never planned to hold a gun again in his life. But here he was, holding one, waiting for his friend, Eddie Vasquez, to duck beneath the garage door and walk into his house.

The garage motor was still going when Hunt put the gun up against Eddie's back. Eddie didn't say anything, and Nora, standing in the light of the side door, raised a hand to her mouth as if to quiet a scream.

'Be calm,' Eddie said, his voice as cool and relaxed as always.

If Hunt had played the part all the way through, he might have knocked Eddie right over with the butt of the gun. But it wasn't in the plan, none of it was, he was making it all up as he went. For all that had happened he had no reason not to trust Eddie. A lot of money was involved, a whole shitload of powder, and it didn't seem to make the most sense to piss anyone off more than he already had.

'Didn't figure you for the gun type,' Eddie said. They were standing there in the garage. The door settled down on its motor, and besides the dull rush of cars on the highway a half mile off, it was quiet.

'Sorry about this, Eddie,' Hunt said, looking up at his wife, Nora looking back at him, completely horrified.

'Hunt,' Eddie said, a note of caution entering his voice. 'No one knows about what happened up there. For all they know, it was just the kid. I can blame it all on the kid and that's how it will turn out.'

'The kid should never have been there,' Hunt said.

'Two hundred kilos is a lot for one man to pack out.'

'I could have done it with an extra horse. No sense in getting the kid involved.'

'He's involved now, isn't he? Just be glad it wasn't you they got their hands on.'

'What now?' Hunt asked.

'You need to relax is "what now."' Eddie lowered his hands. 'Nothing is registered under your name, cell phone, truck, everything under a different name. Let's all go inside, you can put the gun away. We'll figure this out.'

Nora poured the coffee and stood leaning with her hip against the counter, looking the two men over. She had begun to say something and then stopped. If he ever made it out of this, there would be questions; Hunt knew that, but he couldn't do anything about it now, just clean it off and hope it didn't stink.

'Look, Hunt,' Eddie was saying. 'It was dark. No one can say who you were, wearing that hat and riding like you do. It was an aerial drop twenty miles this side of the border. Unless you're out there taking Polaroids and tacking them up to the trees, you should be fine.'

'There's going to be a lot of pissed-off people when you don't deliver,' Hunt said.

'You let me worry about that.'

'Eddie, I'm not trying to be difficult about this, but the kid knows who I am and it's not going to take him long to figure out he's got chips on the table.'

'We all have chips on the table,' Eddie said, taking a draw from his coffee.

The head DEA agent, Driscoll, sat tapping his card on the metal table, tapping lengthwise, then turning the card and tapping it again. He'd been doing it at a near-steady pace for more than an hour. When Drake came in, it was the second time they'd met that day. Just the two of them in the room, Driscoll with his jacket off and tie loosened, sitting there with a stack of paper laid out before him. A man with the posture and thick cut of an athlete, now slumping into his later years, the agent ran a hand through his mustache and off his chin, then leaned back in the chair and looked up. To Drake the motion seemed practiced, almost polite, like the gesture of a lion with a kind of social conscience, cleaning blood from its fur, readying itself for the next kill. 'I've just finished looking through your report,' he said after Drake had taken a seat in the chair across the table from the agent. 'There isn't anything in here about you braining the kid with the dull end of your rifle.'

Drake didn't say anything. The card kept tapping on the table, steady as a metronome. Driscoll's eyes on him, a small, sickly smile lingering at his lips.

'Kids can make up the damnedest stories,' Drake said.

'Yes, they can,' the agent said, giving the card a final tap on the table, then slipping it across to Drake. They were in the federal building in downtown Seattle. From the freeway, Drake had seen the covered bridge, seven stories up, where the prisoners crossed from cell to courthouse without touching the street or coming into contact with the civilized world. 'Is there anything you'd like to add?'

'I wrote it all down as it happened.'

Driscoll looked away, and when he looked back he said, 'Deputy Drake, the truth is that the paper is going to be running a story on this tomorrow.'

'A story on what?'

'Wasn't there a Sheriff Drake up in Silver Lake convicted of smuggling?'

Drake didn't say anything.

Driscoll leaned forward in his chair and looked across the table at Drake. 'I can't guarantee they're going to keep something like that out of the article.'

'My father?'

'I don't know how they heard about all this, but I got them to hold off on running it at least for a day.'

'Thanks,' Drake said. 'What does this mean now?'

'It means you better start answering questions.'

'That was ten years ago. What does the past have to do with any of this?'

'Some would say the past has everything to do with what happens today,' Driscoll said. 'What do you think?'

Drake put his hands up on the table and spread his fingers. Flat, cold, metal. He could feel something inside him working loose. Shame? Fear? He didn't know. He wanted to get up, wanted to leave, but there was nowhere he could go. He'd got himself into this mess, and every way he looked at it he couldn't get himself out.

'You the son who used to play Division One?'

'The paper tell you that when they called?'

'That's what I heard.'

'Had to move back after my father went away.'

'What did you play?'

'Point guard.'

'You were supposed to be some big star, weren't you?'

'Basketball and my father were almost ten years ago.'

'And now you're a deputy up there? Would have thought you'd be coaching or something.'

'Doesn't pay as much as the state.'

'Well, it won't make you rich.'

'No, but I guess that's what my father thought, too.' Drake met Driscoll's eyes for a moment, then looked away.

'Must be hard to be the son and deputy of the

guy who made the sheriff's department famous up there.'

'Like I said, it was before my time.'

Driscoll looked across the table at him. He straightened up in his seat and leaned forward. 'You playing on the right side here?'

'I'm playing on your side, if that's what you're asking.'

Driscoll apologized. 'I can't make much sense of it,' he said. 'I don't know a lot of people who would go up into those mountains. What were you doing there?'

'My job.'

'Sounds like you were doing your father's as well.'

'It was my father's. It's not his job anymore, it's mine.'

'Sorry,' Driscoll said. He did a little wave with his hand, like he was shooing away an odd thought. 'I had to ask.'

'It's fine. I know who my father was and I know who I am. We're not the same.'

'I'd guess you'll never be elected sheriff.'

'No? People can surprise you. There's a few forgiving hearts out there.'

The agent took a moment to thumb the report. 'I can't say if the story running tomorrow in the paper is going to be positive. You might want to start thinking about that.' Driscoll looked through the files in front of him, and when he looked back he said, 'This is pretty big.'

'I realize that.'

'This is really going to piss a few people off. I'm just telling you because I think you should be ready. The people you stopped are not going to take this lightly. About now, their only concern is how to make this all go away. That means silencing those who try to get in their way. The story running tomorrow will have your name in it. Are you ready for that?'

'I suppose I should have thought about that at the time, but I didn't and I don't think I'd have changed the outcome.'

'Taking in the two of them would have been nice.'

'Yes, it would have.'

'Is there anything you can tell me about the second man that could help out my team?'

'There's not much to tell.' Drake knew he wasn't being helpful. Wasn't doing his best. Driscoll was looking for answers and Drake had none to give. All of it was too close to him already. He could almost feel his father's presence, sitting there in the room ten years before.

'You are the only one, besides the kid, who knows anything about this man.'

Drake tried to draw the man's face from memory. The only image he could find was of his father, fifteen years ago, riding slow up a game trail in the West Cascades. His father turning in his saddle to look back at him, face shadowed, church light filtering down through a patchwork of green forest branches, blue and green as stained glass, yellow slanted columns of sunlight, dusted through with tree pollen, floating, ghostlike. 'I'm afraid what I do know is not much,' he finally said.

'Is there anything to add about the second man that I may have skipped over in the report?'

'I'd prefer not to speculate.'

'But if you did.'

'If I did, I would say he was a very fine horseman.'

'Yes,' the agent said. 'I had guessed at that from the report.' The agent waited for Drake to speak on the subject, and when he didn't, Driscoll continued. 'I'm at a loss. I wonder if you might be more familiar with this sort of thing. It's not often we come across something of this caliber. Hippies with backpacks are one thing, but aerial drops and horsemen are something quite different.'

'I'm not the most familiar with this sort of thing either.'

Driscoll gave him a doubting look. 'Where did you learn to ride?'

'My father had a few horses when I was a kid. He would take me into the mountains for rides when he could.'

'How long ago was that?'

'A little over ten years ago.'

'Your father still keep horses?'

'Not where he is.'

'Sorry.'

'You weren't the one to take him,' Drake said. Then, after a moment, he said, 'Were you?'

Driscoll smiled, he looked down at the table,

and when he looked back up he said, 'Riding's not so common these days, is it?'

'Not as common as it used to be.'

'Why would you say that?'

'They're expensive animals, not as utilitarian as they were before.'

'No, I suppose not. How much would you say it is to board a horse?'

'These days it can be expensive. Not something I could afford.'

The agent picked up the report and straightened it on the table. He brought up a leather case and put the report away. 'If you were the second man, what would you do?'

'I don't know anything about that.'

'Speculate.'

'I suppose I would try to get as far away as I could from what was known.'

'This man must work with horses fairly regularly.'

'Yes, I would say he does.'

'I don't mean to pry, but I'd like to ask you something personal. Would that be all right?'

'Haven't you been all through my personal life as it is?' Drake watched the agent and tried to see how he took it. The agent sat there across the table, lips slightly parted, question waiting on the cusp. Then Drake said, 'Does it have bearing on the case?'

'In a sort of fractured sense it does.'

'Why do you say "fractured"?'

'The cracks leading off from the point of impact.'

'I see.'

'Don't take this the wrong way, Deputy. Do you have a wife?'

'I wear the ring.'

'Any children?'

'Not yet.'

'In cases like this, it is common that people go missing before they appear in court. Naturally, we are very concerned about this.'

'Naturally.'

'By this time tomorrow afternoon the paper will have the story out and I want you to be ready.'

'We'll be fine. It's not the first time I've been through something like this.'

'Yes,' Driscoll said, 'that's true. But still, we'd like it if you and your wife would come down to the city for a few days. On us, of course.'

'You make it sound almost like a threat,' Drake said.

'No, Drake, we are certainly not the threatening ones.'

Eddie clapped the phone closed and put it down on the table. He was staring at Hunt.

'I know that look,' Hunt said. The pistol lay in front of him on the table and for a moment Eddie looked at it. Then he looked away.

'I'm not going to tell you it's going to be okay. I think you know that.'

Hunt shifted his eyes over to Nora, who was standing at the window looking out.

'What is it, Eddie?' Nora asked, not turning from the window. 'What is it that he'll have to do?'

'It's not so simple,' Eddie said.

'I'm sorry about this, Eddie,' Hunt said. 'I wish there was a better thing I could say. But I don't think it would make a difference.'

'It's strange how things turn out sometimes.'

'Yes, it is, Eddie.'

Nora came over to the table and sat down. A loose hair drifted into her eyes and she tucked it up. 'There must be something that can be done.'

Eddie looked at Hunt. 'They'd like for you to make a sort of donation.'

'Donation?'

'Yes, of your time.'

'Isn't that what I just did? You don't see me crying because I didn't get paid for my time.'

'You also didn't deliver.'

'Whose fault is that? They were trying to move too much product.'

'Yes, you could say that. But in their eyes it certainly is not their fault.'

'What is it they want from me?'

Eddie turned to look at Nora. 'You should go into the other room now. It's best if you just go into the other room and turn the television on and don't listen to what I need to tell Phil here.'

Nora looked to Hunt.

'I'm trying to help you out here,' Eddie said. 'It's better if you don't know.'

'Please, Nora,' Hunt said.

She looked at both of them in turn, her deep eyes searching. Hunt knew she would ask him later about what Eddie had to say, and he knew he would tell her. She went out of the room and left them sitting there at the table. The television went on and they could hear the midday news.

The kid sat in a holding cell with nine other men. He'd been in and out of the cell all morning, answering questions. At first it was a game to him. It was a tough man's game, it was like going to prison and putting up a good face and hoping it would all turn out okay. But there was no one to prove himself to. They all knew him. They all knew what would come of him, either way. And he didn't like what they'd had to say. Christ, he thought, what am I doing here, what in God's name am I doing here again? He'd been stupid, thought he was smart. The kid had been told it was like playing the lottery. And he supposed he'd won, he'd won himself something real special, something to be proud of.

The back of his head hurt where the deputy had tagged him. He'd heard of cases getting dismissed over such things. It was bad PR. But it didn't seem to matter one bit to any of these guys. The DEA agent had listened. But nothing had come of it. At any point he expected to be pulled out of the holding cell and brought back into the interview room.

All morning he'd been watching as the men in

the cell came and went. None of them talked to him. He'd leave, and when he came back, five of them would be gone and there were another five to take their place. He looked around the cell, careful not to meet anyone's eyes. This is how it had gone for him in Monroe. He wasn't a tough guy. He wasn't that at all, but he'd survived by not trying to be, by minding his own business and just trying to make it through his term.

During his second year he'd caught pneumonia and spent a week in the infirmary. The men talked there and it wasn't like how it was in the cells, with everyone divided by affiliation. He'd known things would all go back to being the same when he left, but it fascinated him then, and he'd thought things might be different.

Several of the men had come from other prisons and they shared stories about what they'd seen. Smuggling anal rock. Tattoo guns made from fan motors. Violence. From the comfort of his bed it had all seemed very safe, almost like entertainment. But when the men showed him their scars, it became real again. 'Five inches,' one man said, pointing to the sliver above his abdomen. 'Just between the lung and the small intestine.' The mark was only a half inch in length, but five inches straight in.

The kid placed his head in his hands and tried to breathe. He stared at the holding-cell floor, gray concrete with flecks of black. He toed one of the flecks and felt his shoe stick. Gum: he hadn't had a piece of that in years. Only eight hours before, he'd been in the mountains. He'd been somewhere that was the opposite of what he'd known. All he could hope for now was that they'd go easy on him. He had been to prison, but for manslaughter. To them, this lifestyle – everything that had led him to this point – would certainly seem to be an accident. One gigantic fluke. He could live with that. He'd lived with it already.

He looked around the cell again. A man in the far corner was staring at him. The kid looked away. He rubbed his hands together and drew his shoulders up. The man walked over and sat down next to him. 'How much do you weigh?' the man said.

The kid looked at him, a shaved pink head, bald at the top where no hair grew, and a broad, punched-in nose that hung slightly askew. The kid looked away. 'Nearly three bills. I can bench a quarter-pounder on a good day.'

'That's a lie.'

'I've been hearing that a lot lately,' the kid said.

'How'd you get in here?'

'Cookie jars.'

'That's about right,' the man said. 'That's always about right.'

The kid felt the man move on the bench and he turned to look the man over. He was leaning away from him on the bench, judging the kid.

'I'd say you were about a buck forty, maybe a little more.'

'Is this your thing?' the kid said. 'You size up other men in your spare time?'

'Among other things.'

'Why don't you take your skills back to the other side of the cell.'

'No reason to be rude, kid. You'd think you'd have learned already to respect your elders.'

'Fuck off.'

'I thought you'd have better manners for a kid from Monroe.'

'Where'd you hear that?' the kid said. He began to sit up and the man bent low and took his legs out from under him. The kid went down hard and the sound he heard was his jaw coming together against the floor. He tasted blood. The man was on top of him. The kid tried to turn over but felt his arm being pulled behind him. He started to yell out for the guard, but his face slammed into the concrete again. A tooth came loose. He could feel more blood.

'I have other skills,' the man said, 'but they say they're not useful skills. I like to think differently.' The kid heard a muffled pop and felt the pain coming from his arm. He tried to yell again, but the man bounced his head on the concrete. None of the other men moved. He was bleeding from the mouth and nose and he could feel the cement growing slippery and warm. He tried to turn over and look up at the man.

'There you go, kid, there you go. Just a little cooperation.' The man bent down and snapped the kid's neck on a quick swivel.

Nora fixed a bed for Eddie on the couch and went upstairs. She ran the shower for a while and stood in the bathroom with the steam collecting on the mirror. After a minute or two she tested the water, adjusted the knobs, and took off her shirt, then her pants. She wiped a hand across the mirror and looked at the reflection there, considering herself. Fifty years old, skin beginning to go with gravity, silver in her hair now. The steam filled the pocket in and she brushed her teeth. Afterward, she ran the tip of her tongue along her gums. She turned and stepped into the shower.

Steam clouded the shower glass like breath on a windowpane. The water ran down her skin, the heat rose from the basin of the shower.

When she'd first met Hunt, she hadn't been scared. She knew about what he did for a living, had heard he'd been to prison. He drank too much, she could see that. Everyone could. She took him home that first night and he woke up shivering the next morning. He woke up like that many mornings, shaking, his mouth dry, asking for another drink, and little by little she brought him back from that place. She could see he felt that he'd never measured up, that everything he touched somehow crumbled. He told her one morning that he'd never set out to be the man he was, it had just happened. One day he was just a kid, and then the next he was what she saw before her. He never set out to be an alcoholic, a murderer, an ex-convict. But he was all of those things, and even if he could get out from under them, he would still be that man. He could never change that.

She nursed him, watched over him, and somewhere along the way he got clean. Other men had taken her to nice dinners at expensive restaurants, but Hunt had been different; bad or good, she knew him for who he was. He didn't need to impress her or feed her lies, he didn't need to sell her. For a month she cared for him, and as a thank-you he took her on a picnic to the state park, a basket between them, jams and deli meats, the smell of fresh bread in the truck as they drove.

It rained that day, which was somehow more appropriate, the two of them parked near the grass, the spot they'd picked just a hundred yards away beneath a walnut tree. Rain falling from the sky, a carton of orange juice taken from the picnic basket and poured into plastic cups on the bench seat of the truck. Heavy rain striking the windshield. She had realized then that there was a little part of her that feared him, that wanted to understand that fear, why she felt the way she did. Rain pattering on the metal roof of the truck, their own breath on the windows like the steam of a shower on a mirror. It was what came foremost to her mind when she thought of their history together, this dangerous man, a man who'd murdered, who'd been to prison, turned gentle, turned into something else, someone only she could see.

When she got out of the shower, Hunt was waiting for her on the bed. He still hadn't taken off his boots, and he sat there on the edge of the bed with his arms at his sides and his boots on the floor. 'What time will you wake up?' she asked.

'Eight at the latest. I need to pull the boat out and give it fuel.'

'That's the plan?' she said.

'That's the plan.'

She walked around the bed and sat down opposite him. She didn't turn to look at him, but instead settled for feeling the way the bed gave with him sitting there. 'You ever think things could have been different if we had kids?'

'We have the horses, don't we?'

'I'm asking a serious question, Phil.'

Hunt looked out the window, toward the tops of the birch trees. 'I can't say anything about that.'

'Yes, you can,' she said. 'You just won't.'

'Nora—'

'Don't start,' she said. 'We both know it was

always me and it doesn't make a difference these days anyway. Even if I could, it would be too late now.'

Hunt didn't say anything. He moved to touch her back but then thought better of it and didn't. She'd thought – only that one time, sitting in the car outside their house with the engine on and the lights playing out along the gravel drive – of a life without him, thinking about what it would be like if she left, if she just left him behind. She thought about it now; she thought about it because she could see some need in him to protect her from the trouble he'd gotten himself into. She could see it, like some distant dust storm, gathering black and full along the horizon. She thought about how it would be, waking in a bed without him, sitting at a table, going day to day alone, knowing the whole while that he was out there doing the same.

'Do you think it's true,' Nora said, 'what they say about having kids: it makes you selfless?'

'I think it makes you something,' Hunt said. 'I don't know what, though.'

'Are you calling us selfish?'

'No, but I think you're calling us something.'

'Maybe I am, and maybe we are.'

'I can't do anything about that,' Hunt said. 'It is and we are, and here we are right now with all of it behind us.'

'You think it was coming all this while.'

'I don't want to think of it like that. I just don't.

It's been a gift to have a life like ours, and I wouldn't have changed it one bit.'

'I want you to promise.'

'What do you want me to promise?'

'If it all goes wrong tomorrow, I want you to promise you won't keep going. You won't. You'll just turn around and come right back here. Do you understand?'

'I don't go through with it, there is no tomorrow, there is no here.'

Nora began to cry. Hunt stayed where he was, motionless, listening to his wife. 'When I saw you this morning, I said, Maybe it's gone already, maybe it's been gone a long time already. I don't like feeling like that, Phil. I don't like it at all. I want you to promise me now.'

'I'm fifty-four years old. It's too late for promises.'

'That's not an answer,' Nora said. 'That's not any kind of answer. If you need to run, you will. Now, you promise me one way or another.'

'This is so exciting,' Sheri said. She was standing at the window looking down on the freeway and the crosscut of the city streets. They were on the twenty-second floor of the Sheraton. Below, she could see the yellow lights from a tow truck swing and touch the cement of a nearby overpass. 'You think they'll make you an agent or something?'

'I don't think so,' Drake answered. He had risen from the bed and come over to the window to look out on the city. He wore a pair of his college basketball shorts and a thin white T. His short brown hair was beginning to go at an early age, and he reached up unconsciously to tousle it and bring it down across his brow. Sheri had her hand up on the window. She stood on her tiptoes looking down. 'Come away from the window,' Drake said. 'You make me nervous.'

'What, this?' She leaned into the window and put her other hand on the glass.

'Stop playing.'

'Don't you live dangerously? Isn't that how you got here?'

'I'd rather be back home where I know what I'm doing.'

'Back home with your two hundred and forty-three citizens.'

He could see she was enjoying this. 'Yes, back home where we belong.'

'Live it up. Treat it like a vacation.'

'It's not a vacation. It's more like protective services.'

'I don't see a guard on the door.'

'I'm your guard.' He picked her up and threw her on the bed. She laughed and rolled off the other side and was back up with her hands held out in front of her, waiting for his next move.

'A little wrestling?' she said, cocking her eyebrow at him.

He threw a pillow at her.

'Play fair,' she said.

He walked over and pulled her sweats to her knees.

'Damn it, Bobby,' she said, smiling. 'I said fair, not perverted.' She pulled her pants back up.

'You asked for it.'

They lay down on the bed and ordered room service. After they had finished their meal, Drake went to stand at the window. The tow truck was still there, the lights going. Sheri called from the bed to ask him what he was looking at. 'Just this accident down here.'

'How many cars?'

'Looks to be about three.'

'That's a bad one.'

'It's certainly not a good one.'

'I feel bad for people like that.'

'People like what?'

'People who get stranded. I hate passing them on the road.'

'Why don't you pick them up, then?'

'I think I would if I saw them out there alone.'

'No, you wouldn't,' he said.

'Well, probably not, but I'd still feel bad for them.'

'I always think maybe they had it coming.'

'That's a terrible thing to say.'

Drake believed wayward souls were responsible for their own salvation. He didn't have any other way of thinking about it, nor did he want to. The scars ran deep, and he thought that if healing was going to come, it would come from within and grow outward. He didn't say any of this to his wife, though he'd been thinking about it. Finally, compromising with a simple statement of the facts, he said, 'Bad drivers cause accidents,' as if he'd been born to believe it.

'Listen to you,' she said. 'Any number of things cause accidents.'

'Well, bad drivers cause most of them.'

'Not very compassionate, are you?'

'It's how I rationalize it,' Drake said. 'If I went around saying all these people are good, I think it would break my heart. It would just tear it all to pieces.'

86

'What do you have to say about those two men in the mountains? Are they good people?'

'I don't know. How can you tell something like that?'

'I don't think you can,' Sheri said.

'Well, maybe that's it then. Maybe I was trying to find out something about them, find out something for myself.'

'About your father?'

Drake didn't turn to look at her. He kept his eyes at the window and didn't say anything. After a moment passed, after the yellow emergency lights spun several times across his face, he said, 'I don't know. I didn't know my father was involved in all that, and then I'm getting notified all about his smuggling down in Arizona. Most of it I had to read in the newspapers. I still don't know what type of man my father is, not now, not then.'

'You know you don't have to make up for him,' Sheri said.

Drake turned away from the window and walked over to the bed. He felt restless. He'd been up all day answering questions for Driscoll. Getting settled into the hotel room. He'd taken nothing more than a thirty-minute nap before Sheri had shown up with all her questions. 'I know I don't have to make up for him,' Drake said. 'But somehow – no matter what I say – I always am.'

87

When he woke in the morning, Nora wasn't there. The clock showed it was a quarter to eight. From the window he could see the horses had been let into the field and Nora was down there in a pair of jeans and a thick work shirt, setting hay out in the paddock. He dressed and went downstairs, where he could hear Eddie's uneven breathing from the living room couch.

Out the back he watched Nora raise the hay and then let it out in a rough tumble onto the ground. They were barely breaking even, between feed and the mortgage on the place. He'd had no way of saying no to what Eddie offered. Quarter horses and stallions out there that cost more than his house, more than his whole operation. From the hook near the door he took the boat keys and stuffed them into his pocket. He was dressed warmly, in a sweatshirt and jeans, white tennis shoes for traction on the boat.

Nora looked up when he stepped outside, but then she went back to her work. He went over to the fence and put his arms over it and stood watching her.

He waited. Nora ignored him, not looking up from her work. He thought about how none of these horses were his. Every one of them belonged to someone else. The two they had owned – raised from foals – had been lost in the mountains. They were gone. No brandings or mark to tell the law whom they belonged to. He felt their loss as he looked out on the field where they should have been, standing out there in the grass among the others. He knew these horses meant too much to him. Knew he shouldn't get hung up on them. He thought of them like children, like people. Sometimes he knew he placed them over people, understood them better, their habits, their needs. The two horses were gone and there was nothing he could do or say to bring them back.

One was dead, he knew this, shot through the head. He couldn't say what had happened to the other, the one the kid had been riding. Now gone, might as well have been dead for all he knew, but he hoped she wasn't.

'Nora,' he said. She wouldn't look at him. He waited another moment, thinking the situation over. He didn't have much time. 'I've got to go.'

She put down the pitchfork she'd been working with and walked toward him. The horses out there with their piles of hay. Several golden piles to choose from and the six remaining horses standing there. He watched one of the stronger horses, a big brown, turn and regard him. This could be it, he thought, this could be all there is and it might be over.

Nora came to the fence and took off her gloves. It was early and the mist climbed off the field as the sun came on. She put her hand on his forearm, and he could feel the sweat and the warmth from her hand come onto him. 'I didn't mean to call you selfish last night,' Nora said. She looked away, back to where she'd been with the horses. 'I'm just angry, that's all. It all just makes me so angry.'

Hunt covered her hand with his. 'I know,' he said, 'but it's part of it. It just means we care enough that it gets under the skin from time to time.'

'We don't have to do this, you know.'

'Yes, we do.'

'No, I mean this. These horses. We don't have to have this business. We don't have to do this.' She looked again toward the horses and then she drifted off for a while, just looking at the end of their property, at something Hunt couldn't see. 'We can find something more suited to us.'

'This is it,' he said. 'I don't know anything else. There is nothing else for me.'

Nora made a face, and he heard her sigh. 'Why don't we just go away?' she said.

It was his turn to sigh. He looked at her, then looked away at the truck waiting for him across the lawn. He would humor her. 'Where do you want to go?'

'Can't we take a trip up to the San Juans? To that resort we stayed at on Orcas. Wouldn't you like that?'

When he turned back to look at her, he could

see the intense look in her eye, like she thought they would actually do it, like he could get away, like it was as simple as just packing up a suitcase and running off to the islands. 'You know we can't do that,' he said.

'Yes, we can,' she said. 'We can order room service, never leave the room, and lie in bed. It will be like when we were there before, spending money we don't have. But we'll be happy, won't we? Just you and I, and none of this trouble to bother us.'

'Stop it,' he said, the anger sudden in his voice. He didn't know where it had come from, but it was there and he could feel it trembling in his vocal cords. He could see he had scared her, too. He was losing it a little. 'I'm sorry,' he said. 'We just can't.'

He watched her, and he knew she understood. He could see she was waiting for someone to carry her away, to make it all better so they could go on with their life, but he didn't know if that person was going to be him. He just didn't know.

'I hate this,' she said with some finality. 'I just want to know we're going to come out of this. I just want to know that.'

'I'm not going to tell you it's all going to be fine,' Hunt said. 'It won't. This is what we're good at, this house, this pasture, these horses. I can't just run away. We can't. But I'll tell you I'd rather be broke and doing something I love than working some minimum-wage job and hating every moment of it. That's no way to live and you know it.'

'No,' she said.

He could sense she wanted to say more, and he waited for it to come, but it didn't. He'd always felt that she had saved him from something. Perhaps she'd saved him from himself in the long-ago time when they'd first met, when they'd begun to know each other. Who knew? He certainly couldn't say. He just hoped that, as it had in the past, everything would turn out for the better. That they could just keep on going. He loved her, he knew this, he loved the horses, and all he could hope for was that he would make it back here, to his house, to his wife, and to his horses.

They watched the pasture for a while. Steam escaped from the horses' lungs and broke into the early morning field and commingled with the rising dew. He rattled the keys in his pocket and pulled his hand away.

She kissed him and watched him walk over to the truck. When he pulled out onto the drive, he could see Nora out there in the field again, feeding the horses, the field rising golden with the sun and the horses all around enjoying it.

G rady had been told where to find the girl, and when he pulled up he could see her waiting there with her suitcase. He honked the horn and watched her turn to look in his direction. She seemed cautious, the morning sun bright on her face, unsure of what he was offering. A Vietnamese girl. When he stepped from the car to take her suitcase, she came nearly to his shoulder. He guessed her to be no older than nineteen. 'Come on,' he said. 'Don't be shy, get yourself in the car and close the door.' He had no way of knowing if she understood him. He didn't know what she'd been told. Probably that there would be a few of her countrymen there to pick her up. There probably should have been, but Grady thought he'd do fine, and it would suit him perfectly to do the job himself.

Grady was always battling that same familiar ache in his heart. He felt it now, throwing her bag in the backseat next to his knife bag and opening the passenger-side door. This ache, this urge, had brought him to prison and had been his salvation. The priest at the prison had always said he had the devil inside him, that it was the devil who had brought him there. Grady had understood this, had understood what the priest was saying, what the doctors had told him before, giving him pills, asking him questions, trying to calm that ache he felt deep down in his insides, humming away like a little bird trying to take wing. They'd said he was almost ready to be back out in society. Young as he was, he shouldn't waste his time in prison. He'd told them all that he intended to kick the devil right out of his body, take him by the head and kick his front teeth right down his throat. They'd said that was a step in the right direction. Grady had grinned then, imagining his foot so far down the devil's throat, he was tickling that devil's heart with his toes.

He watched the little Vietnamese girl get in the car, then close the door. He was already sizing her up. One hundred pounds. He'd read somewhere that the human stomach could expand to hold up to fifty times its resting capacity. He started the car and drove out toward the highway. When he was sure there were no cops around, he put his hand up under her shirt and felt her stomach. She slapped him hard across the hand and said something in Vietnamese he didn't understand.

The skin stretched tight and smooth under his hand. He'd been told to take her to the Vietnamese. It was what he was paid for, what he had been instructed to do. But looking at her, he couldn't help it, a little piece inside him coming loose. The lawyer was paid to deliver drugs, not little things like this. Not little girls like this one. 'Can't wait to get you home,' he said. She didn't say anything back, just kept staring out the front window at the highway, at a world she didn't yet understand.

Drake woke early. He made himself a cup of coffee in the small two-cup pot and watched the city turn from blue to gray. He poured the second cup and sat in the big armchair that faced the television and the dressing table. Sheri was still asleep and he could hear the soft pull of her breathing. He hadn't turned on a light, but the early sun came through the curtain and he saw she was lying half beneath the covers as she always did.

With the cup still in his hands, he dressed. A little under ten years of regular work had gotten him trained on early mornings, and he couldn't sit there, hidden away in the hotel room, for the rest of the day. He didn't like being out of his depth. The city was something he didn't know, but he figured it was just like anything else: he had to experience it to understand it.

He wore a pair of jeans and a button-down shirt with the tails pulled out to hide his gun. Outside the hotel it was warm, and he carried his gun in a holster at the small of his back. He didn't like the feeling of not being in control. It was something he'd grown used to up north and it was something he understood. Down the street was a small coffee shop and he stopped in and bought a croissant and walked on. The morning buses were running and the streets were filling with people. Every once in a while a man in a suit or a woman walking by gave him a questioning look. He was wearing his cowboy hat and he tipped it and mumbled a good morning.

He walked down to the market and sat on a bench looking out on the sound. It was the first time in ten years he'd seen water that big and green. At the ferry terminal he saw a man panhandling for food. He wore a sign saying 'Pregnant and Hungry' around his neck and danced and sang a tuneless ditty on a repeating circuit. Drake watched him for a time and then went into McDonald's and bought the man a breakfast sandwich. 'Here,' Drake said, holding the bag out to the man.

The man took the bag and looked inside. 'Are you trying to kill me?'

Drake didn't know what to say.

The man stepped out onto the sidewalk and surprised a woman walking by. 'Here,' he said. 'You take this.'

At the federal building, Drake called up for the DEA agent, but no one had seen him. He waited in the lobby for an hour, spinning his hat on his finger and watching the people as they came through the metal detectors. At noon he walked back to the hotel and went up in the elevator. In the brushed metal doors, Drake caught a woman staring at him. He took off his hat and held it to his chest.

On the floor of his room there was a note from Sheri written on hotel stationery. He picked it up and read it, then flipped it over and wrote a note and left it for Sheri.

It took him almost forty minutes with the traffic to drive from downtown Seattle to Emerald Downs, where the horses raced in Auburn. He didn't have any clear idea of what he was doing, but he had to do something.

The horses weren't running, but when he flashed his star, the guard at the gate let him through, saying, 'You get that thing out of a cereal box?'

Drake walked the edge of the track, leaning on the railings and looking down on the dirt track. The ground was all smooth as if it had been gone over with a rake. One of the groundsmen came over and pointed him toward the stables.

The stalls were all empty, but Drake found a man hosing down the floors.

'What day they race around here?'

The man looked up and took his hand off the spray nozzle.

'What day they race around here?' Drake asked again.

'Sundays usually, though every once in a while they'll do a few races during the week.'

'They any good to bet on?'

'Not if you want to keep your money.'

'Good advice.'

'Been working here almost ten years and it's the best I've got.'

'How many horses come through here?'

'Two hundred or more on a busy day.'

'You keep them all in here?'

'We end up bringing them in in shifts. Usually, if they lose, it's a quick turnout anyway.'

The man went back to washing the floors. 'You know anyone I can talk to that might know a little something about riding?' Drake asked.

The man released the spray nozzle again. 'What type of riding are you interested in?'

'Jumps and that sort of thing. Obstacles.'

'Best I can think of,' the man said, 'is this place around here. A few of the owners board horses there. It's a small operation, but they're good, decent people. They have a little run on the property and they can tell you a little more than I'd be able to.'

He followed the directions the man gave him, drove the few miles up the highway, and turned off at the next exit. It wasn't the prettiest piece of land he'd seen, but it wasn't the worst either. Freight tracks ran parallel to the highway, and where the road crossed, the rains had taken old newspapers and plastered them to the ground. There were cigarette butts, old soft-drink cups, all of it flung to the side when the gates lowered and the trains came through.

He drove a few miles in, passing a scrapyard and a long expanse of pasture where he could see cows grazing. Where the houses sat, he could see stands of ash and alder and a few bent pines. In the distance a hill rose, and beyond it, he thought, must be the freeway and the sound. The land was all low wetland and grass field. There was a smell of wet sod and foul earth in the air. He could taste it, and he went on down the road wondering what it would take to feel at home in a place like this.

He checked the address before turning in. The house lay below the road in a little depression that seemed to go back a fair ways, where he guessed the horse run must be, and the stables. In the drive outside the garage he saw a black Lincoln parked, and around the edge of the house, a silver horse trailer.

When he stepped from the car, he could see a hand at the blinds. He adjusted his hat and straightened the fall of his shirt so that it wouldn't rise up on the gun. A skinny woman met him at the door. He guessed by the look of her that she was in her forties, in good shape, and he thought perhaps she could have been older but didn't show it. It had taken two rings of the doorbell before she opened. 'I wondered if I might come in,' Drake said. 'I'd like to talk a little about riding.'

'We're not that sort of operation.'

'I know,' Drake said, 'but I asked at the track and they sent me here and I wondered if I could just ask you a few questions.'

The woman seemed to hesitate but then stepped aside and let him pass through. There was a man sitting at the table, wide bodied and unshaven, the black stubble showing on his dark skin. Drake took off his hat, straightening his thinning hair. The woman offered him a seat. He declined. Drake leaned across the table and offered the man his hand. 'Bobby Drake, sir.'

'Nice to meet you, Bobby,' the man said, but he didn't offer his name.

'This really will only take a moment,' Drake said. 'I'm interested in learning a little about the horse business.'

'You look like you know a thing about it,' the woman said. She was looking at his hat.

'Oh, this,' Drake said. 'This is just part of the costume.'

'My husband wears one occasionally, though we don't see them on this side of the mountains often.'

Drake looked to the man at the table. He didn't seem much like the type to wear a cowboy hat, or any kind of hat, his black hair slicked back and a face that could have been Mexican but could have been anything really.

'I'm Nora,' the woman said.

'Bobby.'

'What were you wondering about, Bobby?'

'They told me over at the track that you've been keeping horses for almost twenty years now.'

'That's right.'

101

'You've probably come in contact with a lot of different people.'

'All types.'

'I'd really like to know how someone learns to ride.' The image of the man riding bareback into the thick woods came to him, the pulse of the animal. 'I mean really ride, like they do in the movies.'

Nora laughed and looked away, and when she looked back, her eyes were wet at the edges. 'How old are you?' she said.

'Thirty.'

'Have you ever been on a horse before?'

'My family kept a few horses when I was young, but not anymore. Once recently.'

'Let me show you something.' She took him out back and walked him over to the run. 'This is what's called a triple bar and this is a hog's back. We don't do it here, but I'll give you a number and you can call and get lessons. You live around here, don't you?'

'Up north, but I'll be down here on business for a few days. Do you think they could squeeze me in?'

'You don't seem like you have a problem squeezing in.' Nora laughed. 'Wait here, I'll get you the number.'

Drake watched her go. The Mexican was standing at the back door, looking out on them, and when she came up the steps he went in after her. Drake walked over and offered his knuckles to the stabled horses; he counted six horses for the ten stalls. Two of the six were out in a field farther on.

When Nora came back, he said, 'Looks like you've got room for me when I get serious.'

Nora gave a weak smile. 'Slow month.'

'Sorry to hear it,' Drake said, his face screwed up with embarrassment. He should have known better.

'Don't worry about it, Bobby. I know you were just asking.'

Drake looked out on the two horses in the paddock, and when he looked back he said, 'You seem like a really nice person. I'm sure things will turn around for you. They usually do. At any rate I appreciate the help.'

'Happy to give it,' Nora said. 'It's funny, you know. I thought you were going to be someone else entirely.'

'I hope I didn't disappoint.'

'Not at all. Did you have something like this when you were growing up?'

'No, nothing like this, just a few feet of open ground and a converted garage for a stable. Nothing fancy.'

'We were always planning on having kids, but it never happened. Always thought it would be a wonderful thing for them.'

'Wish I would have known about this place as a kid. I would have been down here every weekend.'

'Nice of you to say. You have any?'

'Not that I know of.'

'That's pretty much what my husband says. He's always giving me little heart attacks.'

'Husbands do that.'

'Yes, they do.'

Drake didn't say anything, and then after a second had passed, he said, 'Thank you, Nora. I'm going to call this number and see what I can work out.'

'They'll do something for you, I'm sure.'

Drake walked around the side of the house to his car. He passed the trailer and, out of habit, looked in at the garage. A late-model Honda sat in the bay, but not the truck he'd been expecting.

The call concerning the heroin came an hour later than the lawyer expected. The driver stopped the car and ran around to open the back. The lawyer held the phone to his ear as he got out of the car. He was big in the belly and wore a shirt and tie, opened a bit at the collar, and fine slacks that fell straight from below the bulge of his stomach. The lawyer had been expecting this call from his Vietnamese clients, but not this late, and as he looked out on his property, at the rhododendron plants and the white gravel drive, he told the man on the other end of the phone not to worry. 'There has been a little holdup, but it will be here tomorrow.'

The driver pulled away and left the lawyer in front of the expansive house, which looked on the far side of the property toward the ocean and was held over the hillside by metal stilts. In truth he didn't know why Grady hadn't delivered the girl. He had never run into a problem like this one before, Grady always being very thorough, always punctual, always clean. Perhaps the lawyer had been unclear with his instructions. Perhaps Grady had thought he'd just deliver when he had both girls. The lawyer didn't know for sure. He could hear the angry tone of the man on the other end of the line.

'I've already sent someone to pick up the first girl from the airport,' the lawyer said, trying to think it over, trying to come up with some sort of answer. 'The other spooked and walked off the plane in Vancouver. My contact in customs was able to find her, and both packages will be delivered tomorrow. Noon, beside the downtown ferry docks.' The lawyer closed the phone without waiting for a response.

He walked to the edge of the rock retaining wall and lit a cigarette. The tops of pine and fir trees climbed out of the landscape. An odor of turned earth came from lower down, fresh manure and wood chips, the faint smell of lemon coming off the pines. He held the burning ember of his cigarette out in front of him, its smoke taken on the wind. He felt the tobacco in his lungs, hot as his own blood. In the far distance he could see the other side of the sound, the blurry shape of land across the water, green and smoldering with mist, like fresh-hewn branches laid across a fire. He still held the phone in his hand, and when he'd drawn deeply from the cigarette, letting the smoke rush back out into the world through his nostrils, he dialed Grady and waited for a response.

ddie's Bayliner was tied at the end of the dock, just fifty feet from the ramp. Hunt had stopped hiding drugs in the thing years before. Taking the example from the old-time smugglers who used to bring it across in the rims of their tires, in the past he'd stuffed each inflatable bumper with wide cylinders of rolled and Cryovaced cocaine and heroin and hung them from the side for all to see. It was the oblong bumpers he stood working with, unscrewing the false bottoms and checking the space into which he would slip the drugs later. The bumpers, really just opaque containers for air, sealed with a lid and a rubber washer, were airtight. It was the perfect place for drugs, easily cut loose from the boat, easy to access, and often overlooked, the same way that smugglers in the Florida Keys sealed their drugs to the undersides of their boats in fiberglass compartments called blisters. Hunt needed something he could ditch with ease and speed.

The Bayliner held two Mercury engines, six hundred horses between the two of them, and enough fuel to get him suitably lost. He'd preferred the privacy of the mountains, but it would do; it was how he'd come into it all those years ago.

A man and his daughter sat on the far dock, picking fried chicken into a crab trap. The daughter, not much older than five or six, stood nearly at the height of her father's waist. At the base of the ramp was another family, the father bringing the trailer down and two teenage boys bringing the boat up until the hull squealed across the carpet pad. Hunt sat and watched them for a time. He cleaned down the cockpit and checked the boat permit. A man passed the family on the ramp, joking with the father, then, after spotting Hunt, walked out along the dock.

From the man's pocket, Hunt heard the pulse of a phone ringing. The man seemed to consider this, pausing to debate whether to pick it up, then, deciding against it, walked forward down the dock as if he and Hunt had some sort of appointment to keep. The man carried with him a small bag that, as he walked, swung from his hand and connected in a rhythm with his thigh. It reminded Hunt of a large cue case, square, with a zipper along its length and a handle in the middle.

'Let me ask you a question,' the man said. He was even with Hunt, looking down from the dock. 'How far can one of these take you? It's a real nice boat. I'd like to have one of my own someday.'

Hunt looked up at him from the bow of the boat, where he stood coiling a length of rope. The man was very pale, with a blond, almost white mustache, and though his eyes were blue, the skin around them seemed thin and dark, as if the blood were coming through very close to the surface. There was something familiar about the man, a passing memory, broken like a bubble as the thing formed in Hunt's mind.

'Hey,' the man said, 'weren't you in Monroe a few years back?'

Hunt gave him a deadpan face. 'I was there.'

'You remember me?'

'Can't say I do.' He didn't want to talk about this, didn't care. He had a few friends from his time in Monroe, a few friends up north he used for stashing drugs, for a place to stay on long trips. He didn't want to make any new friends. Didn't need any.

The man held out his hand. 'Grady Fisher. We did a year together. After that, I didn't see you anymore. Must have got out. Doesn't look like you're doing too bad for yourself.'

Hunt looked up at him. He didn't offer his name or his hand. 'You always prelude a question like that?'

'Like what?'

'By asking the question, "Can I ask you a question?"'

'I didn't want to be impolite.' He closed his hand and let it drop to his side.

Hunt stared back at him. 'This boat will get me just about anywhere when the tanks are full.'

'Sorry if I intruded.'

Hunt didn't say anything. He finished coiling the rope and stuffed it into a low compartment.

'I'm a cook,' Grady said. He patted the case with his free hand, smiling as if Hunt had asked him what the bag was for. 'I was wondering if you might be going fishing?'

He had a funny way of talking, slow at times, almost stuttering, more curious and melodic than anything. Hunt thought about this. The man wouldn't leave; he was just sitting there watching Hunt. 'What's in the case?' Hunt asked.

'Oh, this,' he said, as if he'd just remembered he'd been holding it. 'These are my knives.' Hunt gave him another look. He was ready to leave, but the idea of a man carrying knives around in broad daylight interested him. It seemed completely rational when he thought of it. He probably passed a chef every day of his life, with a collection of knives sitting shotgun right beside him. 'Let me show you.' Grady put the case down on the dock and unzipped the top. 'I've been collecting them for years.'

The only two things Hunt could identify were a hacksaw and a large chef's knife – he guessed the blade to be about twelve inches long. 'Those look very nice,' Hunt said. The man smiled and gave a little giggle. He unfolded the sides until they were laid out as two halves on the dock, the knives fully exposed.

'Go on,' Grady said. 'Pick one up. The weight on them is counterbalanced so it doesn't feel like anything when they make their first cut. You have

110

to be careful sometimes. It's like cutting fish with a laser beam.'

Hunt looked up at Grady, and the whole while, Grady was just looking back at him with the same goofy half smile. The girl behind them on the far dock made a shout of discovery, but the two men didn't look away. 'What's this one for?' Hunt asked, bringing a small knife out of the bag.

Grady looked down at the knife. 'Careful,' he said. 'Witnesses.'

Hunt gave him a look.

'Just a little Monroe humor, that's all,' Grady said. 'That's a boning knife. I use it mostly for small jobs.' He pointed to his own shoulder and showed Hunt where the ligaments and tendons ran. 'They say Jacques Pépin can debone a chicken in five seconds. Do you know who he is?'

'What does your shoulder have in common with a chicken?'

'More than you'd expect.'

Hunt looked down at the knife in his hand.

Grady held out his hand and Hunt passed the knife back to him. 'Just finished gutting a little Asian piglet,' Grady said with that same disfigured giggle. 'Beautiful little thing. Keep your knives sharp and they'll cut through just about anything.' He smiled, and the thin, almost colorless line of hair over his lip flattened.

Hunt held up the hacksaw. 'That thing is sort of a brute,' Grady said. 'Just what you think it is. I use it mostly on the bigger jobs, whole pigs, leg

111

of lamb. Separating the large into the small.' He made a little motion with his hands, imagining the cuts. 'I could do it blindfolded if I had to.'

'That right?'

'That's right.'

'I wish I could talk more, but—'

'You have to go,' Grady finished.

'Yes.'

'It was a real pleasure,' Grady said, holding out his hand for Hunt to take.

The hand Hunt took was thicker than he'd expected, filled with muscle and a little plump. 'Perhaps one day you'll get that boat.'

'Yes, perhaps.' Grady stood watching Hunt as he untied the boat and pushed it a few feet into the water. The engines started and Hunt felt the back dig in. The Bayliner moved out and around, aiming for the edge of the rock jetty. When Hunt looked back, Grady was still standing there, his case of knives in his hand, just staring.

Grady drove an old Nissan with a square body and four doors, registered under an alias. He watched Hunt pull out and make the turn into open water. Then he walked back to his car and opened his bag. Under the seat he had an AR-15 with retractable stock and carbine switched for use as a long-range rifle, measuring about the same length as the hacksaw, a foot and a half with the stock closed. He placed it in the bag.

Watching Hunt handle the knives had given him a thrill the way some animals played with their food before eating it. 'Let him do the exchange, then do it,' the lawyer had said on the phone. It was a shame he'd need to use something like a rifle to do something so simple.

The padlock on the marina gate took him fifteen seconds to pick. He pushed the thing closed behind him and snapped the lock back on the gate again. He was carrying the bag, and when he found a midnight blue boat with twin Volvo engines, he threw the bag over and then stepped aboard.

Twelve hours earlier, Eddie had put it to Hunt like this: 'You run and they'll use Nora to get to you. You take Nora and they'll use me.' Eddie laughed as though something was funny. There wasn't one funny thing about it, but he couldn't stop the nervous laughter. 'The kid is dead. He's fucking gone. It took them about five hours after he arrived to arrange it. The only reason you're not dead is because you had the sense to get out of there. They're not too happy about the lost product, but you're not a liability to them. They figure we owe them. The way it was put to me was that they've invested in us and they want a favorable return.'

Hunt could hear the news playing in the other room. The weatherman warned of showers turning to snow later in the week. Through the doorway he could see the back of the couch and Nora sitting on it. 'Jesus, Eddie. When did we start working with people like this?'

'I'm telling you to protect yourself.'

'He was just some kid. Twenty-two years old.'

'Look, Hunt, these people like to be in control.

If it had been you in there, they would have done the same thing. You're lucky. But we still owe these people some work.'

'Why don't we run now? What's stopping us?'

'How many times have you mortgaged this house? You have anything in the bank? You started out in this business trying to put a straight life together, but now it's more like you use the money to keep the straight life afloat. If you want to run, you're going to need to stay hidden, and that takes money. Because you're not coming back.'

'You would help us, wouldn't you, Eddie?'

'I would help you if I could. I'm just as broke as you. That car out there and my boat are about all I have to show for myself. I'm just like you.'

'But we've made money, haven't we?'

'We've made it, but everything is in cash, the boat, the car. I've been playing it pretty close to the heart. This was supposed to be our big break, our time to really make money.'

'This is amazing,' Hunt said. 'It's just amazing. I get out of Monroe and I can't find a job, I can't even go to school. I'm just scraping by, hoping my bets at the track hold up. So I take this thing with you to make a little money and all the time – twenty years—' Hunt stopped here, his voice caught somewhere deep in his throat like a piece of meat swallowed too fast. Year after year after year, he kept adding, putting the time together in his mind, adding it all up, his life and what it amounted to.

'Two decades,' he said. 'I'm building this life for that long and this is what it comes down to.'

'We owe these people money, Hunt. I don't know what else to tell you. There's nothing else we can do about it. We do this job and we're on our way. It's simple. We both knew how it could be when we started on this.'

'How many more times will there be?'

'As many as it takes.'

'Doesn't it make you uneasy, what they did to the kid? Doesn't that make you want to run?'

'What do you want me to say?'

Hunt placed his hands on the table. He looked over at him. 'They've got us good, don't they?'

'Yes, they do,' Eddie said. 'And the sickest thing is, it makes them happy.'

Hunt pushed the throttle forward on the boat until the speedometer read fifteen knots. Twenty years he'd been making this run. And he could do it now almost without a second thought. It was strange to him that over all those years he had thought of himself as independent. He had Eddie. He always had Eddie, but they were more partners than anything else. At the age of nineteen he'd been a prisoner. Just a year out of childhood, just a year beyond the watch of parents and the guidance of teachers and coaches, people who had at one point or another meant something to him. He laughed a bit at the thought, remembering how they'd all considered themselves prisoners in school. But it wasn't a thing like prison or being held captive. He had disappeared in Monroe. Stood in one place and just disappeared, like a magician doing a magic trick. One moment there, the next gone.

It hadn't started all at once. His lawyer was the first one to disappear. Hunt could understand a thing like that, where a man doesn't come because he's not being paid anymore. That made sense. A few friends would visit. They'd hold their baby pictures up to the glass so Hunt could see. They'd write him letters from exotic places and Hunt would lie in his bed and smell the paper. He would run his fingers along the envelope and look at the postmark. He liked to know where something had been. He liked to see that it had a location and a date and that it had traveled that long distance to him.

The last letter he taped to his wall was dated sometime in the early eighties. What could they say to him anymore: Tough break, better luck next time? There was nothing to say about the thing he'd done, nothing that would ever make it better for him. He felt this, lying there in the cell at night with the pages of the letter drifting there on the wall. He felt that loneliness of disappearing, of fading away. The letter hung there for a year before he took it down.

A high school coach came once to see him, the man dressed not as Hunt remembered him but in a simple pair of jeans, a striped polo shirt. It made Hunt sad to see him like this. To see the expression that crossed his face. Nothing filled Hunt with more despair than seeing a look of pity streak across another's face. That had nearly done it. That had nearly killed him. Beat him better than anyone could ever have beaten him physically. Pride was a mass murderer in prison, and many nights, the men alone in their cells, it took who it could.

His mother would write letters because she could not see him. She tried several times to visit, but every time she came, she cried, and Hunt could do nothing but sit there and watch her pain. To know that he had caused it and that there was nothing he could do about it, no comfort or help he could give, was, of all the things he endured, the worst.

'Why are you still here, Eddie?'

Eddie eyed Nora. She'd just come back in from seeing Bobby Drake off. 'What are you doing, Nora? Giving tours to strangers?'

'He was just a boy looking for some riding lessons.'

'He could be anybody.'

'Him?'

Eddie walked to the window and put a finger to the blinds and looked out on the front lawn. 'Yes, Nora, him.'

Nora went into the kitchen and he could hear her pouring a glass of water from the faucet. When she came back into the room, he was still standing at the window. 'Why are you still here, Eddie?'

'I'm looking out for you,' he said. 'I'm looking out for Hunt.'

'Do we need looking after?' Nora walked over to the table and sat down. She wouldn't meet Eddie's eyes.

Eddie didn't say anything. He was trying to decide if he should leave. If he should just get out

120

now, if he could leave the two of them, leave them like he'd left the kid, waiting in the cell, waiting to get his head smashed in. Eddie couldn't do it. Not to Nora, at least. He couldn't leave her. All she had done to be wrapped up in this was love Hunt. Eddie couldn't punish her for something like that. There would be punishment enough.

'You ever think what would happen if you lost your vision?' Eddie said. He hadn't meant it to sound threatening, but it had, like he was going to do it. 'You know what I mean, go blind. You ever think of that?'

'Doesn't seem like a very nice question.'

'It's not.'

'Not a question, or not nice?'

'Not a question. Forget it, Nora. I'm just thinking out loud, that's all.'

'Well, then no. No, I'd expect it doesn't feel very good.'

'I'm saying I feel like that. I feel like I've gone blind, and I have everything I went into it with but I can't see the walls, and I reach out to touch them and I'm just feeling my way along. That's how I feel. That's where we are, just feeling the walls, and I don't like it, but it's the best thing for us, for you and me, and Hunt. The best way we know how to go on and the only way we're ever going to find our way.'

In the early evening, Sheri answered the phone and, after a quick greeting, handed it across the table to Drake. They were playing Scrabble and drinking red wine out of the water glasses from the bathroom. 'Yes,' Drake answered. He listened for a time, then got up from the chair and wrote down an address.

When they arrived at the restaurant, they realized they were underdressed. And immediately Drake wanted to get back in the taxi and leave. Agent Driscoll was sitting there, and when they approached, he stood up and greeted them, holding his tie back as he leaned and shook their hands. 'No hat today?' Driscoll asked.

'No. I got tired of wearing it. Everyone wanted to know when the rodeo came to town.'

'That's funny. Though I'm not that surprised. You look the part.'

'This is a very nice place,' Sheri said.

'Don't let it fool you,' Driscoll said. 'Company card.'

Drake made the bad joke: 'Crime does pay.' And immediately he was sorry he'd said it. He felt like a fool. But Sheri laughed to be nice, and Driscoll smiled, though Drake got the impression he'd heard it a few times before.

After they'd taken seats, Driscoll asked about the paper.

'I picked up a copy from the lobby,' Drake said.

'Front page of the local section. Not so bad, eh?'

'I didn't read it,' Drake said.

'Why not? It's not every day you get to be a hero.'

'Is that what they're saying?'

Driscoll turned and spoke to Sheri. 'How does it feel to be married to a man like this?'

'Dreamy,' Sheri said.

'I bet,' Driscoll said. He turned back to Drake. 'You didn't read it?'

'There was a lot of that when my father went away. It burned me out.'

'Sheri,' Driscoll said, 'you must have read it?'

'I peeked at it a little.'

'And?'

'I just want to know if my husband has anything to worry about,' Sheri said.

'No,' Driscoll said. 'Nothing.'

They ordered their food, and when it came, Driscoll dropped the news about the kid.

'That's horrible,' Sheri said.

'In the cell? With the guards standing by?'

'No one seems to have seen it.'

'There were ten men in that cell last I saw it.'

'There's nine now,' Driscoll said dryly. 'Not one

of them says he saw anything or heard anything. Nine men in a cell that's fifteen by fifteen.'

'How could that happen?' Sheri asked.

'Unless the kid had a heart attack, it couldn't.'

'Did he?'

'Not unless his heart bounced up and broke his right arm, beat in his face, and then snapped his neck.'

'Easy,' Drake said. He looked at Sheri.

Driscoll gave a quick laugh.

'Is this something we should be worried about?' Drake asked.

Driscoll went on chewing, and when he was finished, he said, 'The only person who needs to be worried is that second man. The case we have is gone. We have some two hundred kilos of coke and no one to charge it on. I'd guess if he hasn't been shot, drowned, stabbed, or otherwise eliminated, it's coming to him soon. It's certainly easier to kill him than it is to kill someone like you.'

'Why do you say that?'

'You're a deputy. That's an automatic death penalty in some states.'

'Not this one,' Drake said.

'Look, there's nothing here to worry about.'

Sheri gave Drake a worried look.

'I'm just trying to say good-bye,' Driscoll said. 'In style.' He lifted his cutlery and gave the room a little homage.

'About that second man, I went down and

checked out a few different stables today. Can't say I turned up much.'

Driscoll paused, fork held in his hand, frozen midway to his mouth. 'Are you a detective now?'

'No. But I can't just sit around with nothing to do.'

Driscoll gave Drake a cold little smile that said just about all Drake needed to hear. 'We have absolutely no case. Unless that man decides to turn himself in, which I'll tell you now would be a tragic idea, considering. We might as well just file this one away and burn the evidence.'

'We still have the horses,' Drake offered.

'One is dead. And unless the other one learns to talk . . .'

Drake chewed his food. Sheri was watching him. 'Did anything come of the saddles?'

'The saddles are too common. The map was unmarked and the GPS looked to be just as clean. No fingerprints from the second man on any of it. There was a set of keys on the kid, just a key ring and an ignition key.'

'I'll bet that key fits the lock of a car up near Silver Lake,' Drake said.

'Already picked it up and brought it down to Seattle. Nothing there. It looks like it was just transportation. The kid had only been out of Monroe for a week when you picked him up.'

'No kidding.'

'It's probably better this way. He would have

been on the return flight for sure. Better not to waste the money on the ticket.'

'That's not a nice thing to say,' Sheri said.

'It's the truth,' Driscoll said, pushing his plate away. He asked if they wanted dessert.

Sheri looked disgusted. 'I'm actually a little tired. I'd like to get back to the hotel.'

'That sounds fine,' Driscoll said, 'but do you mind if I hold on to your husband an hour longer? I'd like to talk him up a bit, see what his thoughts are on the whole thing.'

'If we're leaving tomorrow,' Drake said, 'I think we should get back to the hotel.'

'Don't be like that, Drake,' Driscoll said, cleaning the food from his teeth with a toothpick he'd produced from his pocket. 'Put her in a taxi and we'll talk.'

'I don't think that's—'

'It's fine,' Sheri interrupted. 'You can talk a bit more. I'll be fine. Like he said, there is no danger now that the kid is dead.'

Driscoll waited for Drake to put Sheri in a cab. When Drake came back in and sat down, Driscoll said, 'I don't think she liked what I had to say.'

Hunt slowed the boat and watched in the distance as the ferry crossed on its way to Victoria. The sun had fallen, and for an hour he waited in a small cove south of the border. Light faded slow to the west, and for a while he simply sat and watched it go, the black coming over him, and where the sky and ocean met, a violet haze.

Though Eddie had given it to him straight, Hunt didn't like the idea that he owed someone his life, or that everything they had worked toward had now become someone else's. The thought that someone could just reach out and shake him down like that. Could control him and tell him how things would be. Eddie had told him it was just one man, a lawyer, someone like Eddie, who arranged out-of-the-way deals. It didn't seem that this was the whole story. Hunt had his suspicions. What did one man control that had them doing all this? He knew the lawyer was just the spokesperson for something larger, some international group. People who controlled it all, people who could make him and Eddie disappear.

He wondered about this, watching the sunset and waiting for the dark. He'd never know who the lawyer worked for, and perhaps it was better not to know. And now they would be running drugs for this man, running them whenever they were told, with no particular claim in the deal. The thought of it made his chest crumble. He put a hand to his sternum and breathed in, feeling the air enter his lungs. He was fifty-four years old. What was he doing here? Most men his age had put away their retirement already. Lived good lives, saved, and felt a kind of satisfaction from the family and home he'd never known.

Hunt needed to make a decision. He knew his life would never be the same as it had been just days before, with everything worked out, everything clear. Nora had told him to run. She had made him promise. But he needed a way out. He needed money, he needed Nora to be there with him.

He hadn't felt this way in many years. Not since his time in Monroe, when his life had not been his own and he had answered as best he could for the thing he'd done. It was not a good feeling, and he sat in the boat and felt the rock of the water beneath him. He watched the sun, the faded crown of it on the horizon, the night coming over him and the feeling inside him as heavy as granite.

Driscoll drove him back to the hotel. From the lobby, Drake watched as the unmarked patrol car turned out from the drive and sped east along the length of the lobby windows, as if Driscoll had a plane to catch, though Drake knew he was only headed back up the street to the office. Drake stood there, half-drunk from dinner. He was feeling out of sorts, feeling dismissed and lost. Everything had gone fine. In his half-drunken stupor he actually thought Driscoll could be a nice guy. Driscoll had told him he was still part of the investigation. Where it would go from this point, Driscoll didn't know, but he was happy to have Drake along if he could be of assistance, identify the odd body that popped up, as Driscoll had said, that sort of thing.

There was a funk to him, he smelled this now, something like whiskey mixed with a glass of port he shouldn't have had. He looked around the lobby. He almost couldn't find his bearings, too buzzed and tired to even look for the elevator or the key to his room.

In the elevator he thought to take his hat off when a woman his mother's age entered, but then he remembered he wasn't wearing it. She rode with him for several floors. He studied the woman's reflection in the brushed metal doors. Old as his mother would have been. His mother, an elementary school teacher, lost to leukemia when Drake was just a child, his father standing by, a faraway look coming into his eye. All the time he'd spent with his mother, and this is what he remembered. He couldn't turn it off. He couldn't turn away. Perhaps this was why he searched for his father, the man not there in the way he'd used to be, not the man Drake remembered at all. His mother gone, slipped away in that long-ago time of half-remembered childhood, but his father simply disappearing.

Drake didn't speak to the woman in the elevator. When she exited, he caught her eye looking back at him before the door closed. He wondered how he appeared to her, what rough thing he presented. Had she had a son like him? Someone his age, someone still young, still learning that things could disappear, be taken and never given back. He certainly didn't appear to be an officer of the law, but something wholly different, something of the opposite, more vagabond, more loose, like the kink of a rope after the strength of the knot unties.

When he reached his floor, he used the key card from his wallet to open the door to his room.

Inside, nothing but darkness, the cool, open feel of the windows, the city beyond, and a light drizzle falling through it all. Everything a kaleidoscope of water crystals and light. He heard his wife turn over in bed. 'Bobby?' Filled with sleep.

'Yes,' he said, but nothing more. Knowing she was only looking for confirmation. He took his holster from his belt and laid it across the dresser. His boots he dropped to the floor, and then, walking, his shirt, his jeans, and, as he sat on the opposite side of the bed looking out on the city and its lights, his socks. Getting under the sheets, he reached into the depths with his toes, the feeling almost swallowing him down. The cleanness of it.

Too tired now to brush his teeth, to clean the scum off him, the day, the ruined lives that had been left behind over the course of the past few days. He wanted to but couldn't let it go, brought it all with him to bed, down into the sheets, lingered in it and felt it not on his skin but somehow beneath it, like a layer had been added, thick and gummy, to the insides of his person.

'Sheri?' he said, the city lights like starlight on her turned body. He reached out to touch her, felt his cold fingers on her warm back. She turned and for a moment clutched the sheets to her chest, her eyes looking at him, the dull blue-silver light of the city on her. 'Sheri,' he said again, putting his arm beneath her pillow, his other around the bend of her side, his hand to her back, feeling the warmth. 'Tell me I'm a good man,' he said.

'You are.' Her eyes open, unblinking, looking back at him.

He knew he was drunk, acting foolish, but it seemed to matter to him then, all of it, all of what had passed in the last couple of days. He couldn't explain it. He just wanted someone to tell him he was a good man, that he'd done his job, that somehow it mattered.

He pulled her closer and put his lips to the underside of her chin, his arms tightening around her. Sheri let him, arching her neck until he could put his nose and lips beneath her head into the warmth of her body, clean and smelling of apples and soap. It felt to Drake like two worlds coming together, the past and the present, like his father's small orchard. Shooting apples off the branches with the old .22. All of this before he'd gone away to college, before a lot of things, all of it mixed up together, gun smoke drifting through orchard light, broken apples in the wet evening grass, the smell of cordite and freshly fired rifles.

The lawyer had given Grady the time and location of the meet. He had only a set of coordinates and a GPS. Grady checked the GPS. The wind came bristling over the cockpit and pulled his hair back, his skin red and irritated with the speed. All around he heard the clap of the water underneath the hull. He was doing about thirty-five knots, white water leading off in a trail behind him.

He had wanted to kill Hunt at the dock, but it wasn't what had been asked for. He was to let Hunt do the exchange, kill him, take the drugs, and then sink the boat. Make it look like an accident. It was easy to hide a murder under a half mile of water.

From their talk at the boat launch, he could tell Hunt would never be the type to let him get close. Not offering his name, barely letting Grady get close enough to offer his hand. Not like the last man Grady had killed, an ex-sergeant in the reserves, someone who had shared a beer with him at a bar. Someone who had at one point been in business with the lawyer, who had been a smuggler just like Hunt. Grady had been paid to run him off, scare him, perhaps even take a digit or two and leave him like that. But the sergeant had been easier, drunk, stumbling out to his car to take a piss in the cool night air with Grady following. Someone who Grady could see wouldn't be missed. No children, no wife, just a string of bad decisions, decisions that had cost the lawyer a considerable amount of money. Grady had slit the ex-sergeant's throat behind the bar, the sergeant's pants open and his penis in his hands. Blood and urine collected in a puddle on the cement lot. The lawyer had paid him well for that, simply to make the man disappear. Did it matter how?

Grady's cell phone rested on a grip pad in front of him. The lawyer had called several more times and Grady knew he'd missed the meeting with the Vietnamese. He didn't need the lawyer to tell him this. Soon it would all be finished, Hunt dead, and the heroin delivered. Again, he thought, the how of it didn't matter, as long as the job was done, as long as the heroin was delivered and Hunt was dead. Everyone would have their satisfaction soon.

He thought about that ex-sergeant, throat slit, bleeding out onto the cement, a death rattle going through him, the tremor of it through the pool of blood and urine, like windswept waves passing across a lake. He'd reached down then, pulling at the man's ankles, and begun to drag him across the gravel, a stainless table waiting at his house, a hacksaw and whatever else Grady could imagine.

The memory of the ex-sergeant passed with the bounce of the boat across the water, knife bag at his feet, riding out the waves with Grady, knives and rifle loaded and ready. It would be a shame to use the scope on Hunt, killing from a distance, but Grady knew from experience that it was best not to be seen at all.

unt slowed the boat. The outbound ferry passed, and he could hear the distant pull of the engines, the deep thrumming of the ferry as it crossed in the night toward Victoria. He turned his engines off completely, all around him the lap of the water against the sides of the Bayliner. What could he do but wait and hope and feel the water all around and know this was how it would be and how his life would always be?

From his pocket he removed a pack of cigarettes he'd hidden from Nora. He lit one and felt the familiar wash of the tobacco and his head going up into the air for that brief moment. He brought out a pair of marine binoculars and sat watching the ferry and checked his watch. It wouldn't be long now.

The ferry passed, and in two minutes he felt the dark rise of its wake and the water moving under him. He was sitting in the captain's seat, swiveled around so he could look out on his engines and the waves as they gripped into them. The cigarette was gone, and with it he felt the cool night wash over him, a light breeze feeding off the water and racing inland over the ocean.

He heard the soft drone of another boat, building for a minute until it was a throaty whine, then ceasing altogether. From where he sat, he could see the dark boat come out of the night, drifting almost sideways in the current. Night all around them and the boats drifting together, still and silent, like two shadows resting on the water. The other boat was larger than Hunt's, with a big forward cabin and a raised cockpit. Two men, one at the controls and another waiting on the aft deck. Both watching Hunt.

When the two boats drew closer, Hunt recognized one of the men from past deals. Standing at the gunwale, Hunt called for a line.

'Surprised to see you here,' the man said.

'What do you mean by that?' Hunt said, taking the line as the two boats drew abreast and the gunwales aligned.

'I wouldn't have expected it. That's all.'

'What wouldn't you have expected?'

'This kind of deal. I just wouldn't have thought it would be your thing.'

'I'm finding the available options limited.'

'The whole thing makes me feel a little strange,' the man said.

'Everything lately, considering.'

'Yes, we heard about the kid, the one you were working with in the mountains.'

Hunt was silent for a moment. He hadn't

thought it would be like this and he hadn't expected the guilt he would feel over the kid. 'Did you hear he was dead?'

The man was silent for a moment. 'How did it happen?'

'In the holding cell, before they walked him across the sky bridge.'

The man at the cockpit came down to join them at the gunwale. The dull red light from the cockpit shone on all three of them. Above, a passing break in the clouds focused the moonlight on them, the two-dimensional flatness of light and dark showing how they took the news in the cavernous shadows of their faces. All of them were standing together, and as they talked, Hunt untied the bumpers from where they sat, pinned between the two boats.

'You should feel lucky it wasn't you,' said the man Hunt knew. He was wearing a blue sweater with a light down vest.

The other, who wore a sweatshirt and had a strange smile that never seemed to go away, looked off at a ferry bound for the mainland. Hunt did not look up from what he was doing but continued to work, untying his bumpers, readying them for the shipment of drugs.

'You know you're not going to need those bumpers,' the man with the funny smile said.

'But the drugs?'

The man laughed.

'I'm surprised you're not dead,' the man with the funny smile said.

'I've been saying that for years,' the man in the sweater said, watching Hunt and waiting for a smile to come across Hunt's face. And when none came, the man said, 'You are lucky, you know. We could have been asked to shoot you right here, and no one would have known a thing.'

'Were you?'

'Would you still be here?'

Hunt didn't say anything. He stepped back from the gunwale and stood watching the two men. The man with the funny smile went inside the cabin of the boat, where Hunt heard voices.

'What did he mean, I won't be needing the bumpers?' Hunt asked the first man. He was beginning to feel uneasy about the whole thing.

'Don't you know?' the man said. 'They really are playing you, aren't they? Don't you know what you're here for?'

'I don't know a damn thing,' Hunt said.

'I don't want a part of this any more than you do,' the man said. 'But it's the way things are going. It's the new premium of the business. I don't think I need to tell you what will happen if this gets messed up.'

'They would kill you,' the man with the funny smile said to Hunt, stepping out onto the deck from inside the cabin. 'I'm surprised you're still alive as it is.' He held a young woman by the elbow. The woman was dressed in a long-sleeved shirt and jeans, her eyes bloodshot and a worn look on her face, as if she'd been crying.

The man in the sweater stepped back a ways to let the girl through. 'I'm not used to this either.'

'Not used to what?' Hunt said.

The man with the funny smile nudged the girl forward. 'This is what you came for.'

'What do you mean?'

'This one here. The girl.' The man put his hand over the girl's shoulder. The girl shook it away.

'This is it, this is the exchange.'

'What do you mean, "the girl"?'

'The girl,' the man that was known to Hunt said flatly. 'There were two girls from Ho Chi Minh. But this one got scared. She was supposed to transfer in Vancouver and continue on to Seattle.'

'What happened to the other girl?'

'Picked up, I'd guess,' the man with the funny smile said. 'Probably passed her drugs a couple hours ago. This one's ripe to do the same.'

'How much is she carrying?'

'One point five kilograms.'

Hunt did the math in his head. Ninety thousand dollars.

No one looked at the girl. She stood between the two men; in her hand she carried a small purse that Hunt thought had probably been her carry-on.

'Can you help her over?' Hunt said, holding out his hand. The girl looked at him and then she looked at the man with the funny smile, and he pushed her over.

'Careful,' the man with the funny smile said. 'You don't want her to burst.'

140

Hunt threw the line back to the two men. The one he didn't know was already at the controls. The inbound ferry had passed on its return trip to Vancouver, and as the two men started up their engine, Hunt watched the receding lights of the ferry. He hadn't noticed the low sound of the ferry engines until then, and he sat there in the night and watched the white water come off the back of the other boat and the two men lift up and head into the night.

After the men were gone, Hunt could hear the small breathing of the woman beside him. In the night her hair appeared to be black, pulled away from her face, with thin baby hairs exposed at her scalp from wearing her hair too tight. Hunt thought her to be twenty, though she could have been thirty; he could never tell with Asians. Skinny, she was flat chested and small as a child.

'This is what it's come to,' he said. The girl looked over at him. 'You don't speak any English, do you?'

'A little.'

Hunt was surprised; her accent was heavy but the words were understandable. He felt the blood rise in his face. 'We didn't mean to speak about you that way.'

'I know what I am,' the girl said.

'Yes,' Hunt said. He looked at his hands just for something to look at. The packet of drugs he had expected to receive from the two men would have been good. Better than good, it would have been all he needed to get away. The men had been right about him: if he messed this up, he would be dead. He was surprised he wasn't dead already. How long did he expect to keep working this way? How long before he ended up like the kid?

The girl wasn't what he had expected. It wasn't as clear cut as he was used to, it wasn't clear cut at all, but he thought if Eddie could move the heroin she was carrying in her stomach, there was still hope.

Before he'd known about the girl, Hunt had planned to take the drugs – drugs that should have been in the bumpers of his boat but were in some girl's stomach, some girl who spoke and breathed, who had a mind and a stake in the matter. He'd known he would take the drugs from the moment Eddie had told him about the job. From the moment he'd heard about the kid and what had happened – and what he knew would happen to him now.

That he would be killed was not something he doubted. Maybe not today, but he knew now that it could happen, would happen if he ever found himself in the same position as the kid, locked up, ready to say anything to avoid going back to Monroe.

To have a choice in the matter was all he really wanted. To know that he had some say, though small, over when he died and in what way gave him a little hope. This girl, he thought, what could he do with her? Though he had killed before, he wasn't a killer, at least not anymore, not on purpose.

He needed the heroin she was carrying. Needed it to get free of his life. Because it was not just desperation he felt, but also a strange happiness. The happiness of knowing that he might make it, that at least now he had a chance. The other boat was long gone, disappeared into the night, the men on their way back to whatever hidden slip they worked out of. He showed the girl to a seat and felt the first wave from the inbound ferry hit. It went under the boat, and when he leaned to steady himself he felt the fiberglass dust falling all around him.

Through the scope, Grady watched the bullet hit just over Hunt's head. He saw the black cut of it where it had missed Hunt and gone into the white fiberglass, tinted green by the night vision. He was a half mile off, hidden by the clouded night and the dark water, with only the scope to tell him Hunt existed at all.

Kill Hunt, he thought.

What about the girl?

Gut her.

Yes.

He took aim again and fired.

The glass in the cockpit spiderwebbed as another bullet hit the boat. Hunt lay facedown on the deck, his hands out in front and his cheek to the cold, wet floor. The girl was down, too, crouched in front of the small cabin doors. He told her to open them. He told her to climb down and not to come back up. The whole time the boat was rocking with the ferry wake.

Those two bullets had been meant to kill him. Perfect, well-placed head shots, but the unexpected had happened, a slight drift of the boat as the ferry wake had come under it.

There was a pause, a strange silence, waves running along the hull, the almost imperceptible rocking of the boat as the ocean lifted and then gave it back. Hunt leaned over the edge of the gunwale and looked into the darkness. Nothing moved, and for a second he thought it was all over. He carried the small Browning. It had been there all the time, since he'd returned from the mountains. He held it now and looked in the direction he thought the shots had come from.

Muzzle fire lit in five short bursts, and by the

time he dropped his head, the bullets were already slamming into the side of the boat. *Thwok-thwok-thwok*, like river stones breaching the water from a high bridge, fast and silent. A couple of rounds missed, just inches over the gunwale, and went whistling off over his starboard side. Hunt heard a boat's engine start, something powerful, something with some speed behind it. By the time he reached the cockpit, bullets were boiling across the bow of the Bayliner.

The boat sat there stiff as a corpse on a table, Hunt too scared to rise up and push the throttle forward. With his head ducked, Hunt wedged the muzzle of the Browning into the back pocket of his jeans and grabbed a cotton towel from the side compartment, below the cockpit. He could hear the other boat coming on, the fall and surge of the propeller as it gripped the waves.

He lit the towel with his lighter and lay blowing the flame as another surge of bullets broke over the boat. Fiberglass dust fell everywhere and bit into Hunt's lungs. He felt the cockpit glass fall in a thousand little pieces, crystals of it everywhere and all through his hair. He shook to get them off and blew again into the rising flame of the towel. When the fibers caught and he could see the cotton begin to bend and take the flame, he stuffed the unlit end into the spare gas barrel. He rose and threw the barrel over his port side. He heard the splash but did not turn to see if the towel remained lit. A volley of bullets cut across the cockpit.

A sudden sliver of pain in his calf dropped him to his knees. Something sparked and he could smell the plastic odor of electricity and rubber. He groaned, knew he was hurt, but didn't have time to care. He took a quick look back over the port side at the floating barrel beside him. It was still lit, flame playing at the opening.

Fear gave him courage. He reached up to grab the throttle and pushed it forward; the engines surged to life, the boat lifting up out of the water with the speed. Two seconds later, he could see behind him the giant fireball of fuel spreading into the sky and the dark cloud of a gas fire blotting out the moon and stars. The gasoline spread along the water and for a minute he watched the flames and the lick of the smoke as it rose.

The explosion lit on the night water, and Grady, who had been moving fast, slowed the boat and raised a hand to shield his eyes. He swore under his breath. 'Now what?' he said, looking out on the fire as it rose red, then black into the night, the reflection swept along with the current of the water. The light had fried his retinas, as if he had sat staring into a campfire and then looked away, only to see that night surrounded him, dark and hard as a wall.

Grady brought the throttle down and slowed the boat to a near stop. He heard the rush of the flames as they fed on the night air, and the lap of the water against his hull. Nothing else. One of the bullets must have hit the fuel line, perhaps a spark igniting it all? He thought he'd seen Hunt falter a bit, taking a bullet. Grady raised the scope to his eye and looked into the fire, but the light was everywhere and too much for the night vision.

He eased the throttle forward and circled his boat once through the smoke. Smell of seawater and gasoline, the odor running all through him, over the cockpit and up into his nostrils, where he took it down into his throat and swallowed it whole. No debris. Not one thing. Just a burning lake of flame on the water. He cursed again and raised the scope, running the night vision out onto the surrounding water. A white trail of engine froth a mile off.

The draw of his wake lay behind Hunt in a white trail. Depending on how far behind him the other boat was, he knew it would not be difficult to follow him. The gas explosion had only given him time. He opened up the throttle – the engines roaring behind him – and looked on ahead, with the boat bouncing recklessly from port to starboard as it bit into the chop before him. He heard the Vietnamese girl inside the cabin let out a muffled scream. In that moment he didn't care: they needed to get away and he was trying his best to get them there. The glass that had fallen along the bow now clattered back with the wind and fell all around him. He was standing with his knees bent, taking the chop as it came, trying to anticipate the fall and rise of the water he was running across.

Behind him the white track of the boat spread out until it was lost in the grays and blacks of the night. The motors blared behind him. The wind came full on through the broken cockpit window and whipped him hard in the face and made his eyes water. He'd dropped the Browning somewhere, and from time to time he felt it skitter along the cockpit floor and hit his foot. When he bent into the wind and turned to look behind him, he could see nothing but the white boat wake and the night stretched out dark as wine on the distant water, a horizon of fire where the gas can had gone up. Even this was fading, as if he were rounding the edge of the earth and it were going up over the curve.

Hunt slowed the engine and let it drift in neutral. There was a growing pain in his calf, and he knew something was wrong; he felt the blood and the swelling calf filling up the confines of his jeans. He didn't look down, didn't want to. For fear, or perhaps just out of necessity, he didn't take his eyes off the water behind him, and he listened and waited for whoever was chasing after him.

He could hear the soft gurgle of his engine belt and then, in the distance, the slap of a boat taking waves fast and jarring with the movement. He heard the air wallop under the boat, the smacking sound of the water as it came. In the night, he couldn't tell in which direction the boat was running, but he could see nearly a quarter mile off where his own wake lay and hoped it was not anywhere close.

From Hunt's port side, a searchlight blazed on, and he saw the water in the night and the green of the ocean and how the light sank into it and then disappeared. He knew by the height of the searchlight that one of the big sixty-foot Coast

Guard cutters had been attracted by the explosion. He knew that they would have radar, that he was already a blip on their screen. He knew, too, that if needed, he could outrun them.

The captain of the cutter came on the loudspeaker, the light searching the water, but as Hunt watched he became aware it was not him they were looking for. Still night out there and the amplified, almost mechanical voice of the captain playing on the water, Hunt placed his hands on the metal frame of the windshield and watched as the Coast Guard's tower light scanned the darkness. He turned his engines off completely and listened: the deep thrumming of the cutter's engines, and something else, too, a gurgling of horsepower out there, water lapping at the sides of his boat, and his pursuer shrouded somewhere in the darkness.

The searchlight passed across the surface of the water. A half mile off, Hunt saw the other boat come into focus and be taken up in the light, a midnight blue sixteen-footer with twin engines. The cutter turned, training a steady beam of light now on Hunt's pursuer. As the cutter came on, Hunt watched the small boat rise up out of the water, propelled forward on two powerful motors, light chasing after it, froth spraying in the air, and then the huge bow of the cutter came into view as the searchlight followed. There was the sound of the machine gun again from the smaller boat and the look of sparks flying along the cutter's metal hull.

From the compartment to the right of the throttle, Hunt raised the binoculars and sighted the smaller boat. With one hand on the wheel, the man raised the gun and fired on the cutter, the machine gun bucking wildly in his hand and the bullets spraying everywhere.

Twice the smaller boat circled the cutter, the bullets reaching up toward the light, trying to take it, trying to leave all of them in darkness once again. On the second turn, Hunt could see the man clearly, the thin white skin, with the pale pink around the eyes and the dark, blood-filled bags beneath. He knew him, recognized him from the docks, from their conversation.

Grady charged the cutter and let out a muzzle burst. There was the clatter of bullets ricocheting on the cutter's metal hull. The searchlight went up in a shower of sparks, and Hunt could hear Grady's smaller boat passing through the ensuing darkness, the noise of the boat's engines falling as the cutter came between him and Grady, chasing after Grady. Still, Hunt could hear the sound of the loudspeaker and then gunshots, different from the ones that had sounded before, pistol fire from the cutter, without the reckless sweep of the automatic. In the darkness there was no clear target, and Hunt knew Grady would get away.

Hunt waited, listening as the two boats moved off. When he was sure they had moved far enough away, Hunt started his engine. The Bayliner gurgled to a start and the smell of exhaust came to his nose and tainted the air. Grady had the Coast Guard's attention for now. The muffled sound of pistol fire came across the water, pulled on the wind like distant thunder. Hunt listened for return fire from the machine gun but didn't hear anything more than the water at the sides of his boat. It was as still and calm as it had been before. He breathed deeply, the taste of the air on his tongue, rich ocean air, saline and vegetal. Cold north wind funneled down out of Canada. Hunt opened up the throttle again and sped toward land.

PART III
BY LAND

From where he lay on the couch in the living room, Eddie heard the kitchen phone ring. By the end of the first ring, he could hear the pulse of the phone upstairs, the two phones off by a half second. He knew then that it had not gone as he thought it would and that Hunt was alive.

For a moment he lay there on the couch and listened to the muffled sound of Nora's voice. From beneath the cushion where his head rested, he removed the .22 and disengaged the safety. He wore a pair of Hunt's sweats and an old T-shirt he had been given. With the pistol in his hand he went up the stairs until he could see the light escaping beneath the door. He waited a moment on the stairs, feeling the soft imprint of the gun in his hand.

After a half second, he went to the door and rapped lightly. The pistol he put to the left of the doorframe, and with it hidden, he opened the door. Nora turned to look up at him from the bed, her eyes playing over him for just a second before looking away. She had pulled the phone to her, and the line lay all along the floor and climbed the bed to where she sat. He stood looking down at her from the doorway, the gun held out beyond the frame in the hallway. He didn't want to use it, but he would. It seemed unreal to him that this was what it had come to. He didn't know what Hunt had told her already, but he could hear his voice on the other end of the line and it sounded rushed and a little frantic but not altogether out of control. Eddie looked for any sign of recognition in Nora's face. Again, he hoped to find nothing.

'Eddie is here,' Nora said, and looked up at him. 'No. I'll put it together, but the truck?' She went to look out the window, and Eddie knew she was looking at the horse trailer and he knew exactly what Hunt was thinking.

'Does he want to speak to me?' Eddie asked. He was still waiting at the door, his hand growing tired from holding the gun, and then as he lowered it to rest against the outside frame, he heard the butt skip a moment along the wall. Nora was still at the window, listening to Hunt. 'Let me talk to him, Nora.'

Nora turned to look at Eddie, but when she asked Hunt, her face showed no indication that Hunt cared to speak to him. 'Give me the phone, Nora.' Eddie felt his hand tighten on the grip, and he was careful to raise his finger from the trigger and place it along the guard. Nora gave him a look and turned back to the window. 'Okay,' she said. 'Okay. Yes, I think I can do that.' And then she was saying good-bye and putting the phone back in the cradle of the receiver.

'Why didn't he want to talk to me?'

Nora turned and in the same moment began to move across the room. 'He said something went wrong. He said someone tried to kill him. It was not the Coast Guard, or the DEA, but someone with an M-16 or something big, shooting up the boat. He says he still has the package, but he's hurt. I could hear it in his voice. He wouldn't tell me a thing about it.' Nora drew up next to Eddie and she stood looking up at him, his chin just at the height of her nose and cheekbones. 'I could tell something was wrong. His voice was strained in a way I've never heard before.' Eddie brought his arm around and he hugged her close in the doorframe and brought the gun up until his arm was played back and the .22 rested safely behind him.

'He'll be fine,' Eddie said. 'He'll be just fine.'

Though the Coast Guard had stopped shooting, Grady turned wide, throwing the boat up on its starboard side and hitting the throttle. Close behind, he could see how the cutter ate up the trail of his wake. He saw the green and red beacon lights and the aura of white light produced by the internal cabins. He didn't know where Hunt was; for the moment he didn't care. All he could think about was getting away. In his smaller boat he was certainly faster, but he was sure there would be inflatable Zodiacs and, if he didn't reach the shore soon enough, a helicopter. The lights of a small community lay ahead of him. He had no way of knowing whether the water he was riding through was Canadian or American, and he pushed the boat faster, standing in front of the wheel and feeling the spent shell casings bobble and roll against his feet. There was the hollow metal sound as the casings rolled back with the boat, and when he looked around he could see them all there, building into a small mound against the aft deck.

Behind him, the cutter dropped away. There was

land coming up at him out of the darkness, and the hull hit and scraped against the pebbled beach, the fiberglass splintering beneath him. He was thrown forward. His head hit the console and he felt blood rise and fall into his eyes. The propellers caught – sound of metal twisting, rock scraping. The boat lay down on its port side, its white belly laid out on the beach with the waves rising toward it. Everything silent but the sound of the waves and the wind as it whistled over the starboard gunwale. He wiped an arm across his head and for a moment sat looking at the dark stain on the sleeve of his shirt.

On the shore he could see rocks and a few large pieces of driftwood, then farther in how the grass grew and built up toward a street lined at hundred-yard intervals with yellow overhead light. He wiped again at his head with the sleeve of his shirt. The AR-15 lay at his feet, and he picked it up, releasing the stock and laying it along the body of the rifle. He carried his bag and went stumbling up the bank of grass and out onto the street.

Drake woke to the sound of his phone vibrating on the bedside table. His wife stirred and pulled the hotel bedding over her face. They'd forgotten to close the blinds, and there was a pale moon over downtown. He had fallen asleep immediately. He picked up the phone and went to the window to answer. Below, on the freeway, nothing was left of the accident Sheri and he had watched the night before. For a brief moment he thought of the people involved, of the cars sitting in their driveways, of evidence and things left behind.

Still half-asleep, he listened to what Driscoll was telling him. He closed the phone and for a half second stood at the window looking out on the city. Late-night traffic, yellow cabs waiting outside the hotel doors twenty-some stories below, the golden beams of their headlights playing on the wet cement. He turned back to the room and found his pants, then checked the time, just a little past midnight, fifteen minutes till Driscoll arrived.

He took a shower with the door open so that he could hear the phone ring. When he was done,

162

he toweled down, shaved, and combed his hair as best he could to disguise his thinning temples, then dressed and went back out into the room. He walked back to the bed, the bathroom light leaking into the hotel room and outlining the profile of his wife's body under the sheets. He pulled the sheets back and gave Sheri a light kiss, then stood and fixed his holster on his belt.

Sheri pulled a pillow over her head to block out the light. 'You're leaving again?' she said, her voice cracking with sleep, her auburn hair flattened and mussed by the pillow.

'Sorry.'

'This is some vacation you got me on.'

'I know,' he said, 'but it'll be over soon.'

'I liked it better when you saved cats from trees and wrote reports on cow tippings.'

'I never saved any cats,' he said.

'I was just doing some cheerful thinking.'

Her bare foot was sticking out of the bottom of the sheets, and he went over and gave her big toe a playful tug. 'You going to be okay here?' he said.

'Just tell me all you're going to do is save a cat from a tree, and I promise not to worry.'

'I'm planning on saving a mess of cats, a whole litter.' He bent and kissed her, and he felt her hand come over his neck and linger there for a moment before it dropped away.

'That's good,' she said. 'That's just fine.'

Hunt made no effort to hide himself. The girl sat in the seat beside him. She didn't say a thing, just watched Hunt with her brown eyes. Hunt felt the pain in his calf. He tried to catch his breath, tried to lock the hurt away inside him, thinking the whole time of the distance still to travel.

His boat lay facing inland with the bow out of the water, the waves rising up and splashing over the aft deck. In the distance he could hear the sound of a helicopter rotor. The boat was useless, rifled through with bullets, the smell of burnt wiring and melted plastic. With his seat swiveled around, he watched the red and white Coast Guard Dolphin fly low over the water toward them, the searchlights scanning the water as it came. Soon the lights would be on them. Hunt held his breath, the girl beside him, watching the helicopter until it curved north, veering away from them on some unseen rail. It hadn't seen them, their bullet-torn boat hidden on the radar by the mass of land they had beached on. Had they stayed out there, at any speed, the helicopter would have found them. They needed to get away from the boat. Hunt watched as the flashing helicopter lights tracked up the coast, passing in the night at a mile's distance.

A few drops started to fall. He could hear the rain, the small collision of it on the fiberglass deck, something wet across his forehead and then again on his forearm. His senses were coming back to him, taken up by all the adrenaline, covered up, heightened. He wasn't sure. He looked over at the girl. High cheekbones, skinny, with a few wrinkles around the eyes. She was looking at him. Had she said something? A sudden wash of pain as he tried to stand. He sensed everything at once, and none of it felt right.

He looked down at his leg to where the slim line of blood escaped, and he could feel the pain all through him, shooting up along the nerves like venom in the vein. He tested it, putting more weight than he needed to onto the wound, and he felt the pain come again and something new, almost jellied, slip down his leg. The leg would do for walking, though he did not know for how long or to where.

He had remembered the slip of land from past runs, the long angle of the island, connected at one end by a small ferry dock. It was an Indian reservation two and a half hours north of Seattle. In the past he'd had a friend here, a man he'd known in Monroe, someone who could put him up, could help him out, but that was years ago

165

now, when Hunt had been a different man alto-gether. Hunt didn't even know if the man still lived here, if he still existed – it was a lifetime ago – but he hoped if he could find the house, if he could find his friend, it would do for a safe haven.

The slim line of red trickled down onto the floor, and he could see where the rain was beginning to fall and wipe the color away. Under the silver light of the moon, the deck beneath him was washed with the pink watercolor of his wound. In one of the compartments he found the boat's small orange survival bag. He took from it a roll of gauze, a surgical rag, a pair of scissors, an Ace bandage, the hydrogen peroxide, and the iodine. He placed some of these on the console and the rest he gave to the girl and told her to hold it. He rested in the captain's chair and cut away his pants until he could see the purple hole through his calf, the blood already congealed in sticky red scabs. He let the peroxide fall onto it and felt the cold-ness of the bubbling liquid as it went down into his shoe. When he thought he could handle it, he rubbed the wound down with the rag and winced and saw white-hot spots appear beneath his eyelids.

Had anyone passed in that moment, they would have heard the scream carried with the wind and then suddenly ending. Hunt had not passed out, but it was close. He unscrewed the iodine and let it fall freely, feeling the iron-colored liquid enter into the torn flesh. Quick as he could, he wrapped the gauze, then secured it all down with the Ace bandage, his leg swollen with blood and pumping beneath the bandage like some monster trying to break out.

He felt a moment of nausea pass quickly across him. Then it was gone. Anything of importance he kept in the bright orange survival bag. From the console where he had laid out the medical supplies he selected the iodine, peroxide, bandages, and tape and put them into the bag with the scissors and his lighter. He opened the compartment beneath the console and took out his wallet and cell phone. From a side pocket beneath the throttle he took the flares, cracking open the breech on the flare gun and then snapping it closed again. All of this went into the bright orange bag. He zipped the bag closed and swung it across his back. He searched the floor for the Browning but didn't find it. He took his first painful steps and walked down toward the engines, careful not to slip. He motioned to the girl with his hand. When she came down the deck carrying her bag, he showed her what he wanted her to do.

With her hands she felt the dark water. On the surface the little discarded things of the boat floated – random pens, a coil of rope – and on the bottom, in the shallow parts where the water dimmed to a black murk, Hunt could see coins, broken glass, all of it fallen to the deck and collected there. He saw now the fuel in the water and smelled where it had coated the rope and the pens. A wave came over and washed along the deck; he felt the cold on his tennis shoes. He told the girl to run her open fingers along the corner of the deck until she felt the barrel of the Browning. 'Like this,' he said, spreading his fingers wide. She knelt and, after three sweeps of the water, pulled the Browning up. He undid the orange survival bag and let the gun fall in.

Careful not to bang his calf, he went over the side of the boat, landed with his good leg as support, and hopped forward slowly with his hand on the bulwark. He felt his way along, finding the boat cleats and using these for support.

He checked his watch but found the face broken and the time stopped a little past eleven. The cell phone lay in his bag, but he did not check it and instead began to walk up the beach, holding his leg stiffly beneath him. The girl followed but did not offer to help. To her, Hunt must have seemed near death, his pants torn and his calf swollen as big as his thigh, the blood beginning to soak through the bandage. And on his back, the bright orange bag, like a warning.

Hunt estimated there to be eight more hours before the sun came up and the boat would be found.

Driscoll was waiting just outside the lobby with his cruiser door pulled open and his hand up over the roof of the car when Drake saw him. 'Hey, I'm sorry to have been so blunt when I called earlier, but I think you're really going to like this.'

'What are we doing?'

'I think we got your guy.'

Drake opened the car door and stepped in. He wore his hat again. For a brief moment, he'd thought of wearing the full uniform, but then dressed quickly in a pair of worn jeans and a light henley. Driscoll was dressed as he was earlier, in a brown suit, yellow shirt, and maroon tie. The smell of scotch and steak still clung to him, and Drake could feel it heavy in the air when the doors closed.

'Now you're ready for me to be a detective?' Drake said.

'No, the world's not ready for that.'

'What, then?'

'I just think you'll have a good time with this one. Plus we'll need you to identify this guy.'

Drake looked out on the downtown streets, a light rain falling. He took his hat off and laid it on his lap and gazed up at the tops of the buildings as they passed. Driscoll flipped a switch and the grill lights began to flash, and Drake could feel the acceleration take hold.

'Did you bring your gun?'

'Am I going to need it?'

'Do you ever?'

He was about to say no but then thought of recent days and reconsidered. He slid the weight of it around on his waistband and let it lie against his thigh.

Seeing it, Driscoll smiled. 'Would have thought you'd be more of the six-shooter type.'

'Regulations,' Drake joked.

'Regulations will get you killed,' Driscoll said, bringing the flap of his coat open. 'You know what that is? Desert Eagle, three fifty-seven Magnum.'

Driscoll said it in such a way and with such pride that Drake had a hard time holding a straight face.

'You know what that is?' Driscoll said, tapping the closed fabric of his coat. 'Stopping power.'

'I'm sure it is.'

The car took an odd bounce, and for a moment Drake could feel the vehicle turning through the air, just enough to notice, and then the tires landed and everything straightened.

'What are we doing?' Drake asked.

'Flying.'

Eddie tried Hunt's number again, listened to the message catch, and then hung up. 'You said he was where?'

Nora looked up at the darkening clouds overhead; a few rain-drops had begun to fall, and they could hear them pattering down through the nearby undergrowth. She went back into the stables and grabbed the third saddle. 'Didn't say. Just said he'd call when he found somewhere safe.'

'This is crazy, Nora.'

'I don't know what it is, but I don't really think we should hang around here waiting to find out.'

'We don't know that.'

'Do you know something I don't?' Nora threw the saddle over a small bench. She began to fold the horse blankets for the three horses, and after she was done, she lifted the nearest saddle and put the weight down over the blankets.

'I don't know a thing,' Eddie said, raising the cell phone up in the air and showing it to Nora. 'I just don't like the idea of running off like this.'

'Look, we need to get the truck, in any case. For now, let's think about that.'

'And then what?'

'And then we go somewhere and we figure this all out.'

'I don't like this, Nora.'

'Did I say I liked it?'

'What did it sound like when you talked to him?'

'It sounded like there was a whole lot of wind rushing by, a whole lot of water, and someone was chasing him.'

'We don't know that.'

'He said someone shot at him. What am I supposed to take from that?'

'I don't know. It just worries me that we're rushing off into something we don't know anything about.'

'What do you want to do? What can you do?' Nora said in a rush. She stopped loading the horse trailer and just stood looking at Eddie, her eyes unwavering. 'Do you think they're trying to kill him?' she said. 'Do you think it's the man you're working for? What do you think?'

Eddie raised his hands. 'Slow down, Nora. Just slow down.' He could see her staring at him. She didn't move. The two of them stood ten feet apart. 'Let me try him one more time, that's all, let me just try and see if I can get ahold of him.' He lifted the cell phone and punched Redial.

The first car he'd seen slowed to a near stop, but when it drew closer and the driver could see the bag and the muzzle of the rifle behind, the car bolted away down the road. Grady tried to grab out for it, somehow thinking that if he could get his hands on the car, then he could stop it. The blood was in his eyes again, a slick layer of it from the cut on his forehead. He bounced off the metal, feeling the car slide past him. He raised the rifle and let out a quick burst. The back window blew out but the car kept moving and he didn't see the brake lights flash on.

All around him rain fell from the sky; there was the smell of sea grass, the dirt and seaweed smell of the ocean, and the wind blowing it all off the dunes and up onto the road. He ran on. From somewhere behind, he could hear the high-pitched whine of a boat motor, and he figured two boats for a cutter that size, possibly twelve men. They had fired pistol shots at him from the cutter, perhaps too stunned in those first moments to move for the armory. But he knew now that it would be worse.

He ran on, his lungs beating steadily in his chest, the lights passing overhead in long intervals, and the street filled with black night and the sound of his shoes. He passed beneath a light and watched as his shadow lengthened and grew away from him. The road on which he ran was a long break-water; on one side was the ocean, and on the other, mudflats, where brackish pools of seawater lay and waited for the tide. He could smell the foul tidal pools.

There was the whine of a motor again, then the wind, and he didn't hear it anymore. A quarter mile away, there was the aura of light, yellow and red, and he realized he was looking at the back of a gas station. The rear, turned toward the ocean, was nothing but black shadow, but he could see the front glowing now in the night. There he thought he would get a car, either from the filling tank or from whoever worked there. It didn't matter. He would take what came.

In the morning there had been nothing, only the dead kid. Now there was the girl. Hunt's leg was shot through, but he had the girl and her stomach full of heroin. He couldn't decide if any of it had been a good thing. The limp grew worse, but Hunt walked on. He could feel the blood collecting in his shoe. The rain kept falling and his hair lay matted, wet and flat, to his forehead. His face slackened, then tensed, with each step. He thought of Nora. He thought of the horses and the house and everything that waited for him when this was all over. Behind him, the girl followed. He knew she had some stake in all this. Some right to it. But he couldn't think about that now. Like an explorer of new worlds, he thought only about what came next, what new surprise waited for him. There wasn't time for anything else. The wound in his leg throbbed as he stumbled forward, his legs feeling wobbly as gelatin.

There were no streetlamps, only the lights from the houses. When the yellow light of a flood came on with his movement, he followed it up to the house. He was walking up the drive with the girl a few paces behind.

'Don't be scared,' he told the girl. They stopped for a moment in the floodlight, and Hunt felt his leg pulsing beneath him.

'I'm not scared,' the girl said. 'Never scared.'

He could see a small welt along her cheek that he hadn't noticed before. 'We need a car, but first we need to get those things out of you.'

The girl looked confused. Hunt took his hand and put it to his stomach, then pointed at the girl. She nodded.

As if this was how things always went on these runs, she showed little surprise. From the way she was acting, Hunt thought it could have been her tenth trip, or maybe it was her first. She was either scared shitless or tougher than anything Hunt had seen before. He held out a hand and introduced himself. 'Phil,' he said.

The girl looked at him. He must have looked ridiculous to her, bent with his leg, somewhat bowlegged from horse riding and aged from the sun and a number of sad years. He probably looked more like a man of sixty to her, though his muscles were still as strong as a young man's.

She took his hand and said, 'Thu.' All around them the rain fell, and her shirt and pants were nearly soaked through.

Hunt looked her over, trying to decide what she had just said. He repeated it, and she said it again, and then Hunt let go of her small hand and they continued.

The attendant stood transfixed, upright on his toes, held at the tip of Grady's twelve-inch chef's knife, blood welling from the knifepoint. A man in his thirties with pink skin and brown hair pulled back into a ponytail, he was wearing a green polo shirt with the emblem of the gas station over his left breast. Pop music played softly from the speakers overhead. A drop of blood collected on the man's chin and fell to the floor. Still alive. Grady felt that urge there inside him, tickling at his brain stem, pushing him toward things he could not help. The knife held beneath the attendant's chin, pupils fighting for focus, the dark wall of vision closing in on his life.

In one motion, Grady pushed the blade up into the skin beneath the chin, up through the soft palate, and into the brain. There was a slight tremor on the attendant's face as Grady twisted the handle of the knife and scrambled the man's brains. The attendant's warm blood came dripping down off the knife onto Grady's gloved hand and the sleeve of his sweatshirt.

The weight of the man falling carried him off the

knife, and Grady went around the counter. Like a barber readying the man for a shave, he cleaned the blade on the shoulder of the attendant's uniform. He took from the dead man's pockets a small lighter, a half-empty pack of gum, and a set of car keys. Beneath him was a widening pool of blood. When Grady stepped back he could see the tread of his shoes on the white linoleum floor.

He looked up at the blinking red light of the camera. He looked for the recorder but couldn't find one. 'Fuck,' he said. There was no time for this. He flipped the pump switches from closed to open, took up the AR-15, and loaded a fresh clip into the belly.

He put the knife back into the bag and zipped it closed.

He exited the gas station, carrying with him his gun and the bag, and went quickly to the attendant's car and threw both in. With the door opened he listened to the night air. The rain had moved off and he heard only the tall marshland grass moving in the wind. No sound of boat motors. No clank of armed men, or equipment, or anything.

He drove the car around to the pumps and sprayed the lot down in a wash of gasoline, leaving the trigger on the nozzle locked and the gasoline flowing. He drove the car to the edge of the widening pool of gasoline and lit it, watching the flames suck back along the cement toward the pump nozzle. He was driving when the pumps went.

The houses were all wood sided, some standing two stories, but most one-story prefabs that lay in lines along the street. Hunt couldn't remember which one belonged to his friend. His mind wasn't working right. He stopped, tried to adjust his vision, tried to find his bearings, but the pain in his leg sat on top of him, hot as molten lava. His head floated on a string over his shoulders. Surrounding them, the green pines took the yellow light from kitchen windows and entranceways. The trees and shrubs had grown since he'd been here last. Nothing looked the same. Hunt took the bag from his shoulder and let it down onto the asphalt street. He took out the Browning and slid the clip out. There were droplets of water clinging to the bullets. He blew into the clip, then locked it back in. Next he pulled the slide back and gave the breech a blow. He didn't know if the gun would work if needed, but it was all he had and he held it with a tight grip. He looked up at the houses. One of these was the one he was looking for. He tried to remember. He needed to choose.

Hunt knocked at the door until a light came on. The man who appeared at the door wore sweat shorts and a white jersey top; in his hand was a small bat. Hunt stepped back and the man looked down at Hunt and Thu. In the grainy light from behind the screen door, Hunt could see the rough shave of the man's head, his dark skin, and the almost relaxed way he held the bat in his right hand. Hunt couldn't tell if this was his friend.

'We crashed,' Thu said. The man, who had been studying Hunt, now shifted his gaze to the girl.

A woman appeared in the doorway behind the man, pushing the door open to get a better look at Hunt and Thu. With the screen out of the way, Hunt was sure the man recognized him, ten years older, but still the same man. Hunt shrugged, as if perhaps cold, and in the same movement put the gun into his back pocket, hoping they hadn't seen it.

The man stepped back, letting his wife through. 'Nancy,' the man said to his wife, tilting the end of the bat toward Hunt, 'this is an old friend, Hunt.'

'I didn't know you were married, Roy,' Hunt said.

'What's going on here?' Nancy said.

Thu stepped forward again. 'We had an accident.'

'Is anyone hurt?' Nancy asked.

Thu looked from the woman to Hunt.

181

'If we could come in for a moment,' Hunt said. He shifted his weight, and the pain was evident on his face.

'Oh my,' Nancy said. 'Get out of the way, Roy.' She opened the door wide. Thu grabbed the handle as it swung out.

Roy stepped to the side, forced back into the kitchen behind him. Thu continued to hold the door. Nancy now reached out her hand and said, 'Get in here.'

As soon as Hunt lifted his leg, he knew something was wrong. He felt suction in his shoe, the blood all through it, gumming his toes. The kitchen floor was patterned cream with small ornaments of wheat grain along the edges. It was a prefab, production kitchen, and Hunt bet that if he were to go down the block he might find two or three more with the exact same design.

Wherever Hunt walked, he left a small trail of blood; it was coming over the edge of his shoe and appeared in a line at the ankle and again around the laces, where it filtered up through the eyelets. Nancy pulled a chair away from the kitchen table. Roy put the bat on the counter and directed Thu into the kitchen. 'You've got a good bump, don't you?'

Hunt had forgotten about the gun, and when he sat, it tumbled from his back pocket onto the floor. Everyone stared at it. Hunt felt his head go for a swim. He lowered himself down and picked up the gun. He didn't point it, just sat there with his head down and the barrel of the gun against the floor. It looked almost as if he were using it as a crutch, his hand on the grip and the barrel to the floor.

'What kind of accident did you say you were in?' Roy said.

'Come over here, Roy, and just sit down a moment.' Hunt's words were beginning to falter, 'just sit' coming out like 'jus it.' He looked to Thu, who went over and sat down in the chair beside him. He still hadn't pointed the gun at them. He made a motion with the barrel, rolling it over as if a fishing line were attached at the end and he was pulling the line in. Nancy looked scared and tried to move out of the way of the gun when Hunt rolled it over. Roy just looked angry. 'Come on,' Hunt said.

All four of them sat at the table in the kitchen, with the gun flat in front of Hunt. He was bleeding onto the floor from the wound in his leg, his shoe completely full of it and a thin line of blood escaping near his anklebone. On the floor a syrupy puddle was developing. 'We should do something about your leg,' Nancy said.

'Do you have any laxatives?' Hunt said, his head beginning to nod.

'You need a little more than that,' Roy said. The bat rested on the counter across the kitchen, and whenever Hunt's head rolled, Roy would look over at it.

'Go find the laxative,' Hunt said, speaking to

Thu and half gripping the gun on the table. He was half-intelligible, but he thought 'laxative' had come out clear.

Thu looked at Nancy, and Nancy nodded toward a doorway where the bathroom must have been. 'Second on your left,' she said. She watched Thu get up. Hunt felt the wave of nausea hit him again. 'Let me give it a look,' Nancy said. 'I'm a nurse. The least you should do is let me give it a look.'

'You should let her,' Roy said. Hunt's eyes looked back at them with a dull, glazed look. He didn't blink. 'Is he dead?' Roy said.

'No,' Nancy said. 'He's still breathing.'

In the distance they heard an explosion, far off, and in the silence of the kitchen it sounded like a brief popping, like the first kernel in the microwave. They listened for more but didn't hear anything. It could have been the rain. But then they looked over at Hunt and knew it wasn't. They looked at each other and listened. There was only the sound of the night, the dull ocean sound of waves. Roy leaned across the table and slid the gun out from under Hunt's hand. Hunt kept giving them that glazed, blank stare. He hadn't seemed to notice that there'd been an explosion or that he was no longer in control.

In his mind, Hunt had already left – a weekend he and Nora had spent together ten years ago, the sound of a canoe being shoved into a prairie river. High grasslands all around, rock-and-pebble banks, a big sky above them, blue as a robin's egg.

184

These little things, half-memory, half-dream, came to him as he sat there at the kitchen table, flashing across his vision like pages turned in a picture book. His hand curled around a gun that was no longer there.

When Thu came back into the kitchen, she carried with her a bottle of Dulcolax. She stood in a front of the hallway and looked at the table. Roy held the gun. 'I told you he was going to need more than a laxative,' Roy said.

The helicopter circled once, then landed on the road about two hundred yards from the first line of fire trucks. Drake opened the door and stepped down onto the road. He held a hand to his hat and felt the wind try to take it. It was just past two in the morning, the smoke visible two hundred feet in the air, and the fire lighting it all from below. 'A gas station,' Driscoll said. They were walking up the road away from the helicopter. The first person to meet them was a patrolman holding a radio. They met in stride, and as they walked, Driscoll showed the man his identification.

'It's so hot up there the road is melting,' the patrolman said.

'I suppose there's nothing to do but let those tanks burn off.'

'The water doesn't even seem to touch it, just evaporates before it can even reach the fire.'

Drake could feel the heat now, as they drew up along the fire trucks. He could see the thermals working over the road, the air column traveling up, and how the heat glistened in the air like a

186

current of water. 'What makes you think this is our guy?'

'Not a thing,' Driscoll said. 'I figured it had to be someone real pissed off, and then I figured it must be our guy.'

'You think he did this?'

'Coast Guard said they were tracking a couple of boats. They chased one for half an hour and it beached near here. Broke all kinds of international laws. Either this is our guy or this is someone who knows our guy.'

'Knew what he was doing,' the patrolman added. 'Washed the whole road down with unleaded, then set it on fire. Coast Guard said there was about a five-second delay before the explosion hit. Boom, up goes the road. Boom, boom, the two gas pumps, then about five minutes later the propane in the service station blows.'

'Jesus,' Drake said.

Driscoll walked over to the edge of the road and bent into the grass. The marshland all around looked to be burning, a wash of firelight from the gas station playing across all of it. The light in the air could have been daylight. When Driscoll rose, he held the twisted remains of a soda bottle in his hand, the blue plastic top melted down over the clear green base.

Nora lay on the motel bed. The drive up from the city, over the mountains into eastern Washington, had taken them a little more than three hours. Arriving in the early morning, they'd woken the owner from her sleep in the little one-room office. Eddie had gone to his adjoining room an hour ago and she was glad he'd left. She put her hands to her face, blocking out the dim lamplight from the bedside table. Hunt wasn't dead – she had to keep telling herself this. She didn't know how many times she'd tried his phone. No answer.

Outside, the horses stood penned in the trailer. There was nothing to do with them for now, just let them rest and keep to themselves. She'd parked the trailer around the back in the gravel lot, where the grass was beginning to grow. The river was close. From her bathroom window, she could see the trailer in the gravel lot and the depression of the river beyond. Blackberries grew at the edge of the lot near the water. Someone had built a path there, and if the river bottom was sand, she guessed she would be able to water the horses,

188

lead them out, and walk them along until she found a place to stretch their legs. She thought of how taking a person's horse had once been a hangable offense. She wondered if it still was. None of these horses was hers. Hers had been lost in the mountains. Hunt hadn't explained, but she could guess where they'd gone. It made her sad to think of those animals she'd cared for for so long and how they were gone now.

She picked up her cell phone from the side table and tried Hunt again. They had talked only for that brief moment, when Hunt had sounded hurt and beyond himself, telling her to leave, to get away, and leaving it at that. But she knew adrenaline could do that to you; it could place you outside yourself, and she hoped for that. Hoped that Hunt could get beyond all this. He had told her to take the horses. He hadn't told her why, but she knew he was preparing to run. She just hoped he was alive. Now, with Hunt not answering, doubt was beginning to sink in, and she felt this thought resting there in her stomach, hardening into a sick little ball of pain.

She had gone to bed the night before, thinking that when she woke in the morning he would be there. She didn't know what to think now. Nothing seemed to make sense anymore. She'd made him promise he'd come home, and he hadn't. He wasn't answering his phone. Hadn't she always known about the dangers of the business? Somehow she had been blinded, perhaps by some aspect of her subconscious. Though she'd known about him, known his history, how he made his money, it had never occurred to her, not truly, that he could simply disappear.

Grady pulled the needle through. He was looking at himself in the mirror of a highway rest stop. It was still early and he'd pried the lock off the bathroom door with a tire iron. In his knife case he'd found a six-foot section of coarse butcher's twine, cream colored and thick as spaghetti. With one hand he held the cut on his forehead, pinched together with his fingers, working the string through with the trussing needle. A dull pressure, the thick string grabbing at his skin as it went through. Drops of blood formed and fell. He dabbed at them with the sleeve of his shirt, blotting away the blood. There was nothing to it, and after three minutes he had finished. The scalp turned purple where his head hit. It was so swollen that the pain didn't hit full, but glanced off in little fits as the needle went through and then the string. After he was done he double-knotted the ends and cinched them down, cut the excess away with the small boning knife, and stood looking at himself in the mirror. Besides the small bruised glow from his hairline, he looked just as he had before. His hair covered most of the damage, and in three days' time, he thought, it would be as if nothing had happened.

When Hunt woke he could see the morning sunlight beneath the shades. He smelled smoke, and when he hobbled to the window, he could see Roy out in the backyard burning a bundle of bloodied sheets. Hunt's leg was newly dressed. Though the swelling seemed greater than before, he felt more comfortable with the wound bandaged.

'For a brief moment last night, we thought we'd be burning you out there.'

Hunt turned to look and found Nancy waiting for him, a copy of the Seattle paper in her hands. 'Thank you,' he said. 'I'm sorry about last night. Is Thu still here?'

'I sent her to lie down in the bedroom. She showed us the boat last night.'

'I should go,' Hunt said. 'Thank you. But I should go.'

'We sank it.'

'The boat?'

'Roy towed it out around three a.m. and pulled the bilge plug. It went down easy with all the holes you left in it.'

'It's gone?'

'Water out there deepens quick.'

'Thank you,' he said again.

Nancy considered this for a moment, then threw him the paper. 'Yesterday's paper,' she said. She asked him to open it to the local section. 'I know you and Roy go back, but we don't need this kind of trouble. You understand?' She was standing there, across the room, with her arms crossed, waiting for him to look down at the paper in his hands.

Hunt scanned the article, just a little something, a column of text. He didn't see his name, and after he finished searching through it, he looked up at Nancy and said, 'How do you know this was me?'

'Roy said it was the type of thing you'd be into.'

Hunt looked down at the article again. There was a black-and-white picture of the deputy who had stopped them in the mountains. Grainy, a picture Hunt thought had probably come from his academy yearbook. The last name was familiar to him, Drake. Hunt had known a sheriff by that name a few years back.

'Says there that the deputy used to have a father who did the same thing you do.'

'He was the sheriff up there,' Hunt said.

'The article said that, too,' Nancy said. 'You should read it. You wouldn't want to miss something important.'

Hunt studied the picture of the deputy. Drake had been just a boy when Hunt had known his father, some sort of basketball player. That was all Hunt knew. He'd only spoken with the sheriff a time or two, always concerning business, the man simply competition. 'I'm realizing lately that there has been a whole list of things I've missed in my lifetime,' Hunt said.

He'd been thinking about the boy, how he'd lost his father. Hunt had felt the same, his father gone, but for different reasons. He'd always thought that if he'd had a son, it would have changed him; it would have meant he had someone who belonged to him, family, someone to keep safe, to keep watch over. He thought of Nora; he thought of Eddie, the horses. He wasn't doing the best job of this lately. He was trying, but it hadn't come out the way he'd wanted it to. Not at all. 'Seems like everyone I've had any contact with in the last few days has been hurt,' Hunt said.

'I don't want to be rude, but we don't need that type of trouble,' Nancy said again.

'Sorry,' he said. 'I should go.' Hunt looked out the window at Roy, who was using the end of a shovel to push the blanket into the fire.

'Roy is the one you should be apologizing to. He's the one taking the chances here. Just you being here is enough to put him back in jail,' Nancy said. 'If I had my way, you would have been gone last night. Back out there on the street and out of this house.'

'We would have been fine,' Hunt said, 'but I'm thankful for the help.'

'No, you wouldn't have been. You fell asleep with your gun in your hand. You could barely walk. You can't now.'

'I'll get around.'

'Roy can be as stubborn as you sometimes, and even he wants you to give it a little time.'

'I don't think that'll do me any good.'

She was silent for a while, just looking at him, his calf all bandaged up, the pants cut away in that ridiculous fashion. He was standing there with the pale morning light coming through the window, studying the newsprint in his hand. When he looked up from the article and met her eyes, she said, 'You're wearing a wedding ring. You got a wife, someone you're trying to get back to?'

'I've got a wife.'

'Do you love her?'

'Of course I do.'

'Where is she now?'

'How do you know that isn't her in your bedroom?'

'It isn't.'

'How do you know?'

'A man wouldn't do that to his wife.'

'Do what?'

'Fill her up like that, like a suitcase.'

'You saw it?'

'Figured it out. Wasn't that hard to figure after last night. It's trouble when a man comes to the door half-dead and all he wants is a bottle of laxative. It should have told us something right then, but your mind goes somewhere else when a gun is pointed at you.'

'It's best to get that stuff out of the body as soon as possible.'

'You were protecting her?'

'Trying to save her life.'

'That true?'

'Course it's true.'

'I'd like to think that, though I don't know if it's the truth.'

'What else could it be?'

'How much is she worth?'

'I'm not going to put a price on her.'

'Put a price on her or the drugs?'

Hunt didn't say anything. He looked out the window, the fire dying and Roy standing there watching it.

'Does it seem right to you?' Nancy asked.

'Nothing has seemed right to me for a while now.'

Grady woke and looked to the east, where he could see the auburn sun rising. He passed a hand over his face. He had slept with the seat folded all the way back. With his fingers he wiped the sleep from the corners of his eyes, hard between his thumb and trigger finger. He rose and looked out on the farm road. On the seat beside him was the knife bag, zipper open, with the edge of the rifle stock exposed. He breathed in and looked over his shoulder, then back, nothing there. He closed the bag. A stupid, messy mistake. He looked around again, then started the car. From his pocket he took the half pack of gum he'd taken from the attendant. He was hungry and he chewed a piece of gum to keep his mind off it. He had slept for an hour, nervous and with the memory of the night that had come before.

He had a reputation to uphold: that was the only certainty he had in mind. He was already a day behind schedule, and he didn't like being the one chased, nor did he like doing the chasing. He preferred instead to meet and call it a day right there. But the boat ramp had not been the place. Too early and too public. And the drugs: he didn't have them but could guess where they were.

He started down the road. When he passed a combine, he waved. No reason to be unfriendly. No reason at all. He drove on, thinking about what he would do next.

Nora put her fingers to the edge of the shades. No one could have known where they were, but still she was nervous. She opened the blinds enough that she could see onto the parking lot. Farther down the road was the red glow of a Dairy Queen and gas station. One of those combined things where travelers could fill up and buy a Blizzard at the same time.

Eddie's car sat in front of his motel room, their bedrooms separated by adjoining doors that Nora had long since closed. She could hear the sound of the television, but not enough to tell what he was watching. Her cell phone lay tangled in the sheets. When had she called Hunt last? She was trying to remember. She couldn't think straight. She had barely slept and had watched too much television. She turned the thing off around 5 a.m. And for a while, she had watched the black street, the glow from the gas station. Things seemed to be moving in the night, but she knew they weren't. It was just the wind in the trees. Close to the water there were lines of birch that seemed strange and ghostly at night.

When had she called Hunt last? Nora walked over to the bed and found the phone. When Hunt answered, Nora said, 'What the hell.'

'What the hell?' Hunt said.

'Why didn't you answer your phone when I called?'

'Just didn't hear it, I guess.'

'Where are you?'

'Up north. I barely made it.'

'What do you mean, 'barely made it'?'

'The boat's gone. Sunk.'

'Are you okay?'

'Hurt my leg a little bit.'

'A little bit?'

'It'll heal. Did you do as I said?'

'Yes, Eddie and I are in a motel.'

'And the horses?'

'Three of them are here.'

'Good.'

'Do you need me to come get you?'

'Not yet.'

'I can come.'

'No, I think it's best if you don't. I'm not sure exactly what happened yet.'

'Are you in danger? Why don't you want me to come up there and get you?'

'No, it's someone I'm with.'

'What kind of someone?'

'A girl.'

'You're not messing with me, are you?'

'Not about this, I wouldn't.'

'Well, why don't you ask her if I can come up there?' Nora went to the window and looked out. There was a nervous fear growing inside her. She could feel it down at the base of her throat. She swallowed and tried to rid herself of the feeling, but it was still there. Hunt was taking a long time with his answer.

'It's not that,' Hunt said. 'I would. But she's stopped talking. I'm not sure what to do. She's being watched, but I can't say she'll make it.'

'What are we talking about here, Phil?'

'The girl has the drugs. They're inside her.'

'A mule?'

'Yes, she has the drugs. I don't think I can leave until this gets figured out.'

'How old is she?'

'Twenty? Forty? It's hard to say.'

There was a long pause.

'Nora?'

'What kind of trouble are we in here?'

'The worst kind.'

'Is someone looking for this girl?'

'I think they were looking for me.'

'But now they're looking for both of you?'

'Yes, I'm certain they are.'

'And you think Eddie and I are in danger?'

'I don't know that, but I'd rather be sure.'

'Is this the kind where we shouldn't even be talking on the phone – that kind?'

'No. It's not that. The other kind, like the kid, that kind of trouble.'

'How do you know it's like the kid?'

'Because the Coast Guard showed up and it was probably the only thing to save us.'

'Never thought you'd be saying that.'

'No, never.'

'I can come up there.'

'No, I don't want you up here. You and Eddie should just sit this out. I'm not joking when I say this. I'm already in it. I just can't say how far it'll go.'

She gave him the number and address of the motel.

'I'll call you later,' Hunt said. 'I'm going to keep my promise. Don't worry. I'll call you when I know what to do.'

Nora heard the line quit on her. She held the phone and listened to the dead space.

There was something stuck in the back of his throat. The lawyer coughed, bringing up a hot mouthful of smoke. He wore a bathrobe over the clothes he'd slept in. There was no reason to change. No reason to go out. The people he worked for would not be happy. He didn't know what they'd already heard, but he could guess when it did come out – and it would – there would be consequences. He was just trying to do the right thing now, take the right steps; killing the kid had been first, and now, if Grady could just find Hunt, they would be in the clear.

He'd put all of it in motion, and there was no reason now to watch it all slip away. He put his cigarette out on a small porcelain bread plate. He'd heard nothing and he looked at his watch again. Ten past eleven. The Vietnamese would call soon. They'd want to know why the girls hadn't been delivered. No girls could be explained, but no drugs couldn't.

Grady hadn't checked in. The lawyer looked again at his watch and crossed to the kitchen, where he opened the faucet and watched the water run. He passed a hand through the stream and brought it to his face, running his fingers down along the groove of his mouth and off his chin.

When Grady called ten minutes later, the lawyer wanted to know what had gone wrong, what Grady had been thinking. Not delivering the girl as he was supposed to, Hunt still alive, all of it spinning out of control. The lawyer was standing in his kitchen, looking down into the sink, a whirlpool opening up before him.

It wasn't just Hunt who was in danger now, it was all of them; the lawyer knew this, knew that if the situation couldn't be fixed soon, there would be a lot for him to answer for. He gave Grady the address of Hunt's place in Auburn. He gave him the name of the wife. He gave him a description of Eddie and left it at that.

Two men sat in a tinted Lexus, watching the tourists mill around the downtown ferry docks. One of the men, in an Armani sweater, leaned forward in his seat and checked the dash clock. He blew smoke from a cigarette. Music played softly from the car stereo.

'What time is it?' the second man asked. He wore a similar sweater, rolled neck, with a small horseman embroidered on his left breast. The sleeves were too long for him and he continually pushed them up. The two men were speaking in Vietnamese, both of them in their early thirties.

'Fuck this,' the man in the Armani sweater said. 'We should have just gone up there ourselves.'

'She acted stupid. Acted real dumb, getting off the plane like that.'

'Should have gotten her ourselves.'

'We don't need that trouble. That's what we pay the lawyer for. They would have pulled us over at the border. No doubt about it.'

'At least we'd know something then. At least we'd have some clue what was going on.'

'And what about the other girl? The one who was supposed to come in yesterday?'

'The lawyer is fucking us, that's what.'

'What do you want to do?'

'I don't like working this way. But we do it because we can't do it any other way. You find a better system, you tell me. She was supposed to be delivered straight from the airport.'

'Dumb-ass girl.'

'Fuck the girl. As long as we get what she's carrying.'

'What do you want to do?' the man in the Armani sweater said. He brought a hand to his mouth and removed the cigarette. He sat in the car, relaxed, unbothered by the lateness of the girl. The only thing about him that moved quickly was his mouth.

'Call the lawyer again.'

The man leaned forward and placed the cigarette in the ashtray. He dialed the number. When the secretary picked up, he said, 'I want to speak to the lawyer.' The secretary put him on hold.

The man in the rolled-neck sweater watched him from the passenger side of the car. 'Easy,' he said.

'Two girls got on a plane and neither has shown up. Sounds easy, but nothing about it is.'

The receptionist came back on the line and told him the lawyer hadn't come in that morning.

'Tell him he better find our girls. He better find them fast.'

The only thing Grady knew was that Hunt would run. If Hunt had been smart he'd have stayed in one place and let Grady find him. But he knew Hunt wouldn't do that. He'd been running a long time. Let it end, Grady thought, just let it be over. But still he took a certain excitement from the chase. He didn't like it, but he could appreciate it. The small loose thread, the random element, something he hadn't calculated.

He took the small slip of paper with Hunt's information on it from his pocket and looked it over. The interstate kept going in front of him. Cars turned down past Seventy-fifth and he could see the interstate straighten and the wide view of the city in front of him. He drove on, the address in his head. He placed the paper on the dash, right next to the speedometer, and watched them both.

When he got out of the car, he stood looking at Hunt's house for a long time. He'd driven past it and pulled the car onto a gravel shoulder about a quarter mile off. He could see the downward slope of the roof through the trees. The odor of animals was all around him. Smells of horse manure came to him on the crisp, cold air. From the car he took the bag and went up the road, jogging now and feeling the wind come over him. When he found a small horse path leading into the woods, he followed it, keeping behind the trees to watch the house. He tried to move without being noticed, low and close to the ground. He couldn't see anything in the windows. Not even a light or the flicker of a television.

He knelt and assembled the AR-15. From the bag, he took a few extra clips and stuffed them into his back pockets. With the sight he could look into the house, and he knelt there, watching, for thirty minutes. Nothing moved. The stables were at the far end of the property, and he went there, using the fence and then the building for cover. He could only hope for someone to be inside the house.

Moving through the stables, he saw that the three horses had been brought into the fenced pasture. He stood in the shadow of the stables for five minutes, using the scope to look through the windows of the house from a different angle. Still nothing moved. He went to the fence, in the wide, open backyard, and looked at the house. With age, the siding had turned from white to cream like the surrounding alder bark, the roof good, and windows in every room. He could pick out the rooms by the symmetry of their placement. The kitchen, the back door, the front entranceway visible through it, a living room, and the upstairs bedrooms and bathroom. The horses were watching from a distance, and he called to them but they didn't come. He raised the rifle and sighted them in the scope, their big eyes looking back at him, the constant movement of their long jaws as they busied themselves with their food. He put the rifle down and walked to the house.

With the butt of the AR-15 he knocked out one of the back door's panes and reached inside to turn the lock. Inside, he found a house with wood-panel floors. He listened – nothing besides the sound of his own breathing and the brief shift of his weight on the floor. On the couch he found a bed made. He walked to it and pulled the sheets away, he looked under the cushions, then he knelt and looked beneath the couch. He didn't know what he was looking for. He still carried the AR-15 and he folded the stock now and held the muzzle toward the rest of the house. When he stood up, he could see a car pass on the road just beyond the drive. The shades were open and he watched a child turn in the backseat and look at him. He still carried the rifle but didn't move to hide it. He watched the car pass and then disappear down the road into the trees.

He found the small dining room. Two of the chairs were not pushed in. He pushed them in and then pulled them out and sat in one and faced the other. Upstairs he found a bed that was not made. He looked at it and went into the closet and looked at the clothes. He could smell a woman's perfume. He ran a silk blouse through his fingers. He tried to find a suitcase, but the only bag he found was a duffel. For a short time he lay on the bed with the rifle laid out beside him. Overhead he heard rain begin to fall and patter on the roof. He looked up at the ceiling, then rolled over and noticed the phone. He dialed *69 and waited for the sound of the pulse.

The girl sweated through the sheets. Nancy sat by her with a bowl of ice water. They were waiting now and hoping she would come out of it. Thu's eyes were just slits of white with the small, dark sliver of her irises visible through the lids. Her face was red where Nancy had slapped her a moment before, saying, 'Come on!' Slapping her and then taking her by the shoulders and shaking her till her eyes opened. 'Stay awake, goddamn it.'

Hunt could see the outline of Thu's body beneath the clothes. He took in the sweat all over and the way the pores on her face beaded with water, which collected and then ran down her face onto the bed, making dark patches on the sheets. His phone vibrated again. Nancy looked up. Hunt didn't know where Roy was.

'Who is this?' Hunt said, holding the phone. The call had come from his own house.

'You know who this is.'

Hunt walked out into the living room. He could see the backyard, the big canister in which Roy had burned the sheets.

'What a silly question,' Grady continued. 'Who did you think it was going to be?'

'Do you think you're going to find me?'

'I was thinking I'd start with your wife and ask her.'

'She's not there.'

'Yes, it's unfortunate for me, though I think it's more unfortunate for you.'

'There's nothing unfortunate about it.' There was a pause and then Hunt heard something break; he thought it was glass, though it could have been a lamp or a mirror.

'What's the name of the brown horse with the white notch along the nose?'

'Hermes.'

'Clever,' Grady said.

There was the sound of the rifle, a quick three-shot burst. Hunt didn't hear anything else. He didn't hear the horse, or the bullets hit. The phone just hung there in his hand and he listened, not sure what to say.

'How many horses do you keep in your stables?' Grady asked.

Hunt didn't say anything.

'To me, they're just animals. I'd bet they're something altogether different to you.'

'Why would you do that?'

'You know I'm going to find your wife. I'll find her and we can do this again. Would you like me to call you back then?'

'If you were going to find her, you would

already have done it. You were just hoping she was there.'

'No. I was hoping you were here.'

Hunt heard the rifle fire once more. This time he heard the horse call out. He heard it call again.

'I'll take this one slow,' Grady said.

'I'm going to kill you,' Hunt said, and he thought he really meant it. For the first time he felt he really did. The sound of the rifle again.

'She'll never run in the races.'

'You're sick.'

'You could make it stop.'

'You've got nothing and you're desperate.'

'I can start with your wife, then I can get the girl. I expect I'll need to kill her anyway to get the drugs out of her. I can do this all before I do you. I'll probably make you watch. You want to save someone, you want to save this last horse? You should come over here and meet me. I guarantee it will be fast. You're already dead anyway.'

'The girl is dead.'

'That would be very unfortunate for you. She was buying you time.'

'You don't know a goddamn thing.'

'I know where you'll be very soon.'

'Yes, I bet you do.'

'You're not going to meet me, are you?'

'What do you think?'

'Maybe you'd like to listen? This will become very familiar to you.'

Hunt heard Grady put the phone down. He

guessed Grady was in the bedroom, where the windows looked onto the pasture and the horses. The injured horse was making that whining sound, a sound he'd heard from a horse only once, a horse with a splintered bone lying on its side on the track. Hunt heard the shot, then nothing else.

G rady walked downstairs. There was a certain pleasure he'd taken in shooting the two horses. He trailed a hand along the wall, and as he went, he hummed to himself. It was a song of his own creation, perhaps something he'd heard in the past, though now changed and used in a different context. In his other hand he carried the rifle. When he reached the bottom of the stairs, he went to the small fireplace in the living room and made a fire. He built it up. He sat on the couch and watched television. He relished the idea of taking Hunt's life apart piece by piece, like separating sinew and tendon, skin and muscle, breaking him down.

When the fire had burned for about ten minutes and he could see the coals beginning to develop, he took red, glowing logs and placed them under the couch. He put others beneath the drapes. The smell of smoke and burnt plastic began to fill the room. He went into the kitchen and turned every valve of the range until he could hear gas.

Outside, the rain was still falling. He stepped down onto the yard and he felt the wet earth beneath him. The smell of horses and something new, something of his own creation, smoke and fire, almost claylike. At the pasture, he stopped to look over the bodies of the two horses he'd shot. The first had taken the three shots lengthwise, one to the neck and then the others falling farther back. The second horse he'd taken his time with, a shot at the front quarter, then the back, and the final in the head. Trails of blood ran off the wounds and down onto the ground.

The third horse stood nearby but did not make a move as Grady came to the fence and looked him over. The rain kept falling. There was that faint earth smell to the air, puddles, and raindrops. Grady watched the horse, the light from the house reflected in its big eyes.

The house blew then, startling the horse. Grady raised a hand to look at the house, as if shading his eyes from a strong sun. Flames in all the windows. He wished Hunt could hear the sound; he wanted him to know there was no coming back.

Grady felt the rain's cold touch already soaking through his clothes and on his skin. Streams of water rolled down from his hair and dropped from his nose, collecting along his jawline and falling from his chin. The fire was a brilliant hue of orange and red, alive in the gray falling rain. He saw the horse back there, still running along the far fence, rounding the corner and returning almost to the midpoint of the pasture and looking on. 'Nothing to be afraid of,' Grady said. He was watching the horse. Then with both hands he raised the rifle and took aim.

'What's your reason for coming to Canada?'

The border guard looked into a black Lexus with the two Vietnamese men sitting in it. The man in the driver's seat leaned forward, his teeth stained a cigarette yellow. He spoke with a slight accent. 'Shopping, sightseeing.'

The border guard looked from his face to the passport she held in front of her. She put his name into the computer. 'Where are you coming from?'

'Seattle.'

'Whose car is this?'

'Mine.'

'What line of work are you in?'

'I'm a plumber.'

'Nice car for a plumber,' the guard said.

'You should see my house,' the man joked. 'It's a real dump.'

'Can you tell me your license plate number?' He gave it to her. 'What about you, sir?' She leaned down to see the second man, sitting in the passenger seat. She typed his name into the computer. 'What line of work are you in?'

'I'm his boss.'

'You own the plumbing business?'

'No, I run it.'

'You must do a good business.'

'Not really,' the second man said.

The guard turned back to the driver. 'How long will you be in Canada?'

'Just for the day.'

'Any firearms or drugs in the vehicle?'

'No.'

'Anything you'll be leaving in Canada?'

'No.'

'Have a good trip, guys.'

The Lexus pulled forward.

Eddie left the television running, the volume up high, and all the lights on in his room. Outside, he could feel the cold that had come with the rain and the dull gray of the day as it came on. To the right he could see Nora's motel window, shades drawn, but the light on, and he assumed she was still there. He went to his car and was careful to ease the door shut behind him. From his pocket he dug out his cell phone and dialed the number. All over the car roof he could hear the rain falling. He saw it on the windshield, and he thought that even if Nora looked out the window, she wouldn't be able to tell he was in there.

After the secretary patched him through to the house, the lawyer came on, saying, 'This must be some kind of joke.'

'No joke at all,' Eddie said.

'I thought I'd explained this clearly to you.'

'You did.'

'Then why did your man know about it?'

'I didn't say a thing to him. I just told him where to be and at what time. I didn't say anything else.'

'Don't lie to me, Eddie.'

'I'm not lying.'

'This has been made clear to you, correct?'

'Yes, it is all clear. It's a bad deal, but it's the only deal I was given.'

'It's a good deal, Eddie.'

'Not from where I'm standing.'

'I'd be very happy to be alive from where you're standing.'

Eddie didn't say anything; he was sorry enough as it was, felt shame like he'd never felt before, even knowing from the beginning about the kid. It was shameful, all of it. Nothing would ever make him feel better about what he had done. He thought about taking his own life, but then it wouldn't matter, Hunt was still dead, it didn't matter.

'You know this is turning into a real headache for us.'

'I imagine it is.'

'Don't be smart, Eddie.'

'I didn't mean to be.'

'Sympathy, then? You feel sympathetic for the fuckup your man has put us in?'

'Yes,' Eddie agreed, 'that is what I feel toward the situation.' There was a pause on the other end. Eddie cursed himself, cursed his mouth, but didn't say anything and waited for the man to come back on the line.

'I'm going to send someone to see you. He's an old acquaintance of Phil Hunt's. He should be able to help us out, figure this whole thing out for us. We're not the types to give second chances, Eddie. You should know this. You should feel grateful.'

'I am,' Eddie said, though he didn't feel that way at all. He felt a sickness in his stomach, an ache he could not fix. He gave the man the address of the motel. Then, after it was done, he sat in the car and listened to the rain.

D riscoll walked back into the diner, closing his phone. 'Three dead horses and a burnt-up house,' Driscoll said to Drake. They had spent the night at the gas station, Driscoll going through paperwork, Drake trying to give the place a look but instead just drifting off to look out on the ocean. The boat was there, about a half mile off, beached up on the rocks. 'They just pulled a two twenty-three round out of one of the horses. Same as what they found all over the deck of that Coast Guard cutter.'

Driscoll sat down across from Drake and read him the address.

'Any people?' Drake asked.

'No one.'

'That address,' Drake said. 'I was there yesterday. Doing my detective work.'

Driscoll stared at him. 'You're kidding, right?'

'Didn't seem to be the type to be mixed up in this.'

'Opportunity knocks.'

'Yes, but they just didn't seem to be the type for this kind of thing.'

'Did you meet this man?' Driscoll slid a black-and-white print across the table. 'Just took it off the computer. Owner of the property. Convicted for second-degree murder thirty years ago. Dumb asshole didn't even run, just stayed right there till the cops showed up to take him away. Even pleaded guilty at his own trial.'

Drake held the picture and looked it over, an old mug shot, but he could tell right away it was a picture of the horseman from the mountains. 'Looks like you were right about them wanting that second man dead.'

'You know him?'

'Met him three nights ago in the mountains. He's the rider.'

'You couldn't have identified him yesterday?'

'Wasn't there yesterday. Just a woman and a man, not this one, though, stockier and darker, Mexican.'

'Not Phil Hunt?'

'No.'

'You think the man you met yesterday was this assassin going around killing everything he comes across?'

'No. The wife seemed very comfortable with him. Maybe a neighbor?'

'There's not much down there to be neighborly with, unless you like cow shit and antifreeze.'

'The Lincoln didn't fit.'

'What's that?'

'There was a Lincoln parked in front of the garage, didn't seem to fit that lifestyle.'

'Man, you are a detective. Let me see if we can get you on staff out here.'

Drake gave him a hurt look. 'I tried to tell you about this yesterday. Wouldn't listen to me then.'

'I'm sorry about that. Thought we were saying good-bye, that's all.'

'Thought so, too.'

'You think Hunt is still alive?'

'I don't see why else his house was burned down and his horses killed.'

'Seems like some real cold-blooded thing to do.'

'Seems like it.'

'You got time for a ride over there now?'

Drake looked at the coffee, at the half-eaten plate of eggs in front of him. He needed to call his wife. She'd be wondering about him. About his leaving half-drunk in the middle of the night with this man they both didn't much like, a man who'd come into their lives, just as Drake had stepped into Hunt's. Drake picked up the coffee cup and drained it, feeling the hot liquid in his throat. With his wallet out, Driscoll threw a twenty down and picked up the receipt.

The Lexus pulled to the curb. The Vancouver heat reflected off the city streets and hovered over the cement. In the distance, large glass buildings seemed to float. 'Sixty degrees today, and then forty with a chance of snow tomorrow night,' the driver said. 'Weird weather.'

The man in the passenger seat gave the driver a deadpan stare, then opened his door and stepped out and went into a nearby hardware store.

Inside, he went through the aisles. He found the bin of hose clamps and picked out several of the large metal rings. In the gardening section he found a pair of thick shears with a loaded spring. He held them in his hand and undid the lock. When he came to the bin of bolts, washers, and screws, he took a small screw and held it between the blades and cut it cleanly in half. There was only the sound of the two halves falling to the floor. The clerk at the desk looked his way. The man returned a wave, then bent to pick up the two halves. When he stood up again, the clerk sat at the counter reading.

Outside, the man opened the passenger door

and threw the bag of hardware supplies in before him. When he stepped down into the car, the man in the driver's seat had already opened the bag and given its contents a quick look. 'Ambitious,' he said. 'But not that much for plumbing supplies.'

'Convincing.'

'Sledgehammers are convincing, hatchets, nail guns, saws. Have you ever seen one of those old two-man saws – more teeth than a shark on those things.'

'Can you just drive?'

The driver started the car. 'It should be intimidating.'

'This will be plenty.'

'Do you want to grab some food?'

'How long will it take?'

'Are you in a rush?'

'Just anxious. Drive by the airport.'

Hunt sat on the couch. Outside, the rain had stopped, and he worked his leg and thought the situation over. His father had killed himself over a situation just like this one, small-time loan-sharking with credit that wasn't his. If his mother could see him now, he thought, she might do the same. Hunt had grown up over the years, but the idea of being a continuous failure had stuck with him. He was sure of himself in all the wrong situations. A good man, made up of all the bad things in the world.

The girl's purse lay on the table, and he went over and opened it. A passport fell out, a tube of mascara, a small stick of lip balm, some tissue, a set of keys, her wallet. He picked up the wallet and went through it, money he had never seen before. In one of the card slots he found a picture of Thu and two children. Again, he thought that if he'd had children, his life would have been different. The children were of a dark complexion, tanned, with their hair lightened by the sun. Both wore sweaters, and it made them look funny, out of place, like there was no reason to wear those sweaters. In Thu's coin purse he found a Seattle address. After looking at it for a moment, he put it into his pocket.

The thought hadn't really figured itself out yet. But it did then. He'd been thinking of the girl as a dollar figure. He felt bad for that. The two boys in the picture – Thu's boys – looked up at him from the kitchen table. They smiled. How much was she worth? Ninety thousand? It wasn't enough to start a new life, but it might be enough to get him there. For a second he thought of moving to Vietnam, he thought of Thu, and he thought of Nora. He'd bet that money could do things for them there. It wouldn't be a great life at first, but they'd build it. He felt foolish. He laughed to himself, a desperate laugh, half-choked, and at the end he could feel something slick in his eyes and he blinked it away.

He could hear Roy and Nancy talking from the bedroom. Roy came out and Hunt put the passport and makeup back in the bag. Roy stood looking Hunt over. Hunt held out the picture for Roy to see. Roy nodded, taking the picture and then giving it back. They didn't say anything to each other. Hunt put the picture back into the wallet and put it all away in the purse. He watched Roy fill a bowl of water with ice. After Roy had finished, he followed after him, holding his bad leg and limping through the hallway.

Thu's breath was starting to slow. The girl was almost unconscious, half-dead, her eyes nearly closed. Hunt and Roy were in the doorway looking in. 'She's getting worse,' Nancy said. 'It's time we called someone.'

Roy moved for the kitchen phone, but Hunt put a forearm up and blocked him. Roy was bigger, but the move surprised him and he stopped.

'Come on, man,' Roy said. 'You can't be this cold-blooded. She's going to die. Her pupils look like needle pricks.'

Hunt looked in at Thu. She'd saved his life, they all had, but he couldn't let them do it. There were other things to consider. He knew what turning her over meant, no drugs, no future, just a one-way ticket back to prison. He couldn't have that. There was a lot he hadn't done in his life. There was a lot he'd missed out on – family, fatherhood, safety – because of a past he wanted to take back every hour of every day but knew he couldn't.

The girl's breathing had slowed, and for a while now, she hadn't opened her eyes. The room stank of her sweat. Hunt held his forearm out; he had his fingers up on the wall and his arm out, stiff as he could make it.

Roy put a hand into the crook of Hunt's elbow and folded it back. 'You're lucky I didn't kick your calf out from under you.' Roy went past and Hunt followed.

'You make that call and everyone who is looking for us is going to know exactly where to look.'

Roy held the phone. He thought this over. Hunt knew he was thinking about the boat – even with the rain, he knew it had been a bad sight. Blood all over the deck, the dust from the fiberglass like a paste over everything. Bullet holes and broken glass, it was something serious to consider. Hunt had been considering it; he knew Roy was now.

'I'm already as mixed up in this as I care to be,' Roy said. 'I'm not about to have a heroin overdose in my bedroom.' He put the number into the phone and waited.

'I'll take her,' Hunt said.

'What?' Roy held a hand over the mouthpiece.

'I'll take her,' Hunt said again. 'Give me your keys and I'll take her.' He went over to where Roy stood with the phone in his hand.

Roy didn't answer.

'Come on,' Hunt said. 'Give me your keys. You said it yourself, you don't want to be mixed up in this anymore. We both know how this is going to turn out once they find out you've been to Monroe.' The two men stood very close together. 'Roy, just tell me where to go. I can get her to the hospital faster than if you call an ambulance.'

Nancy came and stood in the hall doorway leading to the kitchen. 'He's right, Roy. Give him the keys. He can get her there faster than if we call it in. One of the capsules she was carrying must have burst in her.'

Roy looked from Nancy to Hunt and then back again. Someone had picked up on the other side of the line, and they were, all of them, listening to the sound of a muted voice coming off the phone.

Roy looked down at the phone in his hand and then hung up.

'Go on, get him the keys,' Nancy said. Hunt could hear her leave and go back into the bedroom. He took Thu's purse from the table and followed Nancy.

Nancy was at the bed, the bowl of water nearby and the rag for mopping at the girl's face. From a side table, Nancy took a pen and wrote down the directions to the hospital. 'Take her into the ER and they'll get her through from there.'

Hunt didn't know a thing about the girl, where her family was from, or how she'd gotten into this. He felt dazed, couldn't believe what was happening or that he was here. He looked down at the sheet of paper in his hand, the directions. Straight ahead till the stop sign, through the center of town, then a right on Blanchard. 'She's going to be all right,' Hunt said. And it was how he felt, how he had to feel. He picked the girl up off the bed and tried to lift her. The pain came immediately from his calf, and he dropped her to the mattress, Thu's eyes shooting open for a moment. He thought for a second she had recognized him, understood what needed to be done. Hunt was still holding her purse, dumbly, unknowingly, like he was holding on to a string and plumbing some hidden depth.

He tried to tell himself this was the best thing for her. It was the only thing he could say to make the guilt go away, though it was still there, waiting for him. How many times had she done this? Just let her go home, he wanted to say. But he didn't know whom he was asking. He thought it was more praying than anything, something he hadn't done in a very long time.

Roy came in and gave Hunt the keys, along with the small orange survival bag he'd come off the boat with. Inside the bag was the heroin, neatly tied up in a clear plastic grocery bag. Thu must have passed the heroin in the night. He didn't know if this was all of it, but he could guess it was most. Lying on top of the small plastic balls was the Browning. He looked at Roy, but Roy didn't meet his eyes as he hoisted the girl in his arms.

Following Roy through the house, Hunt couldn't believe he had the heroin. They came to the door and Nancy held the screen back and they went out into the light and down the stairs to a rusted hatchback.

'You need to try and keep her conscious,' Nancy said. But Hunt could see even then she was losing it. He hoped he could get her there. He hoped that she would make it and that it would mean something, that it would free her and in a way free him, but he didn't know this and he felt the worry all through him like a chill.

He started the car as Roy leaned the girl down into the seat beside him. 'Thanks,' Hunt said.

Roy looked over at him. 'Thanks for what?' Roy said, and then he closed the door.

He watched Roy pass around the car and stand

with Nancy. For a moment he held the wheel and just stared at them. Thu groaned beside him and he looked at her and then backed out, and as soon as he hit the street, he pushed the car into drive and sped forward.

It wouldn't be long now, and he tried to brace himself for the reality of the hospital. But even this wasn't a reality to him. Grady had shot the horses. It scared him. He didn't think Grady would find Nora, but he didn't know that for sure. He realized that he didn't know anything for sure now, and that there had been a point when he could have said he did.

Nancy told him Thu was dying, and he knew there was nothing more he could do for her except drive her to the hospital and hope it all turned out.

The car was automatic, which meant he could drive it with one leg. He rested his injured leg to the side. On his lap the Browning and the heroin stared up at him from the open maw of the survival bag. With one hand he raised the bag to his face and pulled the zipper closed with his teeth. The smell made him gag. He looked back through the rearview mirror at the road behind, then threw the bag to the backseat.

Thu's eyes had closed, and when he looked over he could see a thin line of saliva brim at her lips, then breach and come down along her chin. 'Wake up,' he yelled. He held the wheel in one hand and with the other he shook her till her eyes opened and she turned to him with a sleepy look.

Hunt didn't slow the car when he came to the stop sign. He went on through, the speedometer at fifty on the pressed-gravel road. He could hear the tinging of loose rocks as they caught in the tire treads and sprayed up into the wheel wells.

When they came into town, he caught himself and slowed the car. Thu had nodded away again and he reached out until he had her chin in his hand and shook her face and watched her eyes. They wouldn't open. He went through the main intersection and found Blanchard. With one hand on the wheel, he hit her several times in the face with his open palm. Her head bounced away, then rolled back, but her eyes didn't open, and he swore under his breath and looked for the hospital sign in front of him.

When he found the emergency room, he pulled straight to the entrance and came out of the car yelling for help. It was a three-story hospital surrounded by pine trees and thirty parking spots at most. The sliding glass doors were the only sign that it had seen the modern world at all, and he hoped that they would be able to do something, would be able to help in some way. He was around the side of the car with Thu's door open by the time one of the orderlies came out of the glass doors.

'Help me,' Hunt yelled.

He had Thu under the arms and he could feel the stitches in his leg straining and the pain coming through him. He was dragging her now, away from the open car door and up the slight incline to the hospital entrance. The orderly was there and he was trying to help, but Hunt wouldn't let go, and the orderly was saying, 'Give her here, sir. Give her to me.' And when he saw that Hunt would not, he went in and grabbed a wheelchair from inside the door, and together they got Thu onto it.

The feeling came over Hunt again, like it had the night before, loss of blood, the bandage on his leg dampening. He put his head down and held it between his legs. He closed his eyes. Thu was somewhere inside now, and when he raised his head his vision had gone blurry, but he could see Thu in there and the shape of a doctor standing over her. He was watching this all, and then they were coming for him, and he lurched back into his own reality, his own needs, and he was running around the front of the car. With the doors both still open he sat and pressed the gas pedal, nearly leaving his bad leg to drag outside the car. He bumped out onto the road with both doors open and the engine roaring. When he righted himself and hit the gas again, the jolt swung the doors back onto the body of the car. Things came back into focus. He looked behind him, looked back on the road. Pine trees all around, the small drive leading up toward the hospital, but that was it, no armed pursuit, no chase, just him in the car driving, trying to keep himself on the road.

PART IV

CONFESSIONS

G rady parked the attendant's car in one of the upper lots. Below him he could see the marina where he had left his car. No police cruisers. Nothing. He scanned the lot, looking for anyone who might have been waiting for him. He didn't see one thing out of place, just a few people fishing off the docks. In the mirror he checked the welt on his head. With his fingers he tried to pull the hair down, giving himself a sweep of bangs and covering the gash along his hairline. The purple was getting worse and it looked almost black on his pale skin.

When he'd done all he could with his appearance, he drove the car down to the lower lot and let it idle in neutral. The boat ramp, where he had talked to Hunt the day before, was just in front of him. He tried to remember every bit of the car he had touched, and with his sleeve he went piece by piece through the car, wiping away his fingerprints. When he was satisfied, he left the car in neutral, grabbed the bag with the collapsed rifle, and opened the door.

The rain had passed, and the lot was covered in

puddles. There was little wind and he could see the sky in the water. He put the bag over the top of the car, then, looking around, bent and released the emergency brake. Taking his bag from the roof of the car, he stepped back.

He walked on, making a straight line toward his car, careful not to rush. He could see his car across the lot, sitting there, seagulls on the fence posts, the masts of sailboats, white and bobbing with the movement of the water. Behind him, he heard a woman scream. He walked on. Grady wove through the cars, bumper to bumper. The sound of something hitting the water hard, the burst of air bubbles. When he turned to look back, the attendant's car was no longer where he'd left it.

A crowd had gathered around the ramp, and there in the water, floating out to sea, was the attendant's car. He watched it only briefly, the car bobbing there on the water, air escaping, and the vehicle going under. If Hunt still had the boat, he'd need to find another ramp. He knew Hunt was still out there. All Grady could think about was time. Time to get east of the mountains, find the little motel the lawyer had told him about, and hope for an improvement in his day. He was pulling out of the lot when the car finally went under.

Their man at the airport had told them where to go. They parked the Lexus four spots down and on the other side of the street from the house and looked up toward it. At the end of the block, they could see a city bus pull to a stop, then move off. The cross street above them was busy at all times of the day with cars and people passing. In the late afternoon, with the sunlight directly in front of them on the horizon, the oranges and reds painted the scene like a fire, the figures crossing the street nothing but shadows of coal. The driver lit a cigarette and sat watching the house. Every couple of breaths he released a stream of smoke from the window.

The house sat close to the street, with the front stairs leading almost to the sidewalk. Cars were parked in nearly every space along the street, several with pieces of windblown trash resting against the tires. It was not a well-kept part of town, though perhaps at some time it had been. The plain white house was made of wood boards, the roof cracked and bandaged with tar patches, shingles the color of sandpaper. One central floor looked out over the street, with a window high up that was probably the attic. No one appeared to be home.

Several people walked by on the street, but not the person they were looking for. After forty-five minutes passed, a man carrying a grocery bag stepped from the far curb and crossed the street toward the house. He climbed the stairs and, in the same moment, brought from his pocket a set of keys that the two men in the Lexus could see clearly.

'I wish I had my gun,' the driver said as he opened the door and emerged onto the street. He was careful to push the door of the car closed with his body, his weight shifting to the car, but the door making no sound. He flicked away the cigarette, then crossed the street toward the man, who had reached the top of the stairs and stood with his keys at the lock and his opposing arm wrapped around the grocery bag.

By the time the man opened the door and leveled the bag with his knee, the driver had reached the porch and, without stopping, punched the man in the right kidney. The man buckled, and the grocery bag fell from his arms. The driver then hooked the man's throat with his forearm and rammed his knee straight and with force into the back leg of the man, who seemed to flop over and put his weight full onto the driver, his face caught just above the driver's forearm, a strange smile on his lips. The driver pulled him through the door and into the house.

From the car, the man with the bag full of hardware supplies watched all of this. He waited a beat before he, too, rose from the car, carrying the bag of tools in his hand up the stairs toward the house. The door was open like a mouth, blackness beyond, and into this the man stepped and closed the door behind him.

D rake passed a hand throught the ash. He was kneeling in the wreckage of Hunt's house. All around him the fire still smoldered, pieces of the frame rising out of the black shape. In front of him the bricks of the fireplace stood, painted black with carbon. A water heater that he guessed had been under the stairs was now visible. The house was a complete loss. He looked down at the ash. He put his hands together and clapped the grit from them. Little puddles were everywhere, from the fire trucks and the rain. He clapped his hands together again and stood.

He had been here only a day before. He tried to remember the man's face, brown skin, slight acne scars near the chin, unshaven, his hand in Drake's, strong but well fleshed in the palms. No bodies had been found except for the horses. The fire had burned hot with the gas, and not much was left. But the fire inspectors guessed it wasn't hot enough to burn bones, and they hadn't found any yet.

Nora had been generous with him. He thought of the man watching while Nora went back inside to get him the number, to offer him help. Had she known Drake had taken a shot at her husband just a couple of nights before, aimed to wound him, maybe kill him, would she have acted as she did then? Drake tried to think of taking that same shot now and he didn't think he could. He pictured Nora up there on that same horse. The crosshairs of the sight, the horse coming into view. He couldn't do it. Not now.

He walked over to Driscoll, the grit and ash sticking to his boots, growing on him and caked to his soles, heavy and cumbersome. When he reached the horse fence, he hit them against the wood and watched the gunk fall. Driscoll was leaning over one of the horses. Several men in suits that looked almost like biohazard gear were milling about near another. 'They've cleaned this one off,' Driscoll said. 'Come over here, give it a look.'

Drake stepped through an opening in the wood and ducked his head. He held his hat and walked over to where Driscoll knelt examining the body. 'Quarter horse,' Drake said.

'How can you tell?'

'Strong front legs, short, and a bit stocky.'

'You learn that on the farm?'

'It was the type of horse my father used to ride.'

'Talked with the owner about ten minutes ago. Wasn't happy to hear about this. Says he's been boarding this one here for about three years now, never thought anything of it.'

'It's a shame.'

'Named him Hermes.'

'Good name, must have been a fast horse.'

'Says he was going to sell him this year, sixty thousand. You believe that?'

'Can't say I do.'

'Probably just out for the insurance money.'

'It would be nice to think that was the only thing involved,' Drake said. He knelt and ran a hand along the belly of the horse. He could feel the muscle, the well-cared-for coat. He tried to remember if he'd seen this horse the other day. But then he put it out of his mind.

'This guy, Hunt, better know how to really ride. He's got one hell of a chase coming after him.'

'Wish I'd caught him that first day.'

'No, you don't. He'd be dead in that cell just like the kid.'

'No, I don't,' Drake repeated. 'You think he's got any chance?'

'I think if we get to him first he does. Ask him to give up a few names. I can't say that he'll avoid doing any time, but it's surely better than what's out there looking for him now.'

Drake looked down at the horse, milky eyes, the flies already starting to land. 'Trailer isn't here. Neither is that Lincoln. Honda I saw the other day is charred all to hell back there where the garage used to be.'

'You think any of those vehicles are registered to their right names?'

'Probably not.'

'I can run it through the DMV and see what comes of it.'

'Lincoln definitely didn't pull that trailer out of here.'

'Something big?'

'From what I saw, had to be.'

'How many horses you count yesterday?'

Drake looked around. Far off in the middle of the pasture he could see the third. 'More than this,' he said.

The knock came again on Eddie's door. He checked the slide on the small pistol and put it through the back of his belt. On the bed the case was laid out, foam interior with cutouts for four magazines and a removable silencer. He put it under the bed. He had never used the pistol.

When he put his eye to the door, he could see Nora out there. He cleared his throat. The night was just beginning to come on, and he could see cars passing behind her on the road. She turned to look as one drove by, splashing a puddle, the sound of the wet tires running on the cement. He opened the door, and her attention was immediately on him.

He let her into the room, and when she had gone to the small chair in the corner, where two chairs sat around a cheap wood-veneer table, she said, 'I talked to Phil.'

Eddie went over to the bed and sat on the edge. 'Did he tell you what happened to him?'

Nora looked around the room. When she met Eddie's eyes, he was staring at her, waiting for an answer. 'He said the boat sank.'

'Did he say where he was?'

'Somewhere north, he didn't sound too sure. I think he barely made it down the coast after getting the drugs.'

'So he has the drugs?'

'In a way.'

'In what way?'

'They're inside a girl.'

'Inside her?'

'That's what he said.'

'This isn't at all what I talked to Hunt about.'

'No, I'd expect not. Didn't see yourself in this motel either?' Nora tried to laugh, but it came out strangled and fell away.

'Did he tell you where to find him?'

'No. I gave him the address here. He said he'd come to us.'

'Good,' Eddie said. 'I hope he has those drugs. It could be the only thing saving us.'

'What do you think happened up there?' Nora had her hands on her legs, and when she said this, Eddie could see the worry in her eyes. He looked away.

'I don't know what happened up there.'

'Something went wrong, right?'

'Something went wrong.'

'What is a girl with a stomach packed full of drugs doing in all this?'

'I think she has very little say in it.'

'It's sick, you know.'

'It's how it is, Nora.'

'I don't understand it anymore.'

'It's the same as it's always been. People need a product. We take it from the producer and bring it to the seller. That's how simple it is. This thing isn't going to stop because the government says it will. We're happy when they get involved – drives the price up. We can sell it for anything we want, and people will buy it because they can't not.'

'But a girl?'

'What am I supposed to say to you?'

'You didn't know about this before?'

'Not a thing.'

Nora looked to the window; the shades were drawn, but she could pick out the shapes of things beyond. 'I told him if things went bad to get out of there. I told him to come right back to the house. Now I'm not even there, and I don't know where he is.'

'We just need to wait this thing out a little bit longer. Phil's a smart guy. He'll come here and then you'll see.'

250

The man sat naked in an armchair pulled from his own dining room. It was not this that seemed the most startling to the driver, but the blood that ran from his ankles and from his wrists. The man with the hardware tightened the hose clamps around the naked limbs of the man seated in the chair until the skin tore against the thin metal bands.

Both the driver and his boss stood back and watched as the man raged against the chair and the metal that held him. His arms began to grow slick with blood and finally he stopped, and it was at this time they began to ask him questions.

A litter of kittens had recently been born in the house, and their mother sat in a bin on the warm living room floor. The driver had drawn the shades, and the house had the tin smell of fabricated metal and blood as well as the warmth of the body and the close smell of skin that the pull of the shades only made closer.

As the man answered the questions, the driver sat on the couch and played with the kittens. They were blond like their mother, but a few had black markings, and as they climbed along his lap, he could feel that their new claws had emerged. They were not yet attuned to the screams of the man or the strain of his voice. Life in this house had not yet taught them these things, though the driver wondered if they would ever be well acquainted with this kind of thing.

The driver's boss had come to the point in the questioning at which Thu had arrived at the boat and the two men had taken her out onto the water. The man in the chair had answered as best he could, though at times the driver's boss had tightened the bands on his wrists and around his ankles.

'We waited a full day for the girl,' the driver's boss said. 'It is not a secure feeling, this waiting. To invest your own time in something from the beginning and feel the whole operation has been fouled in the process by an outside force that has been fully out of our control. Do you understand what I'm saying to you?'

The man shuddered, and a thin vein of spittle stretched from his lip and fell to his thigh. 'I don't know what you want me to say. I did what I was told.'

'We expected you would, but in the absence of the lawyer, we have come to you, because you were identified as the one who picked up the girl at the airport. Do you see why we have come to you now?'

'I didn't steal the fucking heroin,' the man said. He was at the point of crying, and the man who was questioning him hit him hard across the face and let the sting sink into the flesh before speaking again.

'You have been identified as the last one to see the heroin. I don't think we can make this any clearer.'

The man in the chair didn't say anything.

'You are accountable in that way. Unless the lawyer tells us different, we have nothing to go on besides this fact.'

Still the man would not speak.

'We are missing ninety thousand dollars of heroin, almost a quarter of a million if you count the other girl, though we know she is not your fault, and I only mention her to show you our obvious agitation. I am only trying to be truthful with you, as I would hope you could be truthful with us.'

The tears came then, and another slim line of saliva, tinted pink with the blood from a cut in his mouth. 'I didn't take the heroin.'

'Yes, that is what you keep saying, but again, we don't have it, nor do we have any other names but your own.' The boss motioned for the driver to get up from the couch. Several of the kittens he had been playing with followed after him and slipped, purring, against his leg where the two men stood together. The boss reached into the hardware bag and brought out the blunt-nosed garden shears and handed them to the driver. The driver seemed to know what to do and he went to the man with the funny smile and pulled up his pinky and stretched it away from his hand.

'This is very simple,' the boss said. 'You have three knuckles on that finger. You will lose one every time you don't give me the right answer. Do you understand?'

The man in the chair did not look away from his pinky.

'Hey,' the driver said, 'do you understand?'

A half nod of the head.

'What happened to the heroin?'

'I gave it to the man in the other boat.'

'Where is this man now?'

'How am I supposed to know that? He should have brought her to you.'

No one said anything, and the driver cut the first knuckle away from the man's pinky. It fell to the floor, the man screaming. The kittens that had been at the driver's feet soon picked up the nub and began to toy with it.

Blood fell freely from the severed finger and pooled on the floor, first one drop, then the next. The pool grew. The man who had been screaming clenched his jaw and held back something that looked to boil inside him.

'Where is this man now?'

'He was older, sandy hair, maybe six feet, he was wearing . . . fuck . . . I don't know what he was wearing. You're fucking crazy.'

The driver made his next cut, and for a moment there was only the sound of the second knuckle falling to the floor, then the scream, and the blood pattering on the floor.

When the man looked down at his pinky, he saw first the red nub and then, farther down, the kittens at his chair and the blood falling. One of the kittens had looked up and was standing with its back legs on the floor and its front on the leg of the chair, and it was licking at the drops of blood as they fell from what remained of the finger.

'Where is the heroin?' the boss asked again.

'Fuck you, fuck both of you.' He was crying again and he wouldn't look up. The saliva dripped from his mouth and slipped in a train along his thigh, where it fell to the seat of the chair.

When the two men left, he was still sitting there. The driver could see the beat of his chest and the defeated way in which he sat in the chair, no longer trying to break free from the metal bands but submitting to them. He was still bound, still naked. The pool of blood had grown to a puddle, and the kittens sat licking at it and mewing to each other. When the driver closed the door, the last thing he saw was the little cat that had leaned upright against the chair with blood all over its face, climbing the leg of the bound man, using its newfound claws to dig into the man's flesh and pull itself up.

Hunt drove away from the hospital. He'd gone through the town fast before, with not even enough time to give it a look. But he looked now. Watched the streets. Sure at any moment that a police cruiser would come after him, that someone would have called him in. Someone from the hospital. Perhaps even Nancy and Roy.

The town was what he expected it to be, houses that looked much like the rest. At the center of town he stopped for a light, and he saw people staring at him. Across the street was a pharmacy. Next to that a diner, then a bank and a post office. He sat in the little hatchback and he figured they knew the car. They might even have known Roy and Nancy. He smiled and gave the people a wave. A father of two kids waved back, but the kids just stared.

How had he gotten here? Hunt had been asking himself this with increasing frequency. He didn't have an answer. He felt a strange pause, looking up at the light, waiting, a pause that didn't seem to belong to the days that had come before. He'd been an office janitor downtown when he left prison, emptying wastebaskets after everyone had gone, he'd worked as a prep cook in a kitchen, he'd even, for a time, worked as a refrigerator salesman. He had a good face, lean, with thick lines that stretched down and outlined his mouth; it was a trustworthy face, a face that said more than it ever could aloud. People bought refrigerators off that face, went home, lived with what they'd purchased, enjoyed. The job had been honest. There had been only a small chance that he would die, that a fridge would fall over and end his life. Now, sitting in the car, with the windows up and the heater spilling in hot engine air, he felt unsure. Something had gone wrong somewhere; despite all his efforts to lead a good life, to support his wife and make a living, he had failed. What good had running bets and smuggling done him? What had been wrong with an honest job? Jobs that paid him as much as he needed, nothing more, nothing less? But he'd never liked the feeling of answering to someone, like he was back in prison, like he was being watched, like he wasn't his own man. He wanted his actions to count for something. He didn't know what that was yet, but he thought that if he could just get free of these drugs, of Grady, maybe he could make a go of it.

The light changed and he pulled through. He knew life just wasn't as simple as loving a job, as making money. It didn't boil down to that. Hunt had chosen his path, known from the beginning what it would be like. Money couldn't buy everything, it couldn't buy his safety or Nora's, it couldn't protect Eddie and the horses. He'd seen that now, he'd heard it, listening over the phone as Grady executed the things he loved, one by one. There was nothing he could have done, and he was working through that, working it out the best way he knew how, just driving, moving forward, hoping everything would turn out for the better, as he'd always hoped it would.

Hunt kept driving, swinging his head down side streets, looking for an exit. He was on an island. There was a ferry, and he pulled up to the ferry booth and tucked his left foot into the door and paid the fee. At the loading dock he waited for the ferry but didn't get out of the car. His pants were half-cut-off, his leg in a bandage. He looked down to see a red stain where the blood had come through. He felt the air from the car vents blowing on his naked thigh. A man in an orange vest directed the other cars into lines. People got out of their cars and waited for the ferry. They stretched, they looked in on Hunt. He was just sitting there. Something strange about him, a man in his car with no book, just sitting there, staring straight ahead.

Hunt lowered the window. He smelled the ocean again. The calls of seagulls, one landing between the line of cars, the yellow feet dancing on the cement. They looked like little dinosaurs the way they stalked after trash, rolling their eyes, their beaks swinging from one side to the other as they two-stepped through the parked cars. He could understand that specific pursuit, that necessity, stalking after what he desired most. Now, to him, it was safety. It was getting away and not looking back.

He thought about Thu. He hoped she'd be okay. On the floor of the car he'd found her purse just sitting there. He didn't know what else to do with it but push it back under the seat. Something suspicious about a man sitting alone in a car with a woman's purse. From the backseat he fished out the zippered survival bag. He could see the shape of the little pellets in there through the orange material. It hadn't occurred to him yet to cover it – the gun in there, the bag thin enough to show the shape of the gun where it met the orange material. In his hand he held the bag, worked it over once in his fingers, and felt the little latex balls. A woman passed near the car and looked in at him. He smiled. And when she was gone, he let the bag drop to the floor, where it fell into shadow.

He wondered if he'd done the right thing back there. What else was there to do? He would have liked to know more about the girl. The pellets on the floor, the heroin, the ninety thousand. He knew some of that was Thu's. He didn't know how much yet. But he felt some of it would need to be hers. He hoped she was okay. He looked at the bag. The ferry blew a horn, and if he looked up he might have been able to see it approach, but he didn't. He kept staring, looking at the bag, sitting there on the floor.

'You feel bad for him?' Sheri said.

'I don't feel good.' Drake put his hand up on the wall. He was outside in the hall looking in on Driscoll's downtown office, talking on his cell phone. The information was coming in, and he could see Driscoll through the glass with the paperwork on his desk.

'You're going to try and help this guy, Hunt?'

'I'm going to see what I can do.'

'What makes you think he's any better than that other one?'

'No one said that other one was bad.'

'You certainly treated him bad.'

'He's dead now. I feel accountable for that. My part.'

'There wasn't a piece of that that was your part.'

'I know. But I still feel it.'

'Just because your father rode horses doesn't make you an expert. There's plenty of other people more experienced than you. Doesn't mean it needs to be you out there.'

Drake didn't say anything. He hadn't talked to his father in ten years, and Sheri knew his father had done a lot more than just ride horses. He took his hand off the wall and pushed his hat back on his head. 'You liking the hotel?'

'Nothing I say is going to change this, is it?'

'No.'

'Will I see you soon?'

'Soon as I can.'

'What if I said I was leaving you?'

'Are you saying that?'

'No.'

'Are you worried about me?'

'Of course I'm worried about you. What business do you have out there anyway?'

'I'm going to be fine. I'm under DEA protection.' He almost laughed but then didn't. He didn't think Sheri would see the irony. He felt bad for the kid.

'I'm pregnant,' Sheri said.

'That true?' he said, without skipping a beat.

Sheri didn't say anything. Then: 'No.'

'You'll be okay, won't you? I'll come by when I can.' He waited, listening to her breath on the other side of the receiver. He wanted to say more, he wanted to tell her it was all going to be fine, it was all going to work out, but he didn't know that, not for sure.

Grady passed the Dairy Queen. There had been a bridge, and beneath it a river, dark blue with the setting sun coloring the trees. At the intersection, just a single dangling caution light. He drove down the street and found the motel but didn't stop. The sun was going and it made everything glow: the lamplight in the office golden, the rooms and the orange shades illuminated from within, car headlights farther down the road. He passed the motel and swung the car into a gravel parking lot a hundred yards off. A girl in a little coffee shack gave him a look but didn't pay him any mind when she saw he wasn't buying.

From the bag he took the small three-inch paring knife and then a little hitch he'd had made in a shop on Aurora. It was a simple thing constructed of leather, button clasps, a spring and a metal slide, and a sort of trigger. With his shirtsleeve unbuttoned, he attached the hitch and then the knife to his forearm. He left his sleeve loose. By shifting the muscle in his arm he could make the knife slide forward on the spring. He'd practiced this, flexing his forearm to release the knife and snap it forward on the slide. It was something he did in his spare time, practicing day after day. The hitch was a little thing of his own design, and he felt proud when he used it. When he looked up from the knife now, he could see the girl watching him. He smiled. The girl looked away. He knew what she had probably been thinking, his arm flexing and his forearm in his lap.

He put the knife away in his sleeve and closed the bag. He opened the car door and the dome light came on. He looked around at the surrounding lot, and with the wind rustling his clothes, he got out and closed the door. The river was audible, a rushing sound of water and rock. Across the gravel lot he could see the sporadic growth of grass from between the pebbled lot and green, leafy bushes of stink currant near the river. Higher along the river, on the opposite side, a band of willow. Grady straightened his shirt and walked the short distance to the coffee shack. The girl slid back the glass panel and watched him come.

'Coffee,' he said.

The girl looked him over. She was a small thing, with brown, shoulder-length hair, combed straight. 'What size?'

'Medium, black.'

The girl turned away and filled a cup for him.

'What time does it get dark around here?' he asked.

The girl put a lid on the cup. She handed it out to Grady. 'It's dark already,' she said.

'Sorry,' Grady said. 'I mean real dark. Does it get that way around here? Like you can't see your hand in front of your face without a light?'

'Sometimes,' the girl said. She looked confused.

Grady held out his hand and looked at it. He felt the knife beneath the cuff of his sleeve. 'I like that,' Grady said. 'Doesn't get like that in the city, too much light all the time.'

'Usually the stars are out, and it's pretty light with that and the moon. Not much else out here. Nothing like the city.' She put the numbers into the register and gave him his total.

He dug a bill out of his pocket and gave it to her. He put the change in for a tip. 'What do you think it'll do tonight?' he said. He held the coffee cup out in his hand at a right angle, and the girl leaned over the counter to look at the sky. He could smell her perfume, a mix of apples and fabric softener. He guessed her to be seventeen, maybe eighteen.

'If it clears, there might be some stars.'

'How old are you?' he said.

'Seventeen.'

'You going off to college soon?'

'Next year.'

'Thinking about the city?'

'If my parents let me.'

'They will,' Grady said. The girl looked at him. He couldn't tell what she was thinking. 'Just be careful,' he said. 'It's nothing like this coffee shack.'

The girl laughed. 'Okay,' she said. 'Thanks.'

'Dark out now,' he said. He smiled at the girl and raised the coffee.

He didn't go back to the car; he walked along the edge of the gravel, where it met the cement of the road. One car passed and he watched it slow into the blinking yellow caution light. The coffee was hot and he sipped at it as he walked.

Around behind the motel he found the horse trailer and the truck. He looked in on the passenger side and then again on the driver's side. Dirt all over the undercarriage and up into the wheel wells. He went over to the horses and stuck his knuckles in and let them nuzzle around on his hand and look for food. 'Nothing for you,' he said.

He took a sip of the coffee and watched the back of the motel. A line of small, square bathroom windows, all of them placed high. The windows would be like mirrors now, the dark outside and nothing to see in them but a reflection. He counted the rooms down. Two lighted windows next to each other.

When he had finished the coffee, he put the cup down in the gravel and walked around to the front of the motel. He watched the woman in the office. She was sitting, looking at her computer screen. The front desk blocked most of her. Grady went down the line of rooms until he found the Lincoln.

He was careful with his shoes, careful not to make noise. At the door, he knocked lightly. A car passed behind him. It was the second car to have passed in ten minutes.

When Eddie opened the door, Grady could see the silenced muzzle of a small gun peeking out at him from Eddie's hand.

'What is that, a twenty-two?'

Eddie stepped aside and let Grady into the room. Grady heard the sound of a television from the next room over. Eddie was standing at the door, holding the gun on him.

'Is that the wife?' Grady said. He was looking at the door leading to Nora's room.

'Would you mind?' Eddie said. He made a circling motion with the point of the gun.

'Round and round,' Grady said. He raised his hands and made a slow rotation so that Eddie could see he wasn't carrying anything.

Eddie pointed at his boots.

Grady raised the right leg of his pants. 'Nothing here.' He raised the left leg. 'Nothing here.' He held out his hands, palms exposed. 'Nothing up my sleeves,' he said. He was smiling. He didn't pull his sleeves up but waited, watching Eddie.

'That's fine,' Eddie said. 'Turn on the television, would you? I don't want Nora to hear us.'

Grady flipped the television on.

Eddie went to sit at the cheap veneer table. He kicked out the other chair for Grady. 'I was told you would be coming here for Hunt.'

Grady sat down. 'That's right.'

'His wife doesn't know anything, so we can leave her out of this.'

'Makes sense,' Grady said. Eddie had dropped the gun, and he let it rest on his lap.

'They said you had a history with Hunt.'

'We were in Monroe together.'

'You don't look like you're old enough,' Eddie said.

'He was getting out, I was going in. Technically, I was a minor, but they said the crime warranted an adult conviction.'

Eddie looked at him. 'That can be rough. How long were you in there?'

'Long enough.'

'You know something about Hunt?'

'I know he's getting to be a headache.'

'He's a friend.'

The light from the television flickered on the wall behind Eddie and hung up in the curtains. An old movie with cowboys and Indians was on. 'This must be sad for you.'

'I don't like it.'

'Did they tell you they would kill you, too?'

'If I made this difficult.'

'Have you?'

'I've tried not to.'

'Can you tell me where Phil Hunt is?'

'I don't know that.'

'You said you wouldn't be difficult.'

'I don't know where he is. I haven't even talked to him. Nora talked to him, not me.'

'Sounds like I should talk to her.'

'I was told that wouldn't be necessary.'

'We're just talking, nothing more yet.'

'Will you be the one to do it?'

'It?'

'Hunt.'

'I'll be the one.'

'Do me a favor?'

'Yes.'

'Don't draw it out.'

Grady had been watching television, nothing but guns and smoke. An Italian actor dressed up as an Indian took a bullet and made a stiff fall. Grady looked over at Eddie. 'Can I ask you a question?'

'Sure.'

'Why are you carrying around that twenty-two?'

'Protection.'

'That thing can't protect you.'

'I think it could do its job if needed.'

'How quiet is that silencer?'

'The whistle of the bullet is the only thing you hear.'

'As well as what it hits.'

'Yes.'

'Looks small enough to fit in a coat pocket.'

'Probably could.'

'This isn't your thing, is it?'

Eddie looked across the table. 'I'm more of the handler.'

'You sit around at bars and make connections, make phone calls, handle things?'

'Yes.'

'I have a bar trick for you, sort of a magic trick.'

'Yeah?'

'Watch.' Grady placed his arms straight out in front of him, flattened his hands, and turned his palms up, then down. 'Nothing in my hands,' he said. Eddie sat transfixed, watching the hands. Grady flexed his forearm, and the knife came forward on the slide. Eddie made a quick movement with the gun, but the blood was already appearing in a line across his neck. The gun went off. It was quiet and the round hit the wall just above the television and made a solid thunk. 'Magic,' Grady said.

The lawyer sat in front of the floor-to-ceiling windows that ran the two walls of his living room. The stereo was on, and the sound of the singer's voice echoed high up in the living room rafters. The ghost shapes of boats and islands took form out of the gray fog in front of him. The smell of smoke from a fire, rich cedar burned into points of glowing embers. Weather calling for snow, the cold coming now and the weather changing. He had sent his driver out for a girl. The girl, half his age, curled in the bed of his lap. A dark half nipple showing from the open neck of the robe he'd given her. Dark hair dyed blond, eyebrows like two sharpened sticks, penned over and held straight. He drank from the glass of whiskey in his hand and sat watching the sound materialize through the windowpanes before him.

A crash of glass, the girl startling. The lawyer watched as one head-size boulder of granite from his retaining wall rolled end over end into the living room. He felt the tremor of it through the floor. The boulder stopped halfway to him, the lawyer too scared to move. Cold wind was coming through

271

the jagged cut the boulder left in the glass, all the warmth in the room sucked back out into the world beyond. No alarm at all. No siren. Nothing. Wires cut. The lawyer still sat on the couch with the girl close by, too dazed and surprised to move. Hadn't he known this was coming? Didn't he know it the whole time?

He saw the dark shadows of men beyond the glass. The wooden handle of a sledgehammer popped through the hole in the glass and swept the frame clean, glass spilling onto the hardwood.

The lawyer stood, holding the whiskey still, dumbly. A living room with a large wraparound couch, the girl on it, a fire, windows letting in the last light of day, some oldies song playing on the stereo, the lawyer just standing there. The two Vietnamese men entered his living room, climbing through the hole they'd left in the window frame. He heard the crunch of glass beneath the men's feet. Saw their cold, untroubled eyes, practiced in the art of terror. He knew these men, knew they'd had a deal at one time, knew it had come to this.

'I was going to call,' the lawyer said.

'Where is the heroin?' the first man said, stopping to pick the boulder up from the floor.

The lawyer stuttered something as he watched the rock rise from the floor into the man's hands. He felt the back of his legs touch the couch, the girl's hand held against his thigh, the touch of her fingers.

'Two girls,' the man shouted. The terrible vein

in his forehead rose under the strain of the rock in his hands.

'Two girls?' the lawyer repeated.

'Where is it?'

'It's on its way.'

'From here to Canada—,' the man said.

'Just a minute—'

'From Canada to here—'

'Just a minute—' He felt his legs give beneath him, his knees knocking together, brittle as petrified wood.

'Looking for our heroin,' the man finished, all the time crossing the floor with the boulder held in his hands. It seemed heavy, looked heavy, and the lawyer watched the strain on the man's face. The eyes clear, held down on him. The lawyer's knees buckled and he dropped onto the couch behind him.

The man raised the boulder up over his head.

'No,' the lawyer said.

The boulder raised high.

'No,' the lawyer begged. 'Please.'

The girl screamed.

The impact carried through the wall. Nora got up from the bed and went to the television and switched the set off. Through the wall, she could hear Eddie's television going. Then the sound of his outside door opening and the brief shadow of someone passing across the shades. The door handle rattled. Nora went to the bathroom. She looked up at the high window and pulled it open. The window was six feet off the ground. She didn't think she could fit. She left the window open and went back into her room. The wood around the door splintered, the knob still there but a jagged hole to the side. She got down under the bed and squeezed herself in. The crack of the wood again. She could see the splinters falling to the floor.

The door opened. She saw it swing wide and a pair of men's boots standing there, the toes pointing toward her, then turning and facing the bathroom. From under the bed, she could see him walk across the floor and disappear behind the bathroom wall. The carpet smelled like water damage and mold, old plastic, and she fought back a sneeze. The space she was in was barely enough room to move her head. The boots reappeared. For a while they stood there in front of her. She imagined he was looking at the television. What had he seen in the back there? The truck? The horses? He'd assume she had run.

The boots walked directly over to her, turned, and faced the dresser and the television. She felt his weight on the bed, the mattress depressing over her, the side of her face pressed into the carpet. Something crustlike on the fibers near her left ear.

There was a brief whistle of air, the television exploded, and she could see the glass fall to the floor. He lay back on the bed, and Nora felt his weight disperse across the mattress springs, his boots leaving the carpet for a moment. She felt him roll back and then roll forward, testing his weight on the bed, and then he was on his feet and he went out the door.

Nora didn't move. She listened for what sounds she could hear. All she saw were the white walls around her, the base of the dresser, the television glass on the carpet, the legs of the table and chairs near the window. He hadn't closed the door on the way out, and she could see the night out there, the way the light from the motel flooded out and lay on the parking lot. There was a cold draft coming from the opening and playing along the floor. Her cell phone was somewhere in the sheeting of the bed. She didn't know if he had found it.

She thought that if she could just get it, maybe she could call Hunt. With her fingers digging into the carpet, she began to pull herself out. She kept an eye on the open door. Where was Eddie? She didn't like the quiet now, no cars passing, nothing happening, no sound of gravel, a small drift of air from the open door. Her legs lay behind her and she tried to use them in the limited space, as if she were swimming, frog-kicking from under the bed.

The door to Eddie's adjoining room shattered out on its hinges. A hand reached down and found her leg. He pulled, fighting her loose, kicking leg. Her fingernails in the carpet, digging in, then her hands on the legs of the bed as she came out from under, then on the bed frame itself. She felt the rug burning wherever her skin came exposed – her chin, her left cheek, her fingernails and fingers. He pulled harder, backing into Eddie's room and pulling her with him.

'You ever pull over someone you know?' Driscoll said. He was sitting at his desk. Drake sat across from him, two coffee cups on the desk between them. They'd been waiting three hours for news from the lab regarding the bullets taken out of the dead horses. There was nothing left for them to do.

'Sure. I pull them over.'

'Even if you know them?'

'It's not that big a place. I know ninety percent of the cars out there.'

'You ever surprised by what they have to say?'

'There's a few wise ones out there, but for the most part it's just what it is. I'm not looking to write anyone up. It's not good to go around pissing folks off if you're just going to see them later on at the bar.'

'I used to think I could be real tough. For the first three or four years, I was serious about this thing. You know, I carried my pager everywhere, I carried my gun. Regulations, everything. My friends always introduced me as the cop. It gets pretty old, you know. Life isn't as much fun. No one wants to do stupid things anymore.'

'Would you have arrested them?'

'No. That's not really what I'm talking about here. It's difficult enough as it is. There's no point. I tend to think those friends of mine are going to do stupid things no matter what. I'd rather be there in case they need a hand up at the end. But I do expect it. I don't go around thinking, I'm going to need to arrest this guy. Even if I know the guy, know he's a real straight edge. It's better to always have that in the back of your head, the 'what if' – maybe his wife left him, maybe he was fired from his job. Even if you know them, I think you need to be prepared. You get what I'm saying?'

'I get that your friends do stupid things.'

'Okay, how about this one. So you pull a guy over, you think you know him, and so you walk over there and you smile and look in the window, and boom, you're blown away. My point is that instead of following your expectations, you try and treat everyone the same. Sure, these guys are my friends, they do stupid things, but what's important is that you're never surprised. The best advice anyone ever gave me was: Watch the hands. The face isn't going to hurt you. It's what's in the hands that will hurt.'

'You worried about me?'

'Deputy Drake, yes, I worry about you. I know these are your people. This guy and his horses and his wife you're so sweet on. But look at it this way. If we're lucky enough to catch him before this other player gets him, you better watch those hands.'

Hunt drove through the intersection, in his rearview the gas station and Dairy Queen. He pulled in and parked next to the motel office. A light was on in the back. When he opened the car door he could feel the cool mountain air. He liked that smell, pollen and sap, like a block of ice evaporating on a kitchen counter, rich and mineral. The wind washed through a thicket of willow, and he looked down the length of the motel and saw the light falling from the room windows onto the walk. The sign above flashed 'Vacancy.'

Again he was aware of the cut pants and the bandage on his leg. He limped over to the office door and pulled it open. A glass door, with a collapsible shade, drawn up. There was no bell and he entered the office without much sound. Two chairs by the window, a small coffee table where a stack of *Better Homes* lay, the Sunday paper from the week before, and in the corner of the room a coatrack. He went to the desk and rapped with his knuckle on the counter. No one came. He could see where the light fell from a lamp in the back room, but could not see the lamp. He turned to look out on Roy's car. He watched the yellow caution light dangling near the Dairy Queen. Even at that distance the light still played on his skin. He turned back to the counter and knocked again. 'Hello,' he called.

He limped around the counter and looked in on the small room in the back. He saw a bed, a dresser, a lamp on the dresser, and in the back a single window, the covers of the bed drawn away, and a book cracked open and laid facedown on the bed. 'Hello,' he called.

No one came from the bathroom, and he stood there in the doorway but didn't enter. The whole feel of it was odd. He backed out and went around the counter and out the door, using his good leg to propel himself forward, his feet moving together in a rough limp as if he had one shoe tied to the other. He went down the walk, stopping at the windows to look in. Nora hadn't given him the room number. He dug out his cell phone and gave her a call. Straight to her voice mail. No answer.

About a hundred feet down the walk, he found the body of a woman in her forties with curly blond hair, laid between two parked cars. There were a number of bullet holes in her body, a final single shot to the head. She wore a kind of smock, a brown vest with a name tag on it. Hunt knew he'd found the clerk. In the parking lot, he could see the scuff marks in the gravel. She'd been dragged from just a few feet outside the office door, through the gravel parking lot, and hidden there between the two cars.

Hunt could hear the televisions on in several rooms, but no one seemed to have noticed this woman in the parking lot or, apparently, the gunshots that had killed her. He left the woman there and went down the line of rooms until he came to one with a busted-out doorknob and splintered wood along the cement walk. The door was partially open and the brown carpet in view. The bathroom light was on in the back and some of that light crept from the room out onto the gravel lot.

He stood waiting outside the door, listening as best he could. There was no sound but that of the televisions in other rooms. Without touching the door, he slipped into the room, moving around the door with caution. What he found was a bed pulled slightly to the right. He could see where it had come away from the wall on its far corner. The television was shot out, and near the bed was an open door, cracked nearly off its hinges, leading to an adjoining room. Nora's clothes were on the dresser, her bag barely unpacked. He went over to the bag and ran a hand through it but found only clothes. He didn't know what he was looking for, his mind empty, no thought but that his wife was gone.

He went into the bathroom and found the open window. He put two hands to the frame and pulled himself up on it and looked out at the river and the stink currant bushes. He saw his horse trailer and truck. After lowering himself, he went back into the motel room and walked to the adjoining door. The television was on. It gave the room a strange feel, like someone was there. No sound except for the television, its light reflecting off the walls.

Something on the screen lit white and then faded. No lights on in the room. With that brief flash he'd seen the shape of a figure sitting within. Eddie.

A minute passed before Hunt could go back into the room. He stood at the door and listened to the television. The eleven o'clock news was on, with warnings of an early snow. When he looked again, Eddie was still there. Hunt could see where the blood had flowed from the cut, like a red bib tied midway up his neck. The blood had come down and caught in his shirt. It looked to be sticky, and when Hunt came closer he could see that it hadn't completely dried.

He called Nora again. Voice mail. Hunt had to turn away, but even then he felt Eddie staring at him. The panic didn't come all at once, but slowly, like an incoming tide. He left the room. He didn't have any clue what to do. Everything had gone wrong. Feeling lost, he went along the walkway, stopping again to look down at the hotel clerk. He stared at her for a long while, longer than he had time for, trying to make up his mind about what to do. He knew he couldn't stand there forever, knew he shouldn't. His wife was gone, Eddie was dead. He stared down at this woman he didn't know, a stranger, someone who hadn't asked for this. He had caused this. Looking at her, he was aware he'd become someone he no longer recognized, someone terrible, something drawn up from the deep abyss, with no real purpose, an unquenchable thirst, a bottomless hunger, searching out some demon inside him.

The televisions were still on in several rooms, and he heard them as he limped past. From his pocket he dug out his keys. He was holding them in his hand as he came to Roy's hatchback. He took the survival bag of heroin from the car floor and closed the door. From above, the red vacancy sign left a layer of dull blood-colored light on everything, like a film of dust in a forgotten room.

With the bag in his hand he walked around to the back of the motel and climbed into his truck. He held tight to the steering wheel, swayed slightly back and forth with his hands anchored to the wheel. 'Fuck,' he moaned, drawing the word slowly up from deep inside. He pounded at the wheel several times in quick succession before starting the truck and pulling forward.

In his side mirror he saw something white on the ground. It was the only thing in an otherwise dark lot. He stopped the truck and got down from the cab. He walked back and looked at the coffee cup lying sideways on the gravel. With his toe he investigated it and watched the cup roll over, then stop. He could hear the river. A horse moved in the trailer, and he turned to the sound and walked back to his truck.

The driver took a rag from under the seat and cleaned the sledgehammer. The two men were sitting with the doors pulled open on the Lexus, looking back at the gates of the lawyer's house. There was sweat on the driver's brow as he finished with the hammer and threw the rag into the shadows at the side of the road. The pits of late-summer cherries everywhere, the cherries themselves long gone and rotted away all around them on the ground, barren cherry trees overhead. Cold, fungal smell of rotting leaves. 'You know the address?' the other man asked.

'I know it,' the driver said, getting out of the car and walking around to the back, where he popped the trunk and put the sledge-hammer away.

The other man watched him, and when the driver came back he asked, 'Grady Fisher?'

'Works as a cook somewhere in South Seattle, does errands for the lawyer.'

'What kind of errands?'

'Errands no one else wants.'

'Those kind of errands.'

'Those kind.'

The driver started the car and they pulled out onto the road and drove south. Neither of them said anything till they reached the interstate. It was late evening and the lanes were all but empty. A lone semi ran past them carrying a double trailer, the sound like a train passing.

'You going to call anyone?' the driver asked.

'Everyone,' the man said.

There was nothing to do but stuff Nora in the trunk. For a while she had made those horrible sounds, punching at the metal, kicking the backseat. For five miles he put up with it, just figured she would get it out of her system. He stopped the car on the side of the road. The night immediately came on, moths and little flying insects drawn to the Lincoln headlights, cold mountain air, the smell of pine. Underfoot small droppings of pine needles, gravel, the rutted side of the road, depressions filled with rainwater. He stood listening to the sounds coming from the rear of the car. When they didn't stop, he brought the key out and opened the trunk to look in at her.

A leg came out at him. He sidestepped and grabbed her ankle as it passed. Holding her with one hand, he gave her a quick punch with the other and hoped that would calm her. She didn't pass out, so he punched her again and this time she went. He hoped Hunt loved his wife. He was counting on it, and he knew people did stupid things for love. They did stupid things all too often.

And he thought this was probably how they had all come into this mess. How it had all begun for them. Stupid.

Hunt drove the big diesel, following the river and waiting for his phone to find coverage. One bar poked up on the display, then quickly disappeared. He didn't know which way Grady had taken her; the road out of town had run east and west. He drove west, toward the mountains, hoping he was right. He slowed the truck, coming to a small town that, like the one he'd just left, ran along the river. Everything was built to look out on the river and everything it brought with it. He tried his phone again and couldn't get a signal. He drove across the only bridge and parked by a closed restaurant.

He got down and walked toward the river, his phone in his hand. He watched for a signal. Nothing. When he reached the river he walked out on the bridge. Nothing moved anywhere, only the water below him. Dark water moving fast. He looked back at the truck. The restaurant beyond was built of painted white bricks, and across the street from that was a general store, with a bench and a few neon beer signs. He toed a loose piece of gravel into the river. He watched the splash and the current take it and the ripples moving out while the water went on.

From the middle of the bridge, he could see the entire town, not much of a sight, a gas station out by the main road and a small, closed-up produce stand. There were a couple of houses farther down on the river. He looked at the phone and waited. He turned it off, then turned it back on. One small blip of a signal popped up, and he tried Nora again. He listened to her voice mail. Thought about leaving a message but didn't.

'Fuck!'

He went back to the truck and put his arms out on the hood and stretched, hung his head between his arms, and breathed in the night air. He looked at the phone again. He checked the time, then walked back over to the bridge and called information. After about a minute, the operator put him through to the hospital.

'There's a Vietnamese woman who came in today on an overdose.'

'Are you family?'

'Only family she has.'

'Do you want to tell me who you are?'

'I want you to tell me about the girl.'

'I can't tell you about the girl.'

'Why can't you do that?'

Silence. 'Who is this?'

'Is she alive? You can tell me that, can't you?'

'I can't tell you anything till you tell me who you are.'

Hunt heard something on the line. He thought it was someone else at the hospital listening in. He hung up.

E ddie Vasquez had been dead almost twelve hours by the time Driscoll pulled into the motel. No one had found him till eight in the morning, sitting there at the table with that curtain of blood drawn across him. The local sheriff had been called, the county paramedics, a group of volunteer firefighters who served one way or another as deputies to the sheriff, and Driscoll.

Drake walked over to the Dairy Queen and looked back at the scene. He could see the EMS ambulance, neon green with flecks of blue. He saw the sheriff's cruiser and about six big-bodied pickup trucks he imagined hadn't been there till the man in room 5 came out and found the clerk sandwiched between his car and the neighboring truck. The drag marks were still in the gravel. Driscoll had picked up some small pebbles clotted with blood from the ground near the office and held them in his hand, examining them.

Best he could tell, the clerk had been shot because she'd seen whatever had been going on in rooms 11 and 12.

'He's the agent,' the sheriff had said. 'What is it you do?'

'Identifying bodies seems to be my specialty these days,' Drake said. They were standing across the room from Eddie. In the opposite corner, Driscoll was using a pen to look Eddie over. Nothing had come back on him, and they didn't know a thing except that he was dead. In one of the dresser drawers, they found a case for a gun that was missing. There were still three clips pressed into the foam, and a slot in the shape of a cylinder.

'For the silencer,' Driscoll said. 'A twenty-two.'

'Kind of light for these guys,' Drake said.

'Perfect for these guys. This stuff started popping up in the fifties and sixties, mostly CIA spooks. Small and light enough to carry without gathering attention, the only production gun that could be effectively silenced. In the seventies it was the weapon of choice for mob hits. Whole series of murders taking place in basements all over America. Neighbors didn't hear a thing.'

Both the outside door to room 11 and the inside door leading from room 12 had been forced open. There were two bullet holes around the lock of the outside door. The inside door had gone much easier, hollow inside and made of wood as light as balsa, cracked right off the hinges. Near as Drake could figure, the woman had been in room 11.

'You think she made it?' Drake said.

'You think she could fit out that back window?'

'I don't even know what she would have stood on.'

'I don't see a horse trailer anywhere.'

'Did you find a Lincoln?' Drake asked the sheriff.

'Only thing we found was that old hatchback up there by the office.' The sheriff was holding a small purse in his hand, and he gave it over to Drake. 'Found this tucked up under the seat. There's some pictures inside. Is that the lady you're looking for?'

Drake gave the bag a look through, a picture of two Asian children standing with a young Vietnamese woman. He looked at Driscoll. 'This isn't the woman I met the other day.'

'Who'd you say that hatchback was registered to?' Driscoll asked.

'A Roy Clemson out in Lummi.'

'Roy Clemson doesn't sound very much like a lady, or an Asian lady at that,' Driscoll said.

'You think he's our assassin?' Drake said.

'Don't know,' Driscoll said. 'I think we better go up there and sit him down for a talk, though.'

'Looking at these two bodies, I'm half-worried what we'll find when we get up there.'

Drake walked around to the back of the motel. There were wide tire tracks in the gravel, same as he'd seen in the mud up by Silver Lake. On the ground he found a paper coffee cup. They were playing catch-up and he knew it.

At the coffee shack, Drake ordered a coffee. The woman in there looked to be about his age, maybe a few years older. 'This your place?' Drake asked.

'Put it up almost three years ago.'

'What kind of business you do out of this thing?'

The woman handed him over the coffee. 'Mostly we get people heading up for the mountains, more in the winter when the lifts open up. But we get a good amount in the morning.'

'Not a lot of people walking up and ordering coffee.'

'No. Mostly it's drive-through.'

'Were you here last night?'

'No,' the woman said. She was using a dish towel to wipe a bit of spilled coffee by the register. 'I have a few girls who do nights for me.'

'Think they know anything about what happened over there at the motel?'

'I don't think they know much about anything yet. They're both a little dreamy at times.'

'Who was working last night?'

The woman paused and gave him a look. 'Are you with the sheriff?'

'In a way.'

'What kind of way is that?'

'If you can believe it, I was told this would be a vacation.'

'Nice vacation.'

'Yeah, that's pretty much how my wife put it.'

'You want me to have the girl give you a call when she gets out of school?'

'Sure, I just want to talk to her. We have statements from everyone staying in the motel, but I'd like to know if she saw anything.'

'We close around sunset. I don't know if she would have seen any of that mess.'

Drake wrote down his number and gave it to the woman. 'Let her know I'd like to talk to her.' He paid for his coffee and thanked the woman.

In the city the rain had begun to come in waves, windswept sheets of water moving up the street like ocean rollers. The two Vietnamese men sat in the Lexus, a half block down from Grady's house. The car was parked on the opposite side of the street, with a clear view of Grady's porch and front windows. The house clung to the back of a small hill, overgrown grass lining the foundation and a set of cement stairs that climbed up from the sidewalk and briefly flattened into a path that led to the porch.

No car in the driveway, just the empty carved-out feel of the house, no lights on, the rain falling everywhere. The patter of water spilling from the sky onto the windows and pinging on the Lexus. The driver watched a cat skitter out from under a torn couch and run half-crazed across the street, where it disappeared into one of the neighbor's yards.

The man in the passenger seat dialed a number on his phone and raised it to his ear. Two hundred feet down the block a light came on, silver blue, through the windshield of a darkened car. 'Anything?'

They were waiting, all of them. The rain falling was the only thing to keep them company. No conversation. No jokes.

The driver slumped down and rested his head against the seat. The rain still falling. Nothing to do but watch the house. Large-shingled siding, scraped gray paint, dull brown in places where it had been swept clean by time.

Smells of the car, the sour, upturned odor of cigarettes, and the old smells of food. Hands still raw from hefting the boulder. Arms still sore. The man in the passenger seat finished the call and clapped the phone closed. Down the block, the other light went off. They went on waiting.

Grady pulled the Lincoln up onto the inter-state, a forest of white pine surrounding him. He pushed the accelerator and felt the engine take him, leveling the car south on the interstate toward Seattle. Nora's cell phone rested on the dash. He watched the phone and waited till a strong signal showed on the display. With one hand, Grady toggled down through the numbers, and when he found Hunt's number he pushed Send.

Hunt answered, and the first thing Grady said was, 'Found her.'

After a moment, Hunt said, 'What do you want to do?' His voice came out shaking and he fought to calm it.

'I want you to come find me.'

'How do I do that?'

Grady gave him the address of his place in Seattle.

'It's that easy?'

'It's that easy.'

'What do I need to do?'

'You'll bring me the drugs.'

'What if I don't have them?'

'Of course you do.'

'They're inside the girl.'

'Get them out.' Grady put the phone on speaker and dropped it to the seat beside him.

'How am I supposed to do that?' Hunt's voice filled the interior of the Lincoln with the hollow, carved-out echo of speakerphone.

'I'd use a sharp knife,' Grady suggested.

'She's in the hospital.'

'I don't know if I have the patience for this,' Grady said. 'If I have to go up there and dig them out of her, I will. But it would be better for your wife if you did it yourself.'

'I'd like to talk to Nora.'

'Might be a little difficult.' Grady picked a small sun-dried fly carcass off the dash and examined it. He put the windows down a sliver, letting in the cold early winter air, wet smell of pine and low farm air, dust and granite. With his finger he flicked the fly out the window.

'You better not have done anything to her.'

'She's still alive, I think.'

'What do you mean, 'I think'? I want to talk to her.'

'Like I said, it could be difficult.'

'Why is that?'

'She's in the trunk.'

'What trunk?'

'The car trunk.'

'I'm going to kill you.'

'I doubt that.'

'No 'doubt' about it.'

'Let's do a little experiment. What do you say?'

'First, I want to talk to my wife.'

'Here is the experiment: I'll let her live if you bring me the drugs. You'll bring them to me and I'll let her live. You put them in my hand, I'll let her go.'

'Yes, I get it.'

'I'm not finished. The drugs are really only the bonus. You can do what you want with them. Really, the question regards you. I am paid to kill you. The loss of the drugs can always be blamed on you. Really, what I'm telling you here is that you're not trading the drugs for your wife, you're trading yourself.'

'What kind of crazy deal is that?'

'The best one you're going to get.'

'That's not any kind of deal at all.'

'What did you expect?'

'Something better.'

'I don't think you understand the situation at all. I am paid to kill you. If you don't die, I don't get paid. It makes complete sense.'

'You're crazy.'

'Okay.' Grady laughed. 'You bring the drugs, and I'll give you a ten-second head start. How does that sound?'

'You really are crazy.'

'That depends on if you think you can get away. I think that you're dead anyway. This is a great deal you're getting here. I think the first one was better, but I'd like to see what you're going to do about it.'

'How was the first one better?'

'Well, let's treat it like an experiment. If we know that the conclusion of the experiment is that you die, then I guess you would have to go back and look at the choices you made to get there. You don't bring me the heroin, you die but your wife lives. You bring me the heroin, you get a ten-second head start, your wife lives, and then when I catch up to you I kill you, and depending on the circumstances maybe I kill your wife, too. You see how the first one is the better deal?'

'What kind of circumstances?'

'Traffic accidents kill thousands every year.'

'You're going to give us a ten-second head start?'

'Yes.'

'What if I said I don't believe you?'

'That's what you'd be saying.' Grady paused to look over at the phone on the seat beside him. Hunt didn't say anything. After a second had passed, Grady thought perhaps Hunt just didn't understand the terms of the agreement, and said, 'There is only one thing certain.'

'I'll die?'

'One way or another.'

'Let me talk to her, Grady.'

'You have the address.' Grady reached over and closed the phone.

Driscoll stopped at a gas station off the interstate. They filled the tank and stood for a moment looking at the wet roads. Drake hadn't caught the exit number or the name of the town they were in. He knew they were getting close to wherever Hunt had picked the car up, but he didn't know if it was an hour or fifteen minutes away. While he waited for the tank to fill, he measured the dirt on the streets with his eyes, like a thin layer of mud from the previous night's rain. He was still in a bit of shock over what they had found at the motel. There was something inside him that didn't want to go on. Some fear of what they might find.

'Can you drive?' Driscoll asked.

'Sure, I can drive.'

'How's your defensive driving?'

Drake gave him a look.

'What?' Driscoll said.

'Just give me the keys.'

Driscoll threw them to him. Drake walked around to the driver's side and got in. After

Driscoll had finished filling the gas tank, he tapped on the roof and leaned down into the open passenger window. 'You want anything?'

'I'll take a black coffee if they have some.'

'I'm sure they have some, I just don't know if you'll want it.' Driscoll smiled, and Drake could see him straighten and put his hands behind his back. Drake heard a crack. Driscoll had taken off his jacket to drive and he wore only his holster and his badge on his belt, the Desert Eagle in plain view.

After Driscoll left, Drake stared off toward the end of the lot. The cement curved down and met the street. The street ran on for a ways until it met the interstate rumbling above. With the windows opened he could smell the spilled gasoline on the cement. The sun broke through the clouds and shone down on the lot, the cement seeming to evaporate under it, water vapor rising in the morning light.

It felt like a bit of peace in an otherwise tragic series of days. What did this woman have to do with all of this? Would they find her dead, too? Though Drake knew it was more than just the wife, that it was more than this. The idea came to him that if he had just let Hunt and the kid through in the mountains, none of this would have happened. What would he have done if Hunt had been his father? Drake honestly couldn't say. He didn't want to think about it anymore, didn't want to make that decision. He hoped he'd never have to. The thought was enough to drop his throat into his stomach, and when he tried to swallow, he felt a little bile rise back up like a bitter reminder.

When Grady got to his house he pulled up in the rain and sat looking down the street. He was a full two car lengths past his driveway, idling the engine with his hand halfway into the knife bag, searching out Eddie's .22. He'd counted two heads in the Lexus behind him and another three in the car up ahead. He didn't think Hunt would have done him like that. He didn't figure Hunt for that sort. No, he thought, Hunt would come at him alone. It wouldn't be like this.

Grady took his hand back from the bag and shifted the car into reverse. He backed it up and angled up the drive with the Lincoln's hood faced out onto the street. With the engine off, he was thinking it over. He guessed them to be the fellows he owed the heroin to. Guessed they'd come after him when he hadn't delivered on time. But he still had only half the drugs. About fifty pellets he'd dug out of the girl he'd picked up at the airport. A real screamer, she'd been a pleasure to put the knife through, just to shut her up. Hell, he thought, if they wanted her back, he could do that. He had her packed up real good in the downstairs freezer, sectioned out and ready for disposal. But he didn't think they were here for her, and he didn't think five of them had come just to collect the heroin. He knew these men had come to do him harm and he thought he'd let them try.

He sat in the Lincoln with the heat going. Better just to keep the heroin. Better for everyone. The heroin was inside the house, in the downstairs freezer. Nothing moved on the street, the rain still falling and the five men just sitting there waiting for him.

When she woke, the trunk was still closed over her. The car had stopped. She heard the patter of rain on the metal above her. Her first breaths brought the smell of asphalt and dampened upholstery to her nostrils. With her hand she felt the swollen skin of her face, the raised cheek, the welt along her temple, skin pulled tight with the swelling.

Nora thought of the woman in the motel parking lot. What had she done to deserve a thing like that? What did anyone deserve? Nora felt she deserved it. Felt she had been deserving it all her life, ever since she'd met Hunt. She'd fallen in love with him, drawn to him and his past, someone hurt, the wounds still visible. Nora there with the salve, with the bandage and the desire to heal.

The motel clerk had come out of the office. She must have seen some of what had gone on. Certainly not the gun, that wasn't possible. No one would have walked out that way had they seen a gun. Nora struggling, her kidnapper with his hands wrapped around her, his big arms holding her, stronger and more solid than he looked for a man of average height.

One, two, three. It was that quick. Still holding Nora by the waist, he reached his hand out, and there was the whisper of the bullet as it left the .22. The woman looked down at herself, at the spread of blood coming across her stomach, and a millisecond later her shoulder sprang back, and then her head. The woman hit the gravel. She had probably put that gravel in, she had probably raked it and filled it in, smoothed it out, cleaned it, made sure it was always welcoming, always professional. Never did the woman picture herself laid out on it. Nora knew that, just as surely as she knew her own situation.

Now something had brought her around, something had woken her. There was nothing but the sound of rain patter on the metal hood above. From somewhere deep inside the car, she heard the sound of water collecting, dripping through the inner workings of the car. Then, half-expectantly, the Lincoln's driver's-side door opened and she felt the springs ease up and the door swing shut. She closed her eyes. Nothing changed, the same black darkness, the same closed-in, shut-off solitude.

'That him?'

'Yeah,' the driver said. 'That's him.'

The two of them slumped down in the Lexus, waiting to see what would happen next.

'What's he doing now?'

'He's just sitting there.'

The man in the passenger seat rose and gave the Lincoln a look. Grady's reverse lights came on, a dull gray in the falling rain, Grady shifting the transmission up into park and turning off the ignition. The man in the Lexus ducked, and when he looked again, Grady had gotten out of the car with his bag and was walking around to the back of the car.

'What's he doing now?' the driver said.

'Looks like he's getting something out of the trunk.'

The driver popped his head up over the wheel and gave Grady a look. 'That our girl?'

'Can't see anything in this fucking rain.'

'Well, who else would she be?'

'You want to wait and see if he delivers?'

'I want to get our heroin.'

'Well, then, how do you want to go about that?'

'You're saying he stole the car?' Driscoll sat on the couch, Drake at the window looking out on the charred edges of the drum in the backyard. Roy and Nancy had brought two chairs from the kitchen into the living room. They kept their eyes on Driscoll. 'But you didn't report it stolen?'

'We were going to.'

Driscoll gave them a doubting look, then wrote something in his notebook. Thu's purse sat on the coffee table between them, contents separated into evidence bags. Nancy picked up the picture of Thu with her boys and stared at it for a long moment, then put it back on the table.

'What do you use the canister for?' Drake said.

Roy looked over at Drake. 'We use it for burning papers, that sort of thing.'

'Things you don't want anyone else to see,' Drake said.

'I don't know if I'd put it that way,' Roy said.

Driscoll waited for the two of them to stop. 'You know your car was involved in a double homicide.'

'You said that,' Roy said.

Nancy, who had been looking at her hands, asked, 'Do you have a picture of the man you're looking for?'

Driscoll gave her the picture of Phil Hunt.

'Are you sure this is him?'

'That was taken about thirty years ago. He shot a store owner with his own gun. It's the only reason he got second degree as opposed to first.'

'Didn't seem like he had much of a plan when he showed up here either,' Roy said.

Driscoll turned and looked at Roy. 'Would you mind looking at the picture.'

Nancy handed the picture to her husband. 'This is the guy?' Roy said.

'This is the first time you've met him?'

'Of course. Why would I know someone like this?'

Driscoll brought out a second packet of paper. On the front was a picture of Roy. 'You and Phil Hunt were both in Monroe together. We could start there.'

'Monroe is a big place,' Roy said.

'Come on,' Drake interrupted.

'I don't know him,' Roy said.

'Relax,' Driscoll said. 'For the moment, let's say you don't know him. We find out otherwise, you could be in a lot of trouble. Do you understand, Roy?'

'Yes.'

'What happened with the drugs?' Driscoll asked.

'We don't know,' Nancy said. 'Thu passed them that night, and Phil took them when he left.'

'Did you see him with the drugs?'

'No, but I didn't see him take my car keys either.'

'Can you tell us what the drugs looked like to you?'

'Little pellets, about this big.' Roy made a circle by putting his trigger finger and thumb together.

'How many were there?'

'Fifty, maybe. Thu probably had one still in her. None of the ones we saw looked to be open.'

'They didn't tell you when you called to check on her at the hospital?'

'They asked us a bunch of questions,' Nancy said. 'Made us feel uncomfortable, made it seem like we were the ones who had done this thing to her. I work there. Doesn't make sense.'

'We saved that girl,' Roy said.

Driscoll wrote something down in his notebook. 'Probably so she can do it again in a couple years.'

'I don't believe that at all,' Nancy said.

Drake walked over and picked up one of Roy and Nancy's framed pictures. He rubbed a smudge from the frame with the end of his thumb. 'How much is that worth, Driscoll? Fifty pellets?'

'Not much. Not enough to warrant all this. A little shy of a hundred thousand, maybe?'

'How much do you think they're paying that assassin to go around doing what he's been doing?'

'More than that.'

'Doesn't make sense, does it?'

'Nothing makes sense when pellets of heroin are involved.'

'What will happen to Thu?' Nancy asked.

'I don't know what the situation is. She'll most likely be deported. But we'll need to talk to her first.'

Hunt sat on the side of a back road. The morning sun warmed his face, and in the field before him the three horses grazed, dipping their necks like oil pistons and tearing at the grass. He could hear their teeth working. He was going after Nora, but first he had to do something about the horses. He couldn't go around with a trailer attached to the hitch of the truck, and he didn't even know if he'd be coming back. He thought he might be dead, and that was no way to leave the horses, like he'd left the others, just sitting there out behind his house to be used for target practice.

Someone owned this patch of field, but he couldn't tell who. The field was on the eastern slope of the Cascades, where the rain would not come and there would be just a few days of protection from the coming snows. The field shone yellow under the sun, the grass already turning with the oncoming winter, all around the perimeter a band of tall fir. At the far end of the field he could see how the forest began, a rise in the earth that seemed to continue into the high peaks. The fence that had once surrounded the patch of land had wilted into the dirt, the wood covered in patches of green cattail moss.

He sat with his legs pushed out in front of him in the grass and his arms held back for support. He had no idea what to do. Leaving Nora wasn't an option.

Ninety thousand wasn't a lot of money to run on; it wasn't anything. He was fifty-four years old. Old enough to know he wasn't going to run. Nora had told him to. But he couldn't, not now, not like this.

He limped out into the field. The horses were staked to the ground and held on ten-foot ropes. They watched him come, ambivalent, their teeth grinding. In the right circles, they were worth about forty thousand each. He went to the big spotted Appaloosa and combed her mane with his fingers. He began to speak to the horse as if he were making confession.

He talked first of the man in the bait shop, the man he'd shot with a spray of buckshot. The man was old, losing his vision. Hunt told the Appaloosa about the old man, how he lived above the store, how he'd heard Hunt down there. It hadn't taken long for him to come down those steps, Hunt standing there, the man carrying the gun with him down the stairs, holding it on Hunt, Hunt side-stepping and grabbing for the weapon. The discharge of the gun. Hunt hadn't meant to do it, the gun going off, buckshot at point-blank range.

All this he told to the horse, the big Appaloosa pulling at the grass, tearing it up, and moving it off the ground in a sideways motion. The wet sopping sound of the man's lungs, the old bag-pipes, the blood at his lips. One of the old man's eyes was shot out and the blood flowed from it like tear tracks on the man's face. Hunt couldn't move, his ears ringing, the power of the shotgun still vibrating in his muscles. The man leveled out there on the floor of his shop. Hunt should have run, should have gotten the hell out of there.

Hunt shuddered, his hand up over the neck of the Appaloosa. Like the two he'd lost in the mountains, he'd raised her from a foal, bringing her up in his own paddock, feeding her, giving her love and time to become the horse she was now. He stroked her mane, his fingers digging deep beneath the hair. 'I'm sorry,' he said, his face pressed into her neck and the words suffo-cated in her skin. He didn't know what would happen now. He didn't know what would happen to any of them.

T he girl from the coffee shack called in the afternoon. Drake could hear the dull sound of the espresso machine, the brush of her cheek and hair against the receiver. He pictured her there in the little shack, the police tape pulled across the motel and the whole thing moving in the wind, stink currant and willow, yellow tape. After their introductions, he asked about the night.

'One strange thing,' she said. 'A man parked in the lot here and sat in his car. He sat for a long time.'

'How long did he sit there?'

'Nearly thirty minutes, it was past the time I usually close.'

'Did he buy coffee?'

'That's why I stayed open. I thought maybe it was one of the owner's boyfriends come by to check up on me. It was near dark by the time he walked over.'

'Did you ask him what he had been doing that whole time?'

'No. I was uncomfortable.'

'Why?'

The girl didn't say anything.

'Didn't you want to know?'

'It looked like he was jerking off,' she said after a while. 'It freaked me out.'

'In the car?'

'Yes, for thirty minutes.'

'Did he say anything to you after he came to the window?'

'He wanted to talk about when it would get dark.'

'What did you tell him?'

'I told him it already was. But he wanted to know if it got pitch black.'

'What was your impression of him?'

'He made me feel strange, he didn't seem right. Very pale skin, irritated around the eyes. He had what looked like a bruise near his hairline.'

The man didn't sound anything like Hunt. 'He was a little rough?'

'He was nice enough. He gave me some advice.'

'What did he say?'

'He said I should be careful about the city. He said it was nothing like this coffee shack.'

'I don't know why you didn't call the sheriff right then.' Drake attempted a joke.

The girl laughed but he could tell it was only to be polite. 'To tell you the truth, he frightened me a little,' the girl said. 'I'm a little scared now. Just jumpy.'

'I don't know if this is the guy we're looking for. I doubt it. You shouldn't need to worry, there's no reason he should come back there.'

'I don't know,' the girl said. 'His car is still in the lot. I don't know why he wouldn't come back for it.'

He'd forgotten about the assassin's car. Hadn't even thought of it. He knew it now. Four vehicles had come to the motel, but only two had left. He'd figured Hunt for taking the Lincoln after ditching the hatchback. The killer back in his own car. 'Can you read me the plate?'

He listened to her voice. He could tell she was leaning over the counter, her diaphragm compressing and the airiness coming into her voice. Drake had probably walked right past it.

He gave the girl the local sheriff's number. 'Don't worry,' Drake said. 'Just procedure.' Drake asked her to call the sheriff for a look at the car. 'Tell him exactly what you just told me.' He thanked her and then hung up.

Grady led Nora in through the back and told her to sit. She looked around for something to sit on but didn't find anything. They were in the basement, and when she didn't sit immediately, he gave her a hard stare till she sat on the floor. There was cold cement all the way back to the water heater, windows covered over with white paint. A dull, claylike glow leaked in through the windows, raindrops and dirt spattering the panes. In the corner, a large standing freezer hummed. There were several workbenches, and a stainless steel prep table by the back door.

He left his bag on one of the benches, walked over to the freezer, and opened it. He pushed a human leg aside and dug out the heroin, frozen through and covered with a thin pink hue. The freezer smelled sour. Though he'd washed everything down and bleached it as best he could, the freezer smelled of stomach acid and human excrement mixed together with all the things the girl had been carrying around inside her. He closed the door and looked back at Nora. She hadn't moved.

Upstairs they heard the front door creak open, the weight of footsteps on the wooden boards above.

Grady looked up. 'Don't worry,' he said.

He crossed the floor with the heroin and deposited it in his knife bag. From the bag he took out the .22 and stuffed it in his pants, then the twelve-inch chef's knife, which he placed on the table, the edge of the metal singing in the empty basement.

'You're in good hands,' he finished, not looking at Nora but at the windows running the length of the basement wall.

The basement was dug eight feet into the ground, and the only things discernible through the windows were the shapes of grass tufts where they pressed against the panes. Rain pattered on the drive, droplets clinging to the outside of the painted glass. Grady could feel an old, familiar urge flood his insides, like the devil pouring kerosene, thick and heavy, down his throat. A shadow passed across the window nearest the street and then, a second later, a window near the basement door.

Hunt left the three horses in the field. He staked them and gave them thirty feet of cord, enough to get beneath the shade of the tall fir trees. The field was not too far off, but remote enough that no one would find the horses for a day or two.

The trailer he hid up an old forestry road. He left it a quarter mile off the field, and when he returned to the back road, he could see that the tree trunks covered the silver trailer just as if it were a boulder in the forest. Down the road he filled a large bucket of water from a moss-covered stream. Once the bucket was filled he cupped his hands and brought the water to his face. He removed his wallet and keys from his pockets and laid them beside him. The address he'd taken from Thu's purse he kept weighted under his keys.

He was hungry, he felt it now, and he let the water run down his cheeks and roll from his chin, the cold of it settling into him. When he had done this several times, he ran the water through his hair and combed it back with his fingers. From the car he got the small survival bag and laid it near the stream. He checked the bandage. Nancy had done a good job, sewing the wound closed on both sides of his calf, and he could see how the scar would be in the pattern of a star, the skin already starting to conceal the wound. He used the water to rinse; then with the hydrogen peroxide and the iodine he cleaned the cut and let it air-dry for a moment before he put on a fresh bandage and wrapped the whole thing once again.

When he finished washing, he collected his wallet and keys from the grass and put them into his pockets. He still wore the same clothes he had left the marina in, jeans cut off on one side and his white tennis shoes, one the vermilion color of his dried blood and the other stained dark as mud. Hunt picked up the Seattle address he'd taken from Thu and held it between his fingers, a subtle breeze working across his wet skin. Grady had guaranteed Hunt would die. It was the only thing Hunt was sure of. There was nothing left for him to lose. He looked at the address again, knowing he needed help and hoping he would find it there.

He brought the bucket to the field and placed it between the three horses. It was not big enough for the three of them to drink from at the same time, but he hoped it would last through the night. The big Appaloosa came to him and drank from the bucket. He gave her his hand and she nuzzled in search of a carrot. 'All right then,' he said, and let the horse run her mouth along the knuckles of his hand. He could smell the dust rise from where her hooves met the earth. 'All right then,' he said again, and limped back to the truck and pulled himself into the high cab.

On the seat beside him was the orange survival bag. He turned the engine over and felt the big diesel rattle and the truck come to life. From the bag he took the Browning, pulled the slide back, and saw the round already loaded. He unfastened the magazine and let it fall into his palm, shucked the bullet from the slide, and loaded it into the clip, then clapped it back together. He checked the safety, and when he was done, he slid the gun beneath his seat.

The fifty capsules of heroin were still inside the plastic grocery bag, the smell coming off it slightly fecal. He opened the passenger window and then his own, feeling the truck beneath him, his hands on the steering wheel, the roll of the engine down along his knuckles and into his arms. He pulled away from the field and went down the dirt road. When he came to the cement, he turned south and kept driving.

N ora sat on the cement floor and followed the overhead creak of footsteps with her eyes.

Across the room, Grady crouched down by the door and waited, holding the chef's knife in one hand and Eddie's silenced .22 in the other. He raised a single finger to his lips. Outside, there was the crunch of gravel beyond the basement door. The handle rattled for a moment and then there was the soft cracking of glass. An elbow came through one of the four painted panes of the door, the only sound that of the glass falling to the cement floor.

A hand reached through and twisted the lock. With the knife still held in a tight grip, Grady made a signal for Nora to stay seated. The door swung open, and a Vietnamese man carrying a small sub-machine gun stepped through. Grady waited. The door swung into the basement, the man on one side, Grady on the other.

Immediately the man's eyes focused on Nora, sitting there on the cement. Behind her, in the middle of the basement, wooden stairs led up to

the main floor of the house. He swept the basement with his eyes – a stainless metal table, several
workbenches, and from the darkness across the
basement floor the dim hum of the freezer's motor.
On one of the benches he saw the knife bag, open
at the rim, pellets of heroin and the stock of the
AR-15 exposed. He took a step forward, hand
held out toward the gun. Nora closed her eyes.

Blood exploded like rough paint from the pea-
size hole in the man's head. The man fell to the
floor with a clatter of gun and bone matter, a dark
pool growing around him. Grady lowered the .22
and kicked the man's legs out of the way before
closing the door. He put the .22 into his pants
pocket and passed Nora at a near run. He didn't
stop when he reached the stairs, just kept going.
The sound of his breathing on the dark basement
steps above her, Nora crawled to a space behind
the wooden stairs. She got in under the shadows
and stayed hidden. The dead man was between
her and the door. She was scared, fear loaded so
tight in her veins she couldn't move. Her eyes
hadn't left the dead man on the floor, the seep of
blood and brain on the cement.

At the top of the stairs, Grady cracked the door
and looked out into his kitchen. He could hear
whispering, but he couldn't tell from which direction it came. He rose and opened the door wide
enough to pass through, that urge already working
away inside him, floodgates open, devil riding
down on a cascade of blood and fire.

He found the first man pressed just inside the kitchen doorway. Without even a word, Grady slid the twelve-inch blade across his throat and severed the man's neck nearly to the spine. Blood in glossy strands, from wall to doorframe, like red waxen candle drippings. Grady caught the body and eased it to the floor. The weight of the man's blood on Grady's shirt, pleasure, wet and warm, on Grady's skin.

In the front room, he saw the door hung open and a shadow waiting on the porch. The cheap metal screen door rested against the wood frame. Grady charged it, and the door swung open with his weight and pinned the man on the porch to the side of the house. Grady stabbed him so hard the knife went all the way through the mesh screen of the door, through skin and skull, out the other side, and nailed the man's head to the wood siding of the house. Pressurized blood welled from the man's head and ran through the mesh screen door.

Grady was struggling to take the knife handle back when the first bullets hit the porch. Grady dropped. Broken bits of wood and potting soil rained down on him. The windows behind him exploded and fell back into the house. From what he could hear, there were two guns on him from the street. With the rain falling, nothing was clear; in the dull, clouded light he could see nothing but dark gray shapes moving in the rain, and the muzzle flash of automatic weapons. He dove back through the doorway and into the house.

A step before he made it to the basement door, he was shot back-to-front through the flesh of his side. Blood, soft and warm on his skin. He opened the basement door and fell through.

Hunt stopped once for gas, paid cash, and was careful not to show his bullet-torn left leg. He bought a bag of peanuts, a large hot dog roasted over an electric spit, and a two-liter bottle of Cherry Coke. While he drove, he drank the soda with one hand, holding the bottle between his thighs when he wanted to take the cap off and then again when the cap needed refastening.

He drove with caution, keeping his truck below the speed limit. He knew he was close to the end; one way or another, it would all be finished soon. There were people out there looking for him. He'd read about the deputy, Drake, trying to track him down. Hunt had known his father, the same age as Hunt. They'd shared a beer once, the sheriff and Hunt, just a friendly meeting, the two of them in the same business, working the same range. It was easy for Hunt to see that the man meant to run him off, and Hunt had told him it would be just as easy for him to do the same.

Still, Hunt had felt bad for the man, his son in school, wife passed away, medical bills and a son two thousand miles away to worry over. Hunt could understand a thing like that. He knew they'd had it hard. Even after he'd heard about the sheriff going away on a smuggling charge, he knew his son would never know the truth of it – that his father had been doing it for him, that in some bemused, half-conscious way his father had seen it as the only way out.

They had met an hour's drive outside Silver Lake, at an empty roadside bar where the two of them could be fairly certain they wouldn't see anyone they knew. Still they had used caution, sitting toward the back at a corner table, Hunt's cigarettes laid out on the wood, two beers beaded with sweat between them. The sheriff had explained about his past, about his wife and son. He didn't want to do the things he did, but he was doing them. Hunt said it was the same for him. Said he was just the same as the sheriff. The sheriff looked him over, waiting to see if Hunt would smile, if he was making fun, but then when Hunt didn't, he said, 'I should run you off.'

'You could do that.'

'It's what I'm paid to do.'

Hunt looked down at the beer on the table. He touched his palm to the glass and felt the cold bead of the water. 'If I said something—'

'What would you say?' the sheriff interrupted. 'No one would believe you.'

'They might not, but still, it would probably get

people talking. I doubt you'd see another term. You make so little as it is.'

The sheriff gave him a cold stare. He glanced around the bar as if looking for witnesses, Hunt expecting to get coldcocked right there. The sheriff reached for the beer in front of him and drained it back in one motion. He stood, chair screeching on the hard tile floor. 'What you do with your time is not my business,' the sheriff said. 'But you put me in a position where I have one of my deputies with me, I'm going to have to act. And I'll make sure you're in no shape afterward to slander me. You understand?'

Hunt nodded. The sheriff straightened his shirt, then walked out of the bar and left Hunt there. Hunt and Eddie had dealt with crooked cops before. But this was different; the man was not looking for a handout or a bribe, he was just trying to do the same thing Hunt had been doing. How long he'd been up to it, Hunt didn't know. All he knew was that he'd caught the sheriff up there in the mountains one time, had seen him from a far ridge, receiving a small load to take down through the mountains. The sheriff had seen him, too, or at least had known about him for some time, pulling him over on the side of the road just outside Silver Lake. No one around, the sheriff could have done anything he wanted, but he hadn't.

In a way, Hunt thought, he owed the man his life. Though it was grudgingly given, he knew the sheriff was not the type to murder him in cold blood. A warning, simple as that, and Hunt with the intention to honor it. He stayed away, picking different routes through the mountains. Careful not to upset the balance drawn between the two of them.

He drove on, drinking from his Cherry Coke. Passing the time by thinking about what he owed this man. Hunt was in rough shape, hole clean through his calf, business gone, wife kidnapped, but he was alive. Everything could have been different had all of it ended ten years before. But he was driving still, heading south, trying to pick up what little there was left of a life that seemed to break as fast as it was being built.

In Everett, thirty miles north of Seattle, he pulled into the parking lot of a hunting goods shop he knew on the east side. He knew there were people looking for him, and he thought someday they'd find him, but not today. He was walking around with pants half-gone around his knee and a bandage wrapped white as a flag around his calf. And he wasn't ready yet to just give up.

He turned the key in the ignition, and the rumble of the engine quieted. He put the survival bag beneath the seat with the Browning. When he walked in, a bell announced his presence, and an employee he knew only by sight waved from the counter. He went over to the pants section and found his size. In the dressing room he eased his pants past the bandage and then fit the new pair on.

From the old pair he retrieved the small slip of paper he'd taken from Thu, and his wallet and keys, and he laid them on the changing-room bench. Standing there in his new pants, he picked up the slip of paper with the address written on it, a North Seattle address that he didn't have any clue about. He didn't know how Thu had come across it, whether it was a friend or a relative. He thought he knew what it was. The address was a good place to drop off ninety thousand dollars of heroin, or at least it could have been for Thu.

Hunt gathered the address and the rest of his things and stuffed them down into the pockets of his new pair of jeans. He didn't have much time. He didn't have any time at all. If someone wanted the heroin more than Grady, it was probably the people waiting at this address.

He looked at himself in the mirror, a tightness in the lower left leg where the bandage was. When he turned to look at the back, he could see where he had wiped his own bloodied hand across the bottom of his sweatshirt. He was running out of time, not even enough time to worry about himself.

He opened the curtain, and on the way to the register, he picked out a cheap rain slicker long enough to hang past his bloodstained sweatshirt. In his hand he carried the old pair of jeans. There was a funk to them, something of the salt water mixed with iodine. At the register he asked if there was a trash can he could throw them in. The man took them from him and dropped them into a wastebasket behind the counter.

'What happened to your leg?' the man asked, taking the cash Hunt offered him.

'Hunting accident.'

'Someone thought you were the deer?' The man laughed. He'd probably said it a million times.

'It was the deer who shot me,' Hunt said. The man smiled and gave Hunt his change.

Outside, Hunt started the truck engine. He turned west and found the interstate, then headed south again.

D rake explained it all to his wife over the phone. He was sitting on a bench outside the hospital doors. Rain fell in the parking lot, and the hospital awning was the only thing keeping him dry. Farther down, where the red painted ambulance lines ended, there were several nurses smoking at the edge of the shaded protection, close enough that he could smell their cigarettes and catch brief fragments of their gossip. Across the parking lot he saw Driscoll's cruiser and beyond that the rounded green of a grass embankment, where bushes had been planted. Lonely incandescent lights sprang like trees from the cement and shone over the cars in a moonlike glow. After he had explained it all, Sheri said, 'What do you want me to say, the couple was lying?'

'I'm not asking you to say that. I just wanted to know your opinion.'

'There's no right or wrong?'

'There's no right or wrong.'

'I'd say they were just doing what anyone would do. Roy and Nancy's problem was not the drugs.

It was the injury. Don't look at it like there's someone to blame.'

'But there is someone to blame.'

'You think that's it.'

'Yes. That's how it works.'

'You know that's not how anything works. To that couple, the man with the gun wasn't the threatening part. It was the girl over-dosed in their bed. You think either Hunt or the couple would have sat by and watched her go like that?'

'Yes, I do.'

'Don't be stupid, Bobby. You've been spending too much time with Driscoll. It's always the injury. You think this guy Hunt was up in those mountains because he's something evil, something just bent on doing wrong. He's like that girl you got in that hospital, just someone with an injury, someone needing to be healed.'

Drake sat on the bench, turning to watch the nurses in their smoke circle. When he turned back, he said, 'What have you been doing, reading the self-help section in the bookstore?'

'Come on, Bobby, when you're hungry, you eat. When you're thirsty, you—'

'When you're broke you smuggle ninety thousand dollars worth of heroin into the country,' Drake interrupted.

'You know that's not how it is.'

'That's what we prosecute them for.'

'Yes, but that's not the problem, is it?'

'No,' he said, taking a while with his words. 'I don't think it is.'

'Did you ever think the girl up in that hospital room needed this more than she cared about her own life?'

Drake didn't say anything.

'You know, if you're going to save that man's life, it's not really about the gun chasing him, or even you.'

'No, I suppose it's not.'

'There's probably something that's been chasing him for longer than you've been alive, and it'll be chasing him longer still, no matter what happens up there.'

'You think you're right on that?'

'I know it.'

'How do you know it?'

Sheri was quiet for a moment. 'I see it on you.'

'What do you see?'

'I see it – anyone who gives you a good look can see it. Why'd you go up there into those mountains in the first place?'

'Hunting. I told you that.'

'That's not true. You know that.'

'All I know is what I did.'

'That's the heroic answer, but I bet the truth has to do with that car, and somewhere deep down your father. But I don't think you'd admit that, would you?'

'Come on.'

'What do you want me to say? I'm telling you

the truth. How come you haven't come home yet?'

'I'm working.'

'When did you become part of the DEA?'

'Driscoll needs me.'

'Where's Driscoll now?'

'Upstairs.'

'Why aren't you up there with him?'

'That's not fair, Sheri.'

'You're still up in those mountains. That's where you are.'

Grady landed face-first on the basement floor. So much blood he didn't know what belonged to him and what belonged to the men he'd killed. He groaned, forced himself up. His hands slick with it. Red handprint on the gray floor. He still carried the .22, pushing himself up on his closed knuckles. He screamed, feeling the torn muscles in his side. White-hot pain all through him. Up through his spine and into his head.

He knew the men were coming after him. The whole situation was fucked and he knew there was no time for Nora. He crossed the room, holding his side, blood between his fingers. The dead man was blocking the doorway. He reached down with his hand and dragged the man out of the way, took his bag off the workbench, and opened the door. Gray, overcast light, rain, and the mossy taste of wet earth.

He rounded the house, holding his bag, clutching his closed fist over the wound, the silenced .22 growing slippery and warm in his grip. Pain anytime he lifted a leg, anytime his muscles moved. It was all through him now.

In the drive, on his way to the Lincoln, Grady flattened himself to the side of the house and listened. On the porch he heard the last of the men enter through the front door, following his path. A neighbor appeared at her window and then quickly disappeared. He pushed forward, got to the Lincoln, and pulled the door open. It hurt to sit. His shirt and pants were covered in a mix of human blood, suctioned to his body and weighted with it. He felt around in his pockets for the keys and brought them out.

This hadn't been in the plan.

The back window blew out. He dropped his head and turned the ignition over. The engine started and he hit the gas, head ducked beneath the dash for cover, not looking, estimating a turn and scraping off a car as he went. Gunshots. A puckering of buckshot along the body of the car.

Gas pedal. Gas pedal.

Nora, he thought.

lready, through the trees, Hunt could see the dark ash smeared like grease across the lawn. All he could see of his house were the bricks of the chimney. He drove past and parked a quarter mile down the road. Rain showers had come through, and the whole place had a look of gloom and growing desperation. He sat in the car and he knew the truth, that it was over, that there had been a point when he thought he might make it out, that Nora and he might have a future, but he knew it was over now. He had seen the yellow police tape stretched around on all sides, like the shape of an imagined house, now just standing in his memories.

He took the survival bag from the truck and walked across the road to the small horse trail that led through the woods and out onto his property. For a while he stood in the trees and took the whole thing in. It looked like a bomb had dropped: where the house had been was nothing but a blackened crater. When he was sure there was no one around, he walked up through the trees and followed the fence toward the house. The patches of blood where Grady had shot the horses were dark holes amid the grass. He stood for a while with his arms up on the fence and stared into the pasture. Even if he did escape, what would be the use? But even as he thought this, he knew that there were still three horses waiting for him in the mountain field. Although they were not his, he could possibly breed them and make a decent profit. He knew, too, that the owners of those horses would never see them again, not unless he was killed, but he tried to put that thought aside.

The closest he went to the remains of the house was the edge of the scorched grass. On the ground he could see the dirt where the fire had burned everything away. And even the earth had the appearance of being baked until nothing could be distinguished except the flatness of the spot he had once walked and the small bits of blackened gravel that had once caught and stuck between the treads of his shoes.

He felt the emotion rise in him again and he took his time and forced it back down into his stomach, where he felt it tighten. He opened the survival bag, took from it the heroin, and went to the stables. On the floor he found the loose board under which he had sometimes kept shipments. With his fingers at the edge of the wood, he pulled it back and sat looking down into the black hole below.

He knew this was either the safest place he could put it or the stupidest. He wasn't sure which, but at a certain point he knew that all that had happened in the past couple of days seemed to be a matter of chance. He thought his chances were better this way, if not very good. Having all the heroin with him felt like death sitting there beside him.

After he was done and the board had been put back and the dust had settled once again across the hiding place, he took his phone from the bag and tried the hospital again.

When the elevator doors opened, Drake exited onto a floor of cream tile, walls the color of eggshells, and rooms consumed by the last light of day. What Sheri had said to him was still there, floating along with him as if pulled by a string. Twice he had brought the phone from his pocket, wanting to call his wife back, but then reconsidered and put it away. At the nurse's station he presented his star and asked about Driscoll.

'Not much reason to be in there,' the nurse said.

'Why's that?'

'I just don't know what information he's going to get out of her.'

'I'm sure she'd be able to say something.'

The nurse gave him a look Drake didn't understand at first. 'She's nearly brain dead with all that heroin in her system.'

'Brain dead?'

'In a coma,' the nurse said shortly, looking down the hall. Drake followed her gaze but saw only the eggshell walls and the cream floors, every ten feet a door, the outdoor light coming in onto the floor.

'When she came in she was already going, and no one to tell us who she is.'

'Her name is Thu,' Drake said. 'She has two kids.'

'See,' the nurse said, 'that just doesn't make one bit of sense.'

'Doesn't that make the most sense?'

'Not if you end up like this.'

Drake looked on down the hall. He needed to see Thu for himself, see if she was the same woman he'd seen in the picture. 'Will she recover?' he asked.

'They've been pumping her full of a medicine that counteracts the drug.'

'Like an antidote?'

'She's absorbed most of it already, but the dose of heroin in her system should have killed her right off. When they brought her in she was showing signs of cyanosis in the nail beds, bluish skin like she wasn't pumping oxygen into the bloodstream. It wasn't a good sign.'

'Would you mind walking me down there?'

'I can do that. But I'm telling you there's not much to see.'

When they reached the room, Driscoll was already inside. The doctor had an X-ray held up and he was circling a white bump near the hip bone. 'You see what I mean,' the nurse said. What Drake saw was a small girl lying faceup in bed; her skin seemed to be drawing away from her, as if the climate had hurt her, something shrinking up inside her and pulling all of her along. She was pale, her eyes closed, the dark fall of her hair on the pillow seemingly the only living thing about her.

Something in the room began to give off low beeping noises, and the doctor and the nurse turned to the bed. Drake stood by, held at the doorway to the room. He was pushed aside and out into the hall as a few more of the staff came to assist. He did not see Driscoll but assumed he was in there, pressed to the corner while the staff tried to save the girl in the bed.

From the doorway it was obvious what was going on, there was no need to watch, but he was drawn to it as one is to an accident passed on the highway, with the same morbid fear of what he might see. Down the hall the phone rang. For a moment it was just part of the background, nurses and doctors scrambling for syringes of epinephrine, the shock and rattle of the crash cart. He felt himself fade back, the outcome now set, the future decided. He was aware again of the phone. He didn't know how long it had been ringing, but he knew there was no one on the floor to pick up. He walked to the desk, reached over the lip of the counter, picked up the receiver, and said hello.

A brief pause, then: 'I'd like to know about the girl brought in a couple days ago, the overdose?'

Drake looked back down the hall, now empty, and all he could hear were the muffled voices of the staff and the constant warnings of the machine in the girl's room. 'I can take a message,' Drake said, feeling foolish, but in the same moment reaching for a pen.

'No,' the voice said, 'there's no need, I was just checking in. If you could just tell me how she is?'

Something about the voice, a roughness, like stones gargled in the throat. 'Hunt?' Drake said.

'I'm sorry?'

A pause. 'Don't hang up. I met your wife a few days ago.'

'What about her?' Hunt said.

Drake could hardly believe it. 'I met her a few days ago. I was looking for horse-riding lessons. It was before we knew anything about you.'

'What do you know about me now?'

Drake told him. 'I was the one in the mountains,' he said. 'You're in a lot of trouble here, Hunt. More than I think you know.'

'I think I've got a pretty good picture of it.'

'You've been to the motel. Have you been to your house?'

'I've been there.'

'Then you've seen—'

'Enough.'

'Yes, I bet you have.'

Hunt didn't say anything. He didn't hang up, and Drake listened. There was something lonely and fractured to the way Hunt hung on the line, and in the air that escaped his lungs and rasped across the receiver of the phone.

'I read about you in the paper,' Hunt said.

'I didn't ask them to print any of that.'

'But they did.'

'Yes,' Drake said, 'there was a good amount written about the past that should have stayed in the past.'

'It's odd,' Hunt said.

'What's odd?'

'I knew your father, Sheriff Drake, up there in Silver Lake.'

'You mean you used to run drugs with him?'

'No, I mean I knew him. Just competition, that's all.' A pause, the sound of Hunt's breathing on the other end of the line. 'We had a beer once, smoked a cigarette, nothing to get friendship rings over. He was nothing to be ashamed of.'

'He was good at running drugs, if that's what you're saying.'

'I meant as a father, not as a smuggler.'

'Well, that ended.'

'Didn't want to take up the family business?'

'Wouldn't know anything about it.'

'No?'

'No.'

'What about now? You know something about it now?'

'I know a little.'

'He cared about you,' Hunt said. 'He took a lot of chances. A lot of what he did, he did because he cared about you. If that matters at all.'

Drake didn't say anything. He couldn't tell if Hunt was trying to manipulate him. If Hunt was lying, if he was telling the truth, there was no way to tell; Drake just had to feel it out for himself.

He heard Hunt on the other end of the line, slow, steady breathing now. Drake didn't know where Hunt was. Didn't think Hunt would tell him. He had hoped that whatever happened in the past would stay there. But he knew that it hadn't and that it never would. The girl down the hallway was dead. Drugs missing. Paid killer out there. Horses and gunmen, OK Corral on an atomic level.

'Do you still have it?' Drake asked.

'What?'

'We've seen the X-rays of the girl, you know what I'm talking about.'

'Is she all right?' The voice once again drifting.

'She just passed, Hunt. I'm sorry.' A long pause: Drake with his ear to the phone, his fingers bent over the edge of the counter, almost holding on. 'Hunt?'

'Yes, I'm here.'

'Do you still have the heroin?'

'No.'

'You could save yourself if you did. We know about your wife, we know she's been taken. We can work something out here.'

Still no one emerged from Thu's room, and Drake wanted to call out, to call Driscoll and have him there to tell him what to do.

'What are you offering, the same thing you offered the kid?'

'That was an accident, it should never have happened.'

'What about your father?' Hunt said. 'What do you think? Did he get a deal? Did he get what he deserved?'

'I can't say anything about that.'

'You mean you won't say anything about it.'

'I'm trying to help you here.'

'Why don't you get my wife back? How about that?'

'We know only as much as you tell us.'

'But I have to give you something, don't I?'

'That's how it works.'

'If I gave it to you, would you drop everything against me?'

'I'd do my best. I can't tell you that without speaking to you further.'

'He has my wife.'

'Yes, I know.'

'Then you'll understand that I can't.'

Silence.

'Hunt?' Drake said.

'Yes, I'm here.'

'Why didn't you run?'

'What are you talking about?'

'After you shot the man in the bait shop, why didn't you run?'

'Why are you asking me this now?'

'I don't know,' Drake said. 'I've been thinking about it. I'm trying to understand it.'

'There's nothing to understand. I shot a man

and I've been paying for it ever since. That's it. I'd take it back if I could, but I can't. There is no taking back something like that.'

'Hunt,' Drake said, 'why don't you let us help you?'

A long pause on the line, then: 'I don't have the heroin, but I can tell you where Thu was taking it.'

'You would do that?'

Hunt read him the address. 'I took it from Thu's purse, figured it's where she was going, where she was supposed to end up. With or without me, in twenty-four hours, the heroin will be there.'

'What about you?'

Hunt laughed, his voice strained, breaking. 'I will be dead.' He hung up the phone, and Drake was left holding the receiver. The pen he'd picked up still in his hand, he copied the address down onto a piece of paper and stood looking at it.

From behind the stairs, tucked back into the darkness, Nora had watched Grady come down the steps, shot through, his ankle rolling until he landed in a mess on the basement floor. She'd thought him dead. The big booming sound of the guns overhead, the house above shaking as the bullets splintered wood, dug through plaster, and lodged themselves an inch deep in the ceiling and the walls. Above, the sound of glass falling, footsteps on the porch and then inside on the wooden floor, the crush of glass underfoot. Grady groaned, half-dazed. Like the walking dead rising from the grave, he stumbled toward the door, his shirt plastered to his skin.

He moved forward, shuffle of feet on cement, grit and the slop of blood falling from his wound. He pulled the body of the dead man away from the door, grabbed his knife bag, and disappeared out the basement door.

Nora sat watching the open door. Outside, the rain, verdant overgrown grass, a back fence gray with age and rot. More sounds of gunfire, the brittle scream of metal on metal, and a car engine racing. Then nothing.

He had forgotten her.

Footsteps above. The door at the top of the stairs opened, kitchen light falling onto the dead man in front of her, a human shadow above on the stairs followed closely by another.

D riscoll drove and the two men sat silent in the cruiser on their way back to Seattle. Drake hadn't said anything about the conversation with Hunt. He hadn't talked to his father in ten years, not since he'd been put away. It felt strange, talking to Hunt. Almost as if he'd opened a door and stepped through to a life a decade before. There had been something to Hunt's voice, something that said it would all be finished soon, and Drake didn't know what to do with that.

The sheriff called over the radio to say they'd run the car and nothing had come back. A dead end, the vehicle registered under an alias, though they'd taken a partial thumbprint off the door handle and faxed it to County and maybe something would come of that. He hadn't heard anything back yet.

'We can check it when we get back to the Seattle office,' Driscoll said.

'Let me know if you want me to do anything with this car,' the sheriff said.

'Impound it.'

'On what charge?'

'Whatever you feel like, street sweeping, fire lane, abandoned vehicle – think of something.'

'I can do that.'

'We've got nothing else to go on.' Driscoll turned off the radio.

Hundred-foot cement sections went by under their car at eighty miles an hour, the throb like a heartbeat beneath the wheels.

'I've got something,' Drake said. He dug the address out of his pocket and gave it to Driscoll.

'What's this?'

'It's where the heroin will be.'

Driscoll looked from the address to Drake with a mixture of shock and disbelief. 'Where did you get this?'

'Hunt gave it to me.'

'Hunt?'

'He called in to the hospital, asking about the girl,' Drake said. 'The nurse's station was empty, so I just picked up. I didn't know it would be him.'

'He just called in,' Driscoll said, holding the address out in front of him over the wheel, 'and you picked up?'

'That's what I said.'

'You got this from Hunt?'

'You can believe me or not, but that is where the heroin will be in a little under twenty-four hours.'

'What exactly did he tell you?'

Drake told him.

'You think he was lying to you?' Driscoll asked.

'Didn't seem to have much reason.'

'You think he's already dead?'

'Could be.'

'Could be he's trying to throw us off.'

'What other choice do we have?'

They were an hour north of Seattle. Driscoll fingered the piece of paper. He picked up the radio and called in the address.

Grady drove. He drove erratically, side-swiping parked cars, his vision closing. He made the turn out onto the main road. Car headlights were coming at him out of the rain. He laid on the horn and swerved back into his lane. A mile up was a retirement home he'd passed earlier, with an ambulance perched on the little rise of a driveway like death itself, just waiting.

He pulled up. Opened the Lincoln's door, half falling onto the street, his bag held in one hand and his other clutching the ragged hole in his side. He didn't pause to close the car door, just left it, the scene inside the car nothing short of horrid disaster, blood-soaked leather, broken glass, dashboard sawed through with automatic fire. He stumbled forward, holding his side.

He tried the handles on the doors first, and when they didn't open he shot the back two windows out of the ambulance and punched the glass in with his hand. He reached inside and worked the latch until the door swung open, and he raised himself inside.

In desperation, he went through the back of the

ambulance, upturning bins of alcohol swabs, gauze, and rolls of medical tape. He found the morphine, filled a syringe, and emptied it into his leg. Almost immediately, the feeling came into him, his heart slowing, almost floating, dreamy pain somewhere out there like the clap of distant thunderclouds. He raised his shirt and inspected the hole. Clean through, a small puckering of the skin. Nothing vital seemed to be punctured, already the muscle bruising and the hole black and full, brimming with his own dark blood. In the tin reflection of the supply cabinet he surveyed the entry hole in his back. The same disfigured blackness. He would be okay, he thought. Just another few hours and it would all be done. He reached for a bottle of alcohol, poured it on, feeling the pain there again. More morphine. Then gauze and tape, a rolled layer of it all around his stomach and back.

He dropped his shirt across his midsection, sopping wet with blood and rain. His vision was drifting again. He slapped himself hard across the face and brought up the knife bag, loading it with syringes and bottles of morphine. The bag was already heavy with weapons and heroin. Outside, the rain still falling.

How had they found him?

He had a good idea who'd given him up. He had every intention of getting Nora back and finishing his business with Hunt. If he could get an address quickly, he might still have a chance.

The Lincoln sat out there on the street but he didn't go to it. He went instead to one of the old cars lining the retirement home, popped the window open, then let himself inside. His back and stomach were on fire but holding. The only blood now was that on his shirt. From beneath the steering column he brought out the wires and dashed them together until the engine started.

Grady was gone. She was on her own. Nora pushed herself farther under the stairs. She could smell the cold mineral odor of cement, damp basement air. Through the openings in the wooden steps she saw one man, then the next, come down the stairs. One of them held an automatic shotgun, the other some sort of assault rifle, the two men standing there at the bottom of the stairs, the open basement door in front of them and the sound of the rain pattering on the grass beyond.

Nora pushed herself back, shoe to cement, until she was against the wall. She heard them say something in their language. One of them bent to look at the dead man on the floor. The other went to the freezer and pulled it open. Dull light escaped from the open freezer door and exposed her hiding place.

They were on her immediately, gun barrels pointed at her face and body. She didn't have any of the answers they were looking for. She didn't know anything. Sirens now in the background, growing closer. Grady might come back for her.

One of the men pushed her face down on the floor, gun barrel to the back of her head, cold feel of the cement against her cheek. The other tore a length of butcher's twine from one of the prep tables and tied her hands behind her. They picked her up by her arms and set her on her feet. They were moving now, out through the basement door, rounding the house. Rain falling, bright daylight, a cold feel coming in the air, the sirens drawing closer.

'What's changed?' Sheri said.

'Nothing. I just—' Drake stopped midway through. 'I don't know what to say here.' He was in the federal building downtown. Driscoll had put in the call about the thumbprint and they were waiting to see what would come back.

'What do you mean?' Sheri asked.

'I don't want to do this anymore,' Drake said. He put his arm up on the wall and rested his head. He was holding the cell phone close into his face, cradling it so that no one could hear.

'Does this have something to do with what Hunt said to you?'

'No.'

'This man you're chasing, he's not your father,' Sheri said.

'I know that.'

'It's not going to bring him back into your life,' Sheri said.

'I know that.'

'Do you?'

'I keep going back to it,' Drake said. 'What if I

hadn't picked them up in the mountains? Everything would be different.'

'That's not any way to talk.'

'What is it, then?'

'You were doing your job, that's all. You can't blame yourself for that,' Sheri said. 'This doesn't have anything to do with your father.'

'Doesn't it?' Drake said.

'Only if you make it.'

'I'm just trying to do a good thing for him. Doesn't mean I'm going to invite him to Christmas.'

'Stranger on the side of the road?'

'Something like that.'

'Thought you said they all had it coming.'

'Doesn't mean I want him to end up dead.'

'Is that what's going to happen?'

'Every way I look at it.'

They said good-bye, and by the time Drake walked in, the phones were ringing in Driscoll's office. Something about a gun battle down south, several dead, and then a mile away a routed ambulance and Eddie's blood-covered Lincoln.

'You're not going to believe this,' Driscoll said. He was staring up at Drake from his desk. 'SPD just found a frozen Vietnamese girl in the basement freezer, belly opened groin-to-rib.'

'They find anything else?'

'Three dead guys. One shot through the head, one throat slit, and my favorite, tacked to the side of the house with a kitchen knife.'

'No Nora?'

'No. But there's a good chance she's still out there somewhere. None of the dead guys match the print taken off the car up by that motel.'

'Whose blood all over the Lincoln?'

'Don't know yet, but I'll bet it matches our thumbprint.'

'What's the name?'

'Grady Fisher, early release from Monroe a few years back.'

'Early release for what?'

'What do you think – murder followed by eight years of good behavior.'

'He the one renting the house?'

'Landlord says he's some sort of chef.'

'More like a butcher,' Drake said.

'Well, come on.'

'Come on' what?'

'Can't say you hadn't been expecting it.'

'I'm done identifying bodies.'

'You're not coming along?'

'I'm heading back to the hotel.'

'What's wrong?' Driscoll smiled. 'You sick or something?'

'This the same address Hunt gave us?'

'No, different.'

'You still got your guys on that house?'

'Nothing's come or gone for the past two hours. What are you thinking?'

'You got that sheet on Hunt?'

'Here it is.' Driscoll handed it over the desk to Drake.

Drake sat studying the face looking back at him, angular, lean, the picture grainy, colors fuzzy. 'What do you think the truth is?' Drake asked. 'You know, about what I told you of the conversation I had with Hunt. Do you think there's anything there to what he said about my father?'

'I can't answer that for you,' Driscoll said. Drake folded the sheet and put it in his pocket.

'What are you doing?' Driscoll asked.

'What do you think.'

'The warden will want to know what's going on. I can call ahead – you might be a little late for visiting hours.'

'It's about time, I guess.'

'Yes,' Driscoll said. 'I've been waiting to see if you had it in you.'

Drake stared down at the printout in his hand, Hunt's face looking up at him. 'You ever get sick of seeing people die?' Drake asked.

'Not yet.' Driscoll got up and walked across the room to one of the file cabinets. He took out his vest and began to strap it on. 'Like I said before, when heroin is involved, nothing surprises me.'

G rady drove through the North Seattle
neighborhood until he found the lawyer's
house. He'd been there once, but that had
been a long time ago, simply a meeting. The view
had impressed him, and the way the lawyer spoke
to him. He'd been offered more for one job than
he was able to make in a year. Since then, everything had been done over the phone, but the
money had always been the same. Grady knew
somehow that it was too good to be true. It was
a good thing to have going, and even from the
first day, he'd known he wouldn't be able to give
it up.

Grady drove past and parked the car. The gate
had been left partially open and Grady squeezed
through, feeling the pain well up inside him. His
shirt was almost dried and stiff as canvas, but the
rain was falling still and his clothes were growing
heavy again. Tall rhododendron bushes grew thick
along the drive and obscured the full size of the
house. Built partially over a hill, it rested on stilts,
with a view of the sound. It was a house built
like most of the other houses from the fifties,

ranch-style front, with vaulted ceilings in the rear and a large, open living area. From what Grady remembered, he could see all the way across the sound to the other side, the snowcapped Olympics rising up past evergreen hills. All of that was gone now, with the dark coming and the rain falling. He felt the water begin to soak into his shirt again, the blood becoming like mud as he passed his fingers across the soiled fabric.

The sound of his feet on the gravel drive was just audible over the patter of the rain. With him he carried the knife bag, and though it hurt, he hunched as he walked, trying to remain unseen.

When he drew near the house, he could see a car shadowed by the front awning, the lawyer's driver at the wheel. Grady paused. Between gusts of wind, he heard music escape the house and carry to his ears. The driver hadn't moved, and after a minute, Grady took a few cautious steps toward the vehicle. When he reached the car, he could see the driver was dead, his head slumped forward on his chest.

Scanning the bushes, Grady crouched beside the car, rain dripping from the awnings and falling onto the drive. A drop of water slowly formed and fell along his face.

Grady followed the sound of the music to where the rock retaining wall held the hill. Light escaped from the living room windows onto a deck. Fifty feet below in the almost black of the underbrush and deep, unforgiving stones, he saw the young girl – an apparition of the falling rain – wrapped like a ghost in a thin white robe, which lay open at the chest to show her naked breasts. She lay with her head downhill, one arm pulled back at an unnatural angle, deep gashes along her body where she'd hit the rocks. Grady stood looking at her, then went in through the broken window.

The guard buzzed Drake through, and he entered the waiting room. Steel picnic tables everywhere. No other visitors but him, after-hours and the visiting room shut down. In the far corner a guard stood but didn't say anything as Drake took a seat and waited. After five minutes the opposite door buzzed, and his father walked in. Drake took the printout of Phil Hunt and unfolded it onto the table.

Drake's father wore the standard one-piece jumpsuit and slippers, his beard grown out and his head shaved to the skin. He looked rougher than Drake remembered him. He looked like a convict. Something about him even scared Drake a little, the rough shave, the dead stare he gave his son as he sat down. He wasn't the man Drake remembered; he was something else that Drake sat trying to understand. Ten years had passed since they'd seen each other face to face. 'Knew it would take something special for you to come see me,' his father said.

The lawyer's mouth had been so broken he could barely speak. Grady knelt, the lawyer trying to find his words. To Grady it looked like someone had gone over him with a meat tenderizer. Busted shins, a foot so broken it looked like gelatin, caved-in ribs, blood-soaked pants, and fingers mutilated and swollen big as carrots. A pool of blood rounded on the carpet beneath him. Grady knelt closer, listening as the air whistled through the lawyer's cracked lips. All Grady wanted was the address for the Vietnamese.

Grady didn't dare touch him, the carpet beneath his body blood-soaked as if the lawyer was melting into the floor. He waited, finding some hidden reserve of patience. The lawyer mouthed the address Grady needed. One more job for the lawyer, one more trip to settle things. All Grady knew now was that his life, or at least the life he had enjoyed up to this point, would change, and that the lawyer had somehow kept him sane. Grady could feel it all changing, cracks beginning to spread across his skin like porcelain breaking in an oven's heat, fissures opening and the fire coming through.

'Kill me,' the lawyer said. 'Don't leave me like this.'

It was the first kill Grady could think of that hurt. He felt no pleasure, didn't feel anything anymore, just the dull weight of the trigger on his finger and the repercussion of the bullet as it went through.

The house was close, near enough to the lawyer's that Grady thought if he was lucky he might even have beat the Vietnamese back to their own house. And though he hoped Nora was still alive, if she wasn't he hoped that she had given them a fight and slowed them down enough to make a difference.

When Grady pulled up a block away from the address, he could see the unmarked police cruiser sitting there just as plain as if the sirens were going. Two men sat in the car, dusky rain falling around them. He parked around the corner, smashed the dome light from the ceiling of the ancient car, and got out. Night all around him. He had on new clothes he'd taken from the lawyer and with him his bag of knives.

For a time he watched the men in there. He didn't know them. Didn't have to. When the Lexus drove down the street, he could see the two men slump down in the unmarked car. He tracked the Lexus till it went past and then up the drive and around the back of the house.

The man on the driver's side of the parked car

had just closed his phone when Grady approached bare handed, tapped on the window, and made a rolling motion with his hand. The two men looked up at him. Grady smiled. He made the motion again with his hand. Grady could see a twelve-gauge pump laid lengthwise between the seats.

The window came down. Grady smiled again, said good evening.

There was the sound of a spring-loaded trigger, and the first man slumped forward on Grady's hand, blood running from the fatal slice across his neck.

'Phone,' Grady said, the silenced .22 taken from behind his back and aimed at the second man. Grady saw the man twitch, think about the gun he kept in a side holster, just at his fingertips. 'Don't be stupid,' Grady said. 'This thing will carve out a hole neater than that twelve-gauge.'

And then it did.

Drake slid the picture across the table to his father. 'Know him?'

His father looked down at the picture. 'Should I?'

'Says he knows you.'

'Personally?'

'On a professional level.'

Drake's father smiled. 'What am I supposed to say?'

'You either know him or you don't.'

'Look,' his father said, 'it's not like I'm going back into it when I get out of here, but I don't want to give anyone reason to come looking for me either.'

'Dad, he's in trouble.'

His father looked at him from across the table. 'Why do you care? He's just like me, just some hustler trying to make some extra money.'

'He's in trouble, and he's got a wife who's gone missing. He's a good person. Wouldn't you have wanted someone to help you if they could?'

'Are you calling me a good person?' his father said, a thin smile spreading across his lips. His father picked up the printout and scanned it. 'Sometimes good people do bad things,' he said.

'Yes, sometimes they do.'

'What do you think?' his father said. 'Are you going to get his wife back?'

'I'd like to.'

'And what about him? What are you going to do about him?'

'You know that's not up to me.'

'If you found him in some back alley, just you, what would you do?'

'It's not up to me.'

'But you say he's a good person.'

'He is a good person. But I can't just let him go.'

Driscoll pushed the door open and stood looking at the interior of the house. Wood splinters all across the floor, broken glass, the air thick with couch dander and a million other things that had exploded into the air. The house in a horrible state, sticky pools of blood, gunshots through plaster, picture frames, and lampshades. There were small yellow markers left by the city cops. It seemed there were thousands, one for every bullet, the bodies gone and the house empty except for the buzz of flashbulbs and the lowered conversation of investigators. A uniformed officer led Driscoll to the freezer.

They followed a trail of blood into the basement, careful to avoid the small pool that had accumulated at the base of the stairs. They found one bloody handprint and the outline of a set of knuckles on the cement floor.

'How many pieces was she in?' Driscoll asked.

'Had to cut her legs off to get her to fit.'

'She still around?'

'They're thawing her out down at County.'

'How frozen was she?'

'At least a couple days.'

'A real stiff, huh?' Driscoll laughed and the officer stared back at him flatly.

Outside, Driscoll sat in the cruiser and went back over his notes. A text came in from one of the agents he'd put on surveillance: 'Black Lexus pulled up. Instructions?'

He closed the phone and stared up at Grady's house, a wash of emergency lights falling again and again on the porch and small front garden. He picked up his radio and called over to the car he'd put on the house. No answer. Then, just a minute later, a new text: 'False alarm.'

The Vietnamese brought her in through the back. Nora tried to remember everything she saw, hardwood floors, peach walls, dim red lighting. They were moving fast. Through a doorway she saw what might have been a sorting table, a small shrine in the corner, incense, and a bowl of fruit. A door opened in front of her and she was thrown in. Two dirty foam mattresses, torn sheets. The door closed. No light. Just a sliver of red from the crack beneath the door. She sat and waited.

The air felt dead and musty. She worked her hands and tried to loosen the twine around her wrists. Five minutes passed, her wrists raw but the twine still there. She could smell garlic, the scent of it cooking in a pan. She knew she was close, a few feet away from the kitchen. The room pitch black, the only sign she was not alone a shadow of footsteps passing beyond the door. A dish fell and broke on the floor somewhere. A brief scuffle, the gagging sounds of someone struggling for air. She waited, hearing nothing else.

The killing of the two men in the patrol car and the killing of the lawyer had lit something inside Grady that he could not stop. At the lawyer's house he had felt like he was breaking apart – the fire coming through and his body cracking and falling in a million pieces to the floor, a black hole opening and ready to suck down anything in his way. He was made whole, stronger than he had been before. The morphine was working away inside him, making his movements more fluid, more practiced, the heat he'd felt merely tempering his fissures, like scar tissue, building him stronger.

He found the first of the two Vietnamese in the kitchen, smell of garlic cooking and the crackle of hot oil working through the air. Grady with a small boning knife taken from his bag, and the man in front of him with his back turned to Grady, facing the stove. Grady stepped forward and plunged the blade deep into the spinal column at the base of the neck and worked the bones free, bringing the knife around on the man's throat. The man fell across the floor, smell of burning garlic, the oil smoking, at the point of ignition.

He waited, crouched near the kitchen doorway, gathering his senses about him. The smoke alarm went then, and he knew it would only be a matter of time now. He bent low and waited, crouched at the doorway with the knife in his hand. The second man entered and Grady reached out with the blade and severed the man's Achilles and watched him totter, his legs gone gummy as he fought for balance, then fell backward onto the hallway floor. Grady was on him immediately, working the knife into the man's flesh.

A minute passed and then another. The smoke alarm sounded, the smell of something burning. Nora heard footsteps go past. Something hit the floor hard outside her door, shaking the wooden boards. She heard a man's voice call out, and then nothing else. Nora didn't dare to move. There was no sound now, just Nora sitting in a pitch-black room with only the sliver of light entering from beneath the door. She waited. Something dark and liquid began to creep beneath her door. She knew already what it was, the light slowly disappearing as the blood spread out along the floorboards.

PART V

SNOW

His father hadn't given up anything but a smirk when Drake asked about Phil Hunt. What had Drake expected? What else was there?

At the end, it was clear Drake hadn't been searching out Hunt but a memory of his father, some humanity he hoped was still there. His father sat on the hard metal bench looking back at him. 'Why'd you come here?' his father said. 'Why did you come all the way out here to search for a man you know better than I do?'

'I thought I might find a change in this. Some small piece I could understand.'

'Did you find it?' his father said.

'I don't know,' Drake replied. 'I don't know if any of this is what it's meant to be. It's just what it is, drugs, kidnap, murder – none of it has ever made any sense to me.'

'We do what we have to,' Drake's father said. 'When they came for me, I ran. I went the other way. I knew what I was doing. I was doing what I was supposed to. I was doing what made sense.'

'I know,' Drake said. 'I read the file. It was the

first thing I did when I got my star.' Drake studied his father for a long beat, shaved head, cold eyes. This man wasn't his father anymore, not like he used to be.

'Here's something you can use,' Drake's father said, leaning back from the table. 'I pulled Hunt over once outside Silver Lake. I had the flashers going, the sirens, the whole deal. Thought I'd be chasing him an hour, thought I'd really run him off.' Drake's father looked to the guard near the door, then looked back. 'Hunt didn't even try for it, he didn't even move. He didn't run. You know?'

Drake was silent. He was waiting for his father to finish.

'You've got the file right there,' his father said. 'You read that part about how they found Hunt the first time, just sitting there with that old man in the bait shop, just waiting for the police to come get him.'

'That was a long time ago,' Drake said.

'He knows what he's doing, one way or another.'

'Why doesn't he just come in, then?'

'He's got a sense of what's right and what's wrong. That's all there is.'

'I can't believe that,' Drake said.

'That's just one of those things you have to learn along the way. They don't teach it.'

'Teach what?'

'That the law used to be about keeping order, it was that simple.'

'You don't think people need to answer for what they've done?'

'I think they answer in their own way. I think Hunt knows that. I think he knows if he comes in now, not one thing will be answered for. You'll have your man, but it's not going to do anyone any good.'

Drake didn't say one thing. His father was watching him to see how he'd taken it.

'And when you get out, what are you going to do?' Drake asked.

'I don't know that yet. I can tell you I won't do anything like what Hunt has going on now. I've already done this once. I'm not planning on doing it again.'

'Surest way to stay out would be to follow that advice right there.'

'I know,' his father said.

The first wet flakes were beginning to fall as Drake reached his car. He sat in the driver's seat with the heater going and watched the Monroe walls. All he could see of the night was the snow falling. Black night out there and the white flecks coming down out of the sky. He checked his phone for missed calls. Nothing. The snow was beginning to stick.

Drake pulled out of the parking lot, the far-off glow of Seattle in the distance. Driscoll hadn't called and there was nothing to go on but the address Hunt had taken from Thu's purse.

When Hunt found the house, he drove by and ran his truck down a couple of blocks, then walked back through the growing snow to the address he'd taken from Thu. He looked normal enough except for the limp and the shoe on his foot colored a dark red in places. He'd stuffed the Browning into the glove box of his truck. The absence of it in his belt made him feel naked. But he thought that if anyone wanted Grady dead more than him, it would be the Vietnamese. It was his only hope, the last thing he had left before he just gave it up and let Grady find him.

The sun had set and it had taken him about thirty minutes after leaving the interstate to find the house in the dark. Still, there was light from the overhead streetlamps, and it was as if he was seeing everything through falling ash, snow in the air and the dull, almost blue lights covering it all. Porch lights shone above doors. Cars passed down the street and continued on. Hunt walked to the end of the block and stood at the corner looking at the house. It was just a normal house in a neighborhood, surrounded by houses of the same muted composition.

The house was painted the color of brick, built in the fifties style, a one-story frame with flat wooden shingles over a cement foundation, the roof almost flat but with that slight rise toward the top and the tin chimney above, from which steam could rise. From the basement he saw the yellow glow of a naked bulb and the bend and curve of piping. When he looked back to the windows on the main floor, he could see the curtains shift and he knew someone had been watching.

Everything said to get out of there. He felt sick, his stomach tight and a feeling of unease all through. When he went to walk, he found his legs did not want to move. The tension inside him made his limbs jitter. At the base of the stairs, he paused to steady himself.

Hunt had expected the door to open. Nothing moved. He went up the stairs and stood on the porch, taking deep breaths and trying to push the air down inside. It was as if he were trying to inflate his arms and legs and make them appear solid. When he knocked, he heard movement behind the door, and then the door opened.

Drake pulled the collar of his coat close around his neck and set out from his car toward the house. There was snow an inch deep now, untouched on the ground. He was looking for the DEA officers Driscoll had put on the house. He adjusted the weight of his service weapon on his belt, then looked on down toward the house. There were cars down both sides of the street, muted, snow-covered mounds, one after another, windshields nothing but a patchwork of fallen snow and glass.

The house wasn't much to look at, but he'd guessed it wouldn't be some big mansion made of drug money. It was painted the color of brick, with shingled siding and cement stairs leading up to a porch half as wide as the house. He paused to look at this.

What had he expected? He had an address written on a sheet of paper, given to him by a convicted murderer, a drug runner, and he, the law, was trying to bring him in. He knew now it was nothing but wishful thinking, something Hunt had told him to get Drake off the phone.

The sight of a single bare bulb in the basement window and the glow of something farther in were the only signs that anyone lived there. He stood in the shadow of a telephone pole and watched the house. Nothing moved. A plane passed overhead, engines shifting as it descended toward the nearby airport. A world softened by snow and the sound of a jet passing overhead, then nothing, snow again and the simple comfort of porch lights going on down the street.

He felt the cold come into his shoes. He was shivering, caught out in this cold without the proper clothing. Drake looked up at the house and then moved off again. His father hadn't told him one thing he could use. He didn't know what he had expected. An answer? Part of him felt the same way he'd always felt, but a little part of him said it was all right. It was how it was, and it was all right.

Hunt was probably dead. Nora, too. The killer gone. The heroin gone. All of it gone. Nothing left but the gray darkness to guess at.

He wrapped his arms around himself and walked a little farther along the row of cars, making fresh tracks in the snow, keeping the house in view across the street. He noticed a shadow, thick as molasses, on one of the snow-covered car windows as he passed, like oil under sawdust. He came closer, looked at the shadow on the window, blue black with the overhead halogens.

There was something seeping from the inside of

the car window out through a hole and onto the fresh-fallen snow, and he put his finger to it and brought it close to his face. The lights overhead made the liquid on his finger a strange, other-worldly color. 'Shit,' he said, dropping to the ground with his hands out in the snow, feeling the cold.

Drake tried the handle, and the dead officer slumped half out of the car, his fingers resting on the ground next to Drake. A bullet hole in his head, neat as if the hole had been drilled through from one side to the other, spiderwebbed glass and the shattered hole where the bullet had come through and disappeared out into the snow-covered world.

He couldn't see the face, didn't want to. The man just lay there on the ground with the snow falling and melting on his skin. Drake checked the pulse. Nothing. The skin was still warm to the touch, snowflakes melting into water droplets on the dead man's skin.

Inside he found the other man, neck gaping, blood down his front and dried onto his shirt collar. Deep odor of blood and the human body hanging in the car. Drake pushed the man back in his seat and reached through until he could get the shotgun out from between their seats. He checked the cartridges, five slugger shells, big and solid enough to stop a bear. He sat panting against the side of the car, his breath heavy and a nervous sweat beginning to dampen his clothes.

He looked back up at the house, the same naked bulb hanging in the basement, and somewhere toward the back another light, an orange glow, just visible through the front curtains.

Grady had Hunt and Nora seated in the kitchen. There was a dead Vietnamese man in the middle of the floor with his neck slit so far open they could see the back of the man's tongue, broken pieces of a white ceramic bowl spread everywhere around the kitchen floor, and a burnt skillet of garlic on the stove. Grady sat in a chair and looked across at them, holding a small boning knife in his hand. Nora was tied by the hands with a length of butcher's twine Grady could see had come from his own basement. Hunt smoldered in his seat.

With his free hand, Grady brought out a syringe from his bag and put it between his teeth, taking the cover off the needle. He brought up a bottle of the morphine, and with the bottle held between his legs, he drew the liquid up into the barrel. After clearing the air bubbles, he injected himself and felt his head swoon. When he looked up, Hunt was staring at him. Grady still held the knife.

The Vietnamese were dead, and the lawyer was dead. Grady was trying to decide what to do. All that was left worth any money was the heroine.

Hunt's half wasn't on him. Grady guessed it was hidden away somewhere, some deal Hunt had hoped to work out with the Vietnamese.

From the first girl, he had about sixty pellets of heroin in his bag, and not a clue what to do with them. He didn't know how much they were worth, but he could guess the amount was enough to warrant all the trouble he'd been through. He looked across at Hunt, then looked away.

The morphine was beginning to work on him again. He felt as he had before, unstoppable. He wanted to yell, he wanted to walk through walls, to plunge his fist through glass and walk on water. He looked over at the dead man on the floor, then at Hunt. 'You ever wonder what it's like?' Grady asked, his vision swinging back to the dead man on the floor. 'What's it like over there?' Grady asked the dead man. He waited for a response. The man stared up at the ceiling, a bloom of red down the skin of his neck, his eyes searching the heavens for an answer.

'What did you expect?' Hunt said.

Grady turned and looked at Hunt. He was having a hard time focusing, the outline of Hunt's face appearing blurred. 'Get up,' he said.

'What?'

'I said, get up. Both of you get up.'

Nora began to snivel a little, and when she didn't quiet, he crossed the room and hit her with his open palm.

'Grady,' Hunt said, his voice going feral.

Grady was standing over Nora, ready to hit her again. '"Grady" what?' His attention focused on Hunt now. 'Thanks to you, everything is fucked. Can't you see that?' He wanted to slice Hunt's face off. He wanted to do cruel things with no real purpose, things he knew he would enjoy. 'Get up,' he said again.

Hunt stood.

Grady hit him hard across the face four times in quick succession. Hunt was still standing, his head merely rocking back after each blow, the blood coming now and dripping in streams from his nose and off his chin and pattering on the floor.

'You're going to show me where that heroin is, or I'm going to carve the two of you up and sell you for your organs. Do you understand?'

Hunt wiped the blood away from his nose with his forearm and stood looking at Grady. He was shamed and Grady knew it. Beaten down in front of his wife. Hunt mumbled something under his breath.

'What did you say?' Grady asked.

'I said I'd take you.'

Drake brought out his phone and called Driscoll.

The snow was still falling and his shoes were wet with it. 'Driscoll,' he said, speaking close to the phone, his eyes still on the house down the street. 'Your guys are dead, and I'm sitting out here with their bodies, watching this house, and I think Grady is in there.'

'Slow down,' Driscoll said. 'Where are you? Wait – you went over there?'

'Listen to me,' Drake said. 'These guys you had watching the house are dead. They're dead, Driscoll.' He was squatting with his back against the side of the car, almost hysterical, the bad situation he'd landed in beginning to dawn on him. His voice was only a whisper, spitting into the phone, the shotgun propped between his legs.

'Don't do anything,' Driscoll said. 'Just stay put. I'm on my way over there now. Just stay right where you are and don't do a thing.'

Across the street the door of the house opened, and a man walked out onto the porch carrying a bag of some sort. Drake held the phone to his chest, whatever else Driscoll had to say lost in that moment. The man on the porch swung his head down the street toward the unmarked patrol car, and Drake dropped down. He held his breath, watching the snow fall, watching it drift down, feeling each flake as it landed on his face, everything clear.

He chanced a look back over the hood of the car in time to see Hunt and Nora, her hands bound, coming down the stairs with the man close behind them. Driscoll was saying something on the open phone, and Drake eased it closed until there was no sound but the scuffle of footsteps across the street. With his elbows he positioned the shotgun over the hood of the car and found a clear sight. He took a breath and felt it go down inside him, felt it fill his lungs and his lungs give it back. Everything in slow motion, snowflakes falling, far off the sounds of wet, snow-covered streets, a plane miles overhead angling in for a landing.

Grady didn't know where Silver Lake was, or why any cop from there would be yelling at him from across the street, telling him to throw down the bag. He looked at the knife bag in his hand. He was feeling the bullet wound now. Somewhere along the way he had stretched it too far, had pulled it open, and he could feel the blood, warm on his stomach, slipping down along the skin and into his pants. He stumbled for a second and then recovered. His thoughts came to him in a jumble, rolling one over the other, like loose rocks tumbling down a hillside with no sense of control. For a second he thought perhaps this cop was something of unrelated interest – a tab he'd forgotten to pay in some country diner, a missed parking ticket – but then the man called Hunt's name, and Grady knew it had something more to do with the latest string of unfinished events.

The cop had yelled for them to stop, and they had. All three of them, Grady, Nora, and Hunt, stopped there in the dusky half-light of the streetlamps. There didn't appear to be anyone else around, just the single cop across the street and no one else.

The knife bag dropped from Grady's hand, revealing the retracted stock of the AR-15.

'Don't,' the cop yelled.

Grady came on with the gun, muzzle flash going, the smell of gunpowder and the hot bullet casings falling to the snow-covered street, steam catching in the wind.

All he could hear were the bullets going past at a million miles an hour, the car shaking. Drake kept his head down, cradling the shotgun. A bullet hit one of the tires, and he felt that side of the car drop, followed by the sound of glass breaking and falling everywhere along the hood and all over Drake's shoulders and head. It was like some hideous carnival ride, Drake too scared to rise up or even move out of the way as Grady came on with the AR-15 switched over to full automatic.

Another tire shot and the car angled dangerously away from him and he felt the shift with his back. He could feel the bullets getting closer. Any minute, he expected the muzzle of the AR-15 to pop over the top and Grady soon to follow, hot death from above. He hadn't known what he was doing. He'd just gone ahead and done it. Hoped that it would all work out and that someone like Grady would just stop, raise his hands, and throw the weapons down.

Fuck, Drake thought. It was him or Grady, and he knew he'd be no use to Hunt or Nora if he was dead. He cradled the shotgun, pumped it once, then put it over the hood without looking and squeezed the trigger. Time slowed, a brief hope that Nora and Hunt had the sense to take cover. Then, as if all of it had been playing on a television screen, the film reel sped back into focus, everything on fast-forward. Big booming of the shotgun barrel. The recoil sent his hand back over the edge of the hood and the gun to him and he shucked a shell. Grady returned fire, bullets screaming over Drake's head. Drake put the barrel back up over the hood and fired again. Sound of aluminum car siding buckling, glass shattering. He didn't have a clue what he was firing at. Couldn't see a thing, just hoped that Nora and Hunt had known to get out of the way.

Hunt figured he had about a twenty-second start before Grady noticed they were gone. An inch of snow had fallen since he'd limped up the stairs and Grady had opened the door to find him waiting there on the porch.

Now on the street, with Grady's attention on Drake, Hunt took Nora under the arm and ran, almost dragging her after him, the bullet wound in his leg pulsing and the blood coming now. His legs were pumping up the street, feet moving, the sound of automatic gunfire behind him, bullets tearing through car siding, through house boards, clunking their way into wooden telephone poles. He ran, his feet slipping through the snow, off one curb and up the next, the big diesel parked at the end of the block and his only hope that they would make it.

He didn't have time to think about the kid back there, Drake, the deputy he'd recognized by sight. The same stupid kid, half his age. The deputy had saved him, he knew that. Hunt knew he and Nora would have been dead as soon as Grady got the heroin. Drake had saved them.

Grady saw the big shotgun go up over the hood like some demented ship breaking through a giant wave, up and then over, sliding down onto the hood. Grady turned, threw himself over the nearest car, and came crashing down onto the ground as the first boom of the shotgun came tumbling through the line of cars. Pain all through him. The dry ache of the wound in his stomach, like he was hollow, like there was nothing left there to give. He sat and wiped the snow off his face and jacket. His hand felt like a lead weight. He put the muzzle of the AR-15 over the hood of the car and squeezed the trigger. Car alarms rattled on with the vibrations of the bullets, the sound almost deafening. Another booming of the shotgun, the cars rattling again. Grady looked around, but Hunt and Nora weren't there.

He waited, looked up over the car, and, when he didn't see the cop, went at a near run, pinched over with his legs going, following Hunt and Nora's fresh tracks in the snow. He could see them up there in the street, dipping from one light to the next. Grady stumbled, slamming hard into the side of a parked car but still moving. He was having a hard time focusing his vision. He'd lost the knife bag somewhere, his final clip loaded into the belly of the AR-15, and him running, holding the gun with both hands, his legs pumping after them, his side on fire, and the pain of his belly wound coming now and jabbing at him with every stride.

Drake waited, gathering himself for another look over the top of the car. He clutched the shotgun in his hands and breathed in. Time seemed to slow, everything brightening, snowflakes falling, ashy light, the sound of a car on a snow-covered road some distance away, adrenaline-filled senses seeding his mind.

The phone in his pocket began to vibrate. He didn't pick up. Nothing was happening. No shots fired back at him, nothing. He popped his head over the hood and looked at the street. No one was there, just the line of cars covered in a thin layer of snow and busted up by his shotgun. He kept his head down and crossed the street, broken glass in the snow, no blood, empty AR-15 casings dropped everywhere. An engine started up down the block, and there was the sound of the machine gun on it immediately.

When Grady reached the second block, he saw they were already in the truck. He steadied himself, snow falling and landing on his eyelashes, the cold wind at his back. The truck engine started and he took aim, his first cluster of bullets tearing down along the line of cars and skimming across the side of the truck, bullets playing on the metal bodies of cars like firecrackers.

He was too far away for anything but a lucky shot, the truck moving away too quickly for a shot with the scope, his head swimming. He pushed himself up and took aim again, this time letting the bullets go where they might. He didn't care anymore, didn't care whether he got the heroin or not. He just wanted to be done with it. He wanted Hunt dead. Wanted him dead and nothing more to do with the whole bloody business.

The truck tore out onto the street. A cloud of snow dragged out behind the tires, the wheels spinning. One last volley of bullets, sparks rising off the metal as the truck sped on. Grady stepped out onto the street with the gun going, back windows breaking on cars. Hunt's truck fumbled in the snow, then spun around the corner, Hunt's face visible for a moment in profile as he took the turn, the big wide-bodied truck fishtailing, and then he was gone.

Hunt pulled to the side of the road. The airport lay on one side, an empty four-lane road out ahead of them. Barbed-wire fence as far down the street as he could see. He checked Nora for bullet wounds. 'Are you bleeding?' he said. 'Are you hit anywhere?' He was frantic. Nora didn't even have enough time to respond as his hands played over her.

'I'm okay,' she managed to say. She gave him a look and he could see the cut on her lip where Grady had slapped her. He touched it with his hand, the blood dry and smooth on her lip, a small swollen bump over her teeth. There were several more welts along her forehead and cheek, he couldn't say from what. Nothing seemed to be bleeding. She turned her back and he untied the twine from around her wrists.

There was still the soreness in his calf. He'd hit the gas hard, worked the brake and slipped the transmission into drive. It had all hurt, but he hadn't registered it at the time, his bad leg bracing for everything, torn muscles tensing. He was sure he was bleeding beneath the bandage, wound ripped open by all the excitement.

Behind, in the rearview, the streetlights continued down for a mile without breaking. They were parked next to a long fence that ran the length of the airport. Nothing but airplane hangars and metal containers to look at.

Hunt put his arm back over the seat and watched the road behind them. Nothing came out of the darkness, just the night back there and the falling snow. He'd seen Drake, shotgun out, running up on Grady as he'd fired on them. It was the last thing he'd seen before his truck took the corner.

Somewhere above, he could hear an airplane circling. He leaned over in the cab of the truck, took the Browning from the glove compartment, and held it in his hand.

'It's done now, isn't it?' Nora said, her breath in steamy tendrils.

Hunt looked down at the gun. There was about ninety thousand dollars' worth of heroin to get back to. Ninety thousand dollars he didn't want a thing to do with. He looked over at Nora. 'The horses are up an old Forest Service road on the east side of the Cascades,' he said. He gave her the mile marker and made her memorize it. He told her where to find the trailer, how much he thought each horse was worth, and who to contact about them.

'Why are you telling me this?' Nora said. Night out there, and the darkness closing in on them, snow tapping against the window as if it wanted to get in.

Hunt looked down at the Browning. He looked at his hands for a long time. 'The heroin is hidden in the stables, in the little cubby under the loose wooden board.'

Again, she wanted to know why – why was he telling her this? He wouldn't answer. 'It's done, isn't it?' she asked. 'Please tell me this is all done.'

Drake jogged forward in a state of disbelief.

He held the shotgun in his hands. There was the sound of sirens in the near distance. He knew this would be Driscoll, though he didn't know how far off he was or if he would arrive in time to help.

Nora and Hunt were gone, Grady just standing there in the night with the snow falling all around him as he listened to the oncoming sirens. Drake raised the shotgun and called for Grady to throw his gun down. Grady took one half turn toward Drake and then he was off, running as best he could through the snow. Drake fired and missed, the spatter of the slugger shell, big as a meteor strike, on a nearby cement wall. A gust of snow obscured Grady's running figure. The landing lights of a plane overhead illuminated Grady's profile before the plane turned toward the airport, then nothing again.

Drake clutched the gun close to his body. He was running, following the imprint of Grady's footfalls in the new snow. In the dark he could see only about thirty feet in front of him before the prints disappeared into the night.

The footprints went on, and he was running blindly. No sound, just the wind bringing the snow, then the shadow of someone running in the distance. He stopped in the street and raised the shotgun. A dull click of the trigger, the shotgun jammed and Drake just holding it useless in his hands. No time to dig the shell out. He threw the shotgun down and, running, brought out his service pistol from the holster at his belt.

Drake came to the perimeter fence, barbed wire all the way along it. Tall grass poked up through the new snow, a buffer area of about a hundred yards between the perimeter fence and the last of the neighborhood houses. There were no streetlights now, just the distant blinking of the runway lights to guide him to Grady.

Hunt turned the truck around and followed the road to the edge of the airport fence. He found a small alley, where he parked the truck under cover of shadow and sat looking out at the world beyond. A strange stillness out there, a light wind working the falling snow, everything white.

Hunt asked Nora again about the horses and told her to repeat the information back to him. When he was satisfied, he took the Browning and slid it down into the pocket of his rain slicker.

'You shouldn't be doing this,' Nora said.

'I can't just leave him out there,' Hunt said. 'There's been too much taken away because of me.'

'What if he's dead already?' Nora said.

He opened the door and felt the cold night come through the cab of the truck and mingle with the steam of their breath. Hunt didn't have any more to say. Nora tried to tell him something, but he didn't wait for her. He left the keys in the ignition and closed the door.

He limped to the edge of the alley and looked

down the street, not a single car, just clean white snow, the perimeter fence across the street, stretching on into nothingness. He took a deep breath and plunged forward through the wind, his bad leg dragging against the drifting snow.

He didn't have any clear idea where he was going, but he knew he'd find his way. He kept to the middle of the road where cars had passed and flattened a path before him. Running, half hopping to avoid injuring himself further, he almost tripped over the shotgun in the street. He was two blocks off the main road, the gun just resting there in the snow. He put his hands on the gun, the metal cold as the air around him. Hunt knew it had been Drake's gun. Scanning the nearby snow, he soon found the track of Drake's footsteps.

The chamber was jammed, and using his finger, he pried out a disfigured shell and dropped it into his pocket. One shell left. He held the gun in his hands, eyes searching through the storm-filled blackness. There was no sign of Drake but the footfalls in front of him, leading off toward the airport and quickly filling with snow.

Drake ran on. The sirens had faded away and now he could hear his own breathing, feel his heart pumping, sweat cold on his forehead. He stopped with the snow beneath him. He was in a wide field before the perimeter fence with the house lights a hundred yards back. Farther down the fence stood a series of shadowed dampening walls, built to block out the airport noise.

A set of guidance lights flashed on with a quiet intensity, brilliant white light everywhere and the thunder of jet engines overhead. The dark underbelly of a plane passed in the air above him at an incredible speed, and moments later he heard the scuff of the tires as they took the runway. Lights out, and Drake back in darkness, his pupils struggling to make sense of the quick shift from bright daylight back to the blackness of night.

The whistle of a bullet in the air, sound of bone and tissue tearing, his right knee collapsing, warm liquid down his shin and into his shoe. He fumbled forward. Blood splattered on the snow. His blood. He took another step, his body weight on his wounded leg, hot white pain. He gasped, held it, felt his lungs burn with it, his knee thumping. He fell and lay in the snow, eyes open, the tips of grass poking out of the fresh-fallen white field.

He heard the crunch of footsteps, tried to get up, his body not doing what he wanted it to. He got up on his elbow and pointed his pistol into the night. Beneath him he could feel the snow growing warm with his own blood. The crunch of footsteps. He took aim and fired toward the sound. Another bullet hit him in the right forearm. He yelled out, dropped the gun, his hand held over the new wound in his arm.

Crunch of snow again, the shuffle of it as it parted. Grady came out of the night holding the AR-15 on Drake. Grady's breathing was irregular. A patch of blood was forming on Grady's right side. Drake didn't think he'd shot him, but he couldn't be sure.

Drake panted, his face covered in a growing sweat. He felt light headed. He tried to keep his vision straight, but it was going and he couldn't seem to help it.

Grady kicked Drake's gun away. He tapped the scope on the rifle. 'Could have taken off your head, but it'll be more interesting this way.' Grady put a hand under his jacket, and when he brought it out, there was blood on his fingers. He looked at it. Felt the texture of it between his trigger finger and thumb. It seemed to amaze him.

'For who?' Drake managed to say.

'For me.' Grady let the rifle slip down through his hands into the snow.

Drake lay there, looking up, wet snow beneath him, the ground hard with the cold, his knees pulled in and his good hand over the hole Grady had torn in his forearm. He closed his eyes. He couldn't find the energy to move. Grady placed a hand around Drake's throat and held him down. Drake just lay there, feeling the inevitability of what would come next.

There was the sound of a spring releasing, something pulled forward on a slide. Drake opened his eyes and saw the blade come at him. Instinctively, he put out his hand and felt the knife slice in. The new pain surprised him. He found some reservoir of energy and pushed back in the snow with his good leg, his knee on fire and Grady on the ground slashing after him. Drake reached out again, his hand bloody, and grabbed for Grady's sleeve. He felt the mechanism under there. He felt the handle of the knife and he tried to twist it off Grady's arm. Grady put his whole weight on top of Drake, pushing the knife down.

For a moment it was just them in the snowfield. Nothing but their gasps, teeth clenched. Spit falling from their mouths, snow crushed beneath them. Grady on top of Drake, trying to drive the knife in, Drake trying to lever him off. Snow falling. The dim red flash of the lights from the runway. Drake landed his good knee in Grady's gut, and both men called out in pain. The tip of the knife dropped into Drake's shoulder and he felt it there throbbing in the muscle. He forced Grady's hand back up.

A plane passed overhead, blinding landing lights, dragging a human shadow across the two of them. The snowfield bold and flat all around them. The landing lights flooded the scene in pure white light, and suddenly Hunt was there, pulled from the darkness like a magic trick.

Drake heard the click of the hammer a split second before the shotgun went off. He heard it but didn't turn his face, didn't even think to shield his eyes. The barrel was a foot away from Grady's temple. Grady looked up, his face taking it in, realizing what was coming, for a half second his eyes widening, looking down the length of the gun. Hunt let his finger down onto the trigger, and Drake watched as the bullet took teeth and gums, tongue and throat, all the way back through Grady's head and left it in a splattered mess on the snow-covered field.

A jet touched down, the thick sound of rubber meeting tarmac, the scuff of wheels, and the rise of smoke off the runway. Drake felt every muscle in his body give way. He felt the cold beneath him, welcomed it, let it soak in. Hunt stood there with the gun half-raised over Grady's body, as if perhaps Grady might come back, as if he might still pose some threat. The lights dimmed around all of them until there was nothing but the faint red pulse once again.

'He was going to kill you,' Hunt said. He didn't look at Drake as he said it. He just said it.

'I know.'

'I just shot a man,' Hunt said, his voice in a fog, turning to look at Drake, the shotgun still held in his hand.

'I know,' Drake said.

'I never wanted to.'

Drake coughed. He was watching the gun in Hunt's hand, the pain in his knee aching and his vision going milky. He leaned over on his side and tried to focus, snow falling and accumulating on his lashes, the red-lit profile of Hunt's face the only thing there to tell Drake he hadn't imagined it all. 'Even if I wanted to arrest you,' he said, 'I'm in no condition to do it.'

Hunt gave Drake a blank stare, gun faced out toward him. Drake couldn't read him.

Drake brought out his phone and toggled down through the numbers until he found Driscoll's. The gun was still pointed at him. 'Do you mind,' Drake said, motioning to the twelve-gauge pump.

Hunt threw the gun down in the snow and watched as Drake pushed Send and waited for Driscoll to come on the line. Drake lay back in the snow and watched the flakes coming down. Driscoll was saying something, but it didn't matter to Drake. He wasn't ready for it, though he knew he couldn't wait any longer. He felt his head swim for a moment, the dizziness coming over him. When he turned back to find Hunt, he saw only his rough shadow jogging across the field, the far-off lights of houses behind his limping figure, the path he'd taken already filling in behind him. Everywhere the soft fall of snow, a distant crunch of footsteps, and then no sound at all.

After they had rested, Hunt told her about the house. He said that it wouldn't have made sense to go back there anyway, that the place didn't exist for them anymore. It was all gone, all of it, and to go back there – even just to pick up the heroin – would have risked arrest, would have meant jail time, and he couldn't do that.

They were sitting in the little pasture up the forgotten road. There was frost in the grass, but no snow. A day had passed and it was night again. Hunt had built a fire against the cold and hidden it as best he could with a wall of rocks, but no cars passed, nor did they ever seem to, and he knew they would be safe here, just like the old times, before all this. And he told Nora that he knew it would all change, but he didn't know the future as he'd thought he did, and the only thing he knew with any certainty was that it was coming and he hoped it would be good.

Out of the darkness, they listened to the sounds of the horses in the pasture, the hard-soled hooves, the lap of their tongues as they bent into the bucket and drew water. Hunt and Nora had washed in the little stream, and Hunt had cleaned Nora's lip and lifted her shirt to look at the bruises left on her body from the trunk. They had stood there next to the stream for a long time, just like that, half-naked, bruised, goose bumps on their skin, but happy. Hunt put a hand to Nora's stomach and eased his palm around onto her back and embraced her and felt her warmth close to his.

'Don't worry,' he said. 'We'll figure this out and we'll be all right.' She had cried then, but he didn't know what to do except to hold her and run his hand along her head, down onto her neck, and then begin again.

He didn't tell her that these were his words from twenty years ago. That he had told himself these very same things. He'd said them then because that was what he believed. He'd said them because he knew that he couldn't go back to jail, that he would never go back, and he'd known then, just as he knew now, that he would make something happen and they would be all right. That they might not have everything, but they would have something, and the only thing he could hope for was that it would be something good.

When Drake saw Driscoll again, it was in the hospital room. Drake's surgery had taken five hours. His kneecap was partially shattered, pieces of the patella everywhere, the muscle so torn up that the doctors said he'd probably walk with a limp for the rest of his life. Sheri sat in the little chair near his bed. She'd pulled it out from the wall so that they could see each other around the IV drip, and from time to time she would hold his hand and tell him not to be so stupid again.

Drake could see the sour look on Sheri's face when Driscoll walked through the door. 'I'll get some ice chips,' she said. Then, as she passed Driscoll: 'No more adventures.'

Driscoll opened his mouth but didn't say anything. He watched her walk past, and then when she was gone he said, 'You read the paper today?'

'I never read the paper.'

'Can't say I blame you.'

Drake coughed. 'Stopped reading it after my father went away. Kind of strange reading about your family in the paper like that. It's like reading a review of the life you're leading while you're living it. Never made me feel too good.'

'Your name came up.' Driscoll smiled and then said with obvious sarcasm, 'You're famous again.'

'Seems like I can't go a week these days without my name in print. I already know what happened, I was there.'

'Still no sign of Hunt. Know anything about that?'

'What does the paper say?'

'Bag of knives, bag of heroin sitting in the snow. Two dead Vietnamese men inside the house. Nothing on Hunt.'

'You think that's it, then?'

'Almost a hundred thousand in heroin.'

'The girl was carrying that much?'

'A little less,' Driscoll said. 'But we found evidence they had been bringing in girls on an almost monthly schedule.'

'Any girls?'

'No.'

'You think they got smart after what happened to Thu?'

'I don't know,' Driscoll said. 'This story will never reach across the Pacific. They'll just say it never happened, that Thu is still alive, living the good life somewhere.'

'The good life, huh?'

'Yes.'

'That's a crazy way of putting it.'

'What's crazy is it will start all over again.'

425

'And Hunt? Anything?'

'Nothing.'

'What about the drugs? What about the stuff he took off Thu?'

'I don't know. Probably shot up in the vein by now, junkies from here to Montana.' Driscoll sighed. 'I can't say really.'

'Do you think he'd have sold it?'

'He's your best buddy now. You tell me.'

Drake made a face. 'I'll just give him a call. You got your cell phone on you?'

'Come on, Drake. I don't know. I'm just giving you some shit. Can't I do that? Who knows where those drugs are now. Hunt knows. But who knows where he is?'

'So that's it, then?'

'Found another dead guy in a house in North Seattle. Executed right there in his front room. Nice place, a view out over the water. The guy was supposed to be some sort of lawyer, seems to have done just about everything, you know? A little of this, a little of that. The bullet we took out of his head matches the twenty-two we found in Grady's knife bag. We're looking into it, but we're pretty sure this dead guy was the one putting the whole thing together.'

Drake coughed, looked out the window, the pain in his muscles tensing his body as his lungs filled. The wound in his arm was just a thick line of stitching, but nothing broken, nothing beyond repair.

Driscoll walked over to the IV and fingered the bag. 'What's in here?' he said. 'Anything good?'

'Saline. Vitamins. Superpowers.'

'No joke?'

'No joke.'

'There's one thing,' Driscoll said. 'It was hard to tell with all the snow out there, and the struggle. Footprints from the medics, from the cops, from our guys. I mean, there was blood everywhere, covered over by snow – half the time we didn't even know we were stepping in it. But it looked, from what I saw, like Grady was shot from a standing position.'

Drake thought about this for a moment. Almost from his subconscious, he moved a hand to his thigh and worked the muscle. He'd had an old basketball injury there once, a bruise the size of his hand, too big to hide. 'I can't really say how it happened,' Drake said. 'The adrenaline was going, I could have done anything, stood on two busted knees if I had to. All I knew was that he was coming after me and I could only stop him one way.'

'What did you say was in that IV?'

'Superpowers.'

Driscoll smiled but didn't say anything. Sheri wasn't back with the ice, though Drake knew there wasn't going to be any. 'What I said to you when we first met, about your father,' Driscoll said. 'I'm sorry if I implied anything. You did a good thing out there.'

'I know that—'

'I didn't mean anything by it.'

'Don't worry about it, Driscoll. I'm looking at six months of paid vacation time.'

'Vacation time, huh? Just like your stay downtown this last week? That worked out well for you.'

The doctors released him when he could walk to the end of the hall and back again without resting. He knew there would be physical therapy, and lots of it. Twice a week he would need to drive down from Silver Lake and come to the hospital in Seattle, where the state paid for his rehabilitation.

When he was eighteen he thought he'd have his own place, live out a ways and buy property the way his father had. But when his father went away, the property he'd grown up on became his. Twenty acres of land, a fence made of chopped alder and set in a frontier-style A-frame around two acres of the property, the soft wood rotted in many places. And the horses that his father had once kept – confiscated and sold. He was lucky even to have the house.

Sheri drove him to the bottom of their steps and helped him walk up the stairs to the door. 'Are you going to be okay here?' she asked, leaning him up against the porch railing.

He'd been in the hospital a month, and just standing there in the open with his property all around him felt better than anything he'd felt in a long time. 'I'll wait for you here,' he said. He adjusted his balance a little, taking the strain off his bad leg and putting his weight on his good.

'The doctors told you not to do that,' Sheri said.

'The doctors told me not to do a whole lot of things. You just go park the car and come back over here and I'll show you a few other things I'm not supposed to do.'

She scolded him with her eyes. 'Is that all you've been thinking of?'

'Not all the time, just most of the time.' He smiled and watched her walk back over to the car and drive it around near the converted garage, where his father once stabled his horses.

While she was getting the bags from the trunk, he opened the door and went inside. Using the cane the hospital had given him, he went to the kitchen and ran the water from the faucet and splashed it over his face, one hand on the counter and the other cupping the water. It tasted of the earth, a little bit alkaline, like water drawn up from deep below, hard and cold as rock.

All along the kitchen window were old jam jars Sheri had pulled from the dirt when she'd made rows for their garden, the glass discolored and chipped from its time in the earth. He'd thought of visiting his father then but hadn't gone. He didn't know anything about these jars, didn't know where they had come from or if his father had known about them at all. The only thing he knew was that they were old, filled with dirt and history, and he'd put them up on the windowsill to remind him of that.

The limp was nearly gone when Driscoll called, just a little half step added every ten feet, as if his bad leg was slowly losing a race with his good.

'What is this, an anniversary call?' Drake said. He was driving around Silver Lake in his cruiser, and when Driscoll called, he pulled the car into a grocery store parking lot and turned off the engine.

'I guess in a way it is,' Driscoll said. 'I was wondering if you could do me a favor.'

'I'm not going to get shot again, am I?'

He heard Driscoll laugh. 'I hope not.'

'So there's a possibility?'

'There's always the possibility, isn't there?'

'Only when I'm working with you.'

Driscoll didn't say anything, and then: 'What do you say? Can you run over to the next county and see a sheriff for me?'

'Which town?'

Driscoll told him.

'That's twenty miles south of Canada.'

'I'm not trying to get you into any more trouble here.'

'What's this about, Driscoll?'

'The sheriff over there says he's got a woman in custody who matches the description of Nora Hunt.'

Drake paused. He watched a woman about his age pass in front of the cruiser with her shopping cart, a little girl two or three years old in the toddler's seat.

'Did you think I just forgot?' Driscoll said.

'I just don't think it's her, is all. Wouldn't have figured they were even in the country anymore.'

'Yeah, well, maybe they're not. Or maybe Hunt cut her loose and ran. I'm not sure. All I have to go on is an old photo from the Department of Licensing. I never met her in person. Never saw what she looked like. I've got nothing to go on here. But you've seen her, talked to her even. You could give me a positive identification.'

'This is a stupid question, but I'm going to ask it anyways. Why don't you just check the woman's ID?'

'Doesn't have one, or at least didn't have it on her. Even had the sheriff send me a digital photo. Based on this old photo I have, I can't say either way.'

'What do you think?'

'I think it would be nice if you wanted to go over there.'

Drake sighed. 'Yeah, I can go over there. How long can they hold her?'

'It's not even legal as it is.'

The drive took Drake a little more than an hour. He used back roads until he could get onto the highway and take the cruiser over the mountains and down into the next county.

When he pulled up at the sheriff's office, he adjusted his gun and put his hat back on his head, then went in through the front doors. He was wearing his brown deputy's uniform, and he hoped that if it was Nora, she wouldn't recognize him with his star on. He gave the deputy at the desk his name and stated his reason for being there. The deputy led him around to the sheriff, and the sheriff took him back to the holding cells.

'You're that one, right? Drake from Silver Lake?' the sheriff said. They were going in through the back office, finding the holding cell.

'You're probably thinking of my father,' Drake said.

'You were the one who shot that psycho a year back?' the sheriff asked. 'Heard you took something like five bullets.' The sheriff was smiling. He was a big man with a nice overhanging gut that Drake didn't think would do him any good if he had to run anyone down.

'Just two,' Drake said.

'Goddamn!'

'Just lucky, I guess.'

'Yeah, well . . . it's two more than I'd like to take.'

They came to a stop in front of the little ten-by-ten cell with the woman in it. Drake looked through the bars to where she sat on a small bench. 'What did you say her name was?'

'Joan Thomas,' the sheriff said.

'She got any type of ID?'

'Just a few twenty-dollar bills on her, a grocery card, and a movie-rental punch card for the convenience store we got here in town.'

'What do those say her name is?'

'Joan Thomas.'

Drake looked in on the woman. She didn't look up at either of them, kept her face to the floor. 'Hey,' Drake said through the bars. 'What's your name?'

The lady looked up at him and then quickly looked away. He could see it was Nora Hunt, the gray roots grown out, hair cropped close around her face, but the same thin features, a nose as small and delicate as crystal.

Drake took his hat off and scratched his temple. Then finally, after he'd straightened the hat back on his head, he said, 'That's not her.'

'Shit,' the sheriff said. 'I thought for sure we had something here.'

'Sorry,' Drake said. 'Do me a favor and call Driscoll over at the DEA and tell him it's not her.'

'Yeah, I can do that.'

'What are you going to do with her now?'

'I think we better release her,' the sheriff said.

Nora was watching them now, listening to everything they said.

'Sorry,' the sheriff said through the bars. 'I

thought you were someone else. Do us a favor and carry some ID next time.'

Nora didn't say anything.

'You want to press charges against the sheriff's department?' Drake said. He smiled a bit, and the sheriff looked uncomfortable.

'No,' Nora said. 'I just didn't think walking around without an ID could cause such a fuss.'

The sheriff went over and undid the lock and opened the gate to the cell. 'Come on out,' he said.

'You going to give her a ride back to wherever you picked her up from?' Drake asked.

The sheriff gave him a hurt look, then said under his breath, 'Honestly, she wasn't so much fun to get into the car the first time.'

'I can give her a lift,' Drake said. He looked at Nora. 'If that's all right with you?'

They drove up the road, past the town hall, past a Mexican restaurant with a green awning and neon beer signs in the window. Drake pulled over a half block down from the convenience store.

'You going to get a couple movies with your rental card?' Drake said.

They hadn't spoken at all in the car.

'That and go buy some groceries,' Nora said.

Drake leaned into the windshield and looked up at the store awnings that appeared in a line down the street. They were parked next to a Laundromat, and he read the signs all down the

436

block. At the end of the street, he could see the big diesel. 'What happened to the trailer?'

'Oh, you know,' Nora said. 'It's around.'

'Just around?'

'Here and there.'

'Hopefully more here than there,' he said. 'Please tell me I did the right thing back at the sheriff's office.'

'You did the right thing.'

'Don't tell it to me just because I want you to.'

Nora made an ugly face, then looked out the window. He thought she'd just get out then, just get out and leave him there in the cruiser. And he didn't know what he'd do about that, what he could do, or what he'd want to if it did come down to it. When she turned back, she said she couldn't remember his name.

'Bobby Drake.'

She looked away, looked into the Laundromat, at the people in there with their spinning clothes. 'Bobby, I'm not going to take you up there and show you we're doing fine. But I'll tell you we're okay, we're raising horses and leasing a bit of land. And it's been good to us so far.'

'What kind of horses?'

'Quarter horses.'

'Are you racing them?'

'Not yet.'

'You must live pretty hand to mouth?'

'We do all right. Two foals this spring, and I give lessons on the weekends.'

'Maybe I should come by.'

Nora smiled. 'No, I don't think Phil would like that.'

'No, I don't think he would either.'

Nora leaned over in the seat and gave him a hug. The smell of pears, something else, too, sweat possibly, fear. 'Thank you,' she said.

'Wait,' he said. She had the door halfway open. She turned back to look at him. 'Why up here? Why so close to Canada? Why not just move up there?'

'Phil knows this area. Knows the hills and knows the mountains. We weren't going to move somewhere we didn't know anything about.'

'You could have, though. It probably would have been better.'

'We're too old for that, too old to start again.'

'You could have avoided incidents like today if you had. I'm glad I was called to come take a look, but I may not be the one to show up next time.'

Nora looked up the street for a while; she seemed to be thinking this over. 'Are you going to say anything?'

'No. The way I see it, you're both good people, it's just bad things that happen.'

'They certainly do.'

'Just tell Phil not to make any cargo deals across international borders.'

Nora smiled. 'I don't think it's crossed his mind.'

'I don't think it's something I could look the other way on.'

She made a little motion to get out of the car.

He put out a hand to stop her. 'What happened to the heroin Hunt got off Thu?' He said this quickly, as if it had just come into his mind, but the truth was he'd been thinking about it for a year. Thinking about it and in a way regretting it. 'What did Hunt do with it?' he asked.

She looked back at him, her hand on the door handle. 'Bobby, you don't have anything to worry about,' Nora said. 'As far as I know, it's gone. Just the way Grady went, dead and gone.'

He couldn't question this. In any case, he didn't say anything as she opened the cruiser door.

She got out of the car and walked up the street. And for a moment she turned and looked back at him. He raised his hand. Nora smiled, then looked away and kept walking. When she reached her truck, he saw her climb into the cab. The brake lights went on, and she shifted the transmission down through reverse and into drive. He watched the truck pull out and go up the street, and when it was out of sight, he started his car and pulled a U-turn, heading back the way he'd come.